"Do you expect me to be Spider-Ma[...]

She and Black[...] [...] of trees on the we[...] mansion, look[...] four stories ab[...]

"I expect you to follow my lead, dear heart. If the two of us can break in, then the place isn't as secure as it should be." He swung himself up into a tree and then began climbing.

She could hear the distant noise from the circus on the great lawn on the eastern side of the building; she could hear the muffled roar of the big cats. Ferris grimly reached for the first branch. "Are you up there?" she called. "I'm coming."

He was waiting for her, miles away from the safety of the thick-limbed oak tree, lounging indolently on the third-floor balcony.

"I won't let you fall. Jump! Trust me at least that far."

"I don't trust you, Patrick. I thought we made that clear."

"Come on," he said, and his hand closed over hers, yanking suddenly. Caught off guard, she had no chance to do anything more than shut her eyes and leap.

ABOUT THE AUTHOR

Anne Stuart is the much-acclaimed author of four Intrigues as well as ten American Romances. In 1985 Harlequin published her *Catspaw*, Intrigue #9, which was enormously popular, and we know her readers will be delighted that she has brought back her intrepid Ferris and Blackheart for another exciting adventure in *Catspaw II*.

Anne lives in Vermont with her husband and two children.

Books by Anne Stuart

HARLEQUIN INTRIGUE

HARLEQUIN AMERICAN ROMANCE

CATSPAW II

Anne Stuart

Harlequin Books

TORONTO • NEW YORK • LONDON
AMSTERDAM • PARIS • SYDNEY • HAMBURG
STOCKHOLM • ATHENS • TOKYO • MILAN

Harlequin Intrigue edition published December 1988

ISBN 0-373-22103-7

Partitioned off exhibit rooms

Venetian Bedroom

Greek Columns

Wire strung across balconies

Balcony

Fabergé Eggs

San Francisco Museum of Decorative Arts

Balcony

Front Entrance

CAST OF CHARACTERS

John Patrick Blackheart—A retired cat burglar now running his own security firm in San Francisco. But was he *really* retired?

Ferris Byrd—Could she make a life with a man she couldn't trust?

Danielle Porcini—All she cared about was escaping her abusive partner-in-crime and wreaking a belated vengeance.

Stephen McNab—A cop with his own ideas of vengeance.

Senator Phillip Merriam—He was willing to do anything to gain national power, including selling out his own mother.

Marco Porcini—He possessed the cunning of a fox and the intellect of a soap dish.

Chapter One

Vertigo
(Paramount 1958)

Francesca Berdahofski, alias Ferris Byrd, stood in a pool of water outside her apartment, staring in frustration at the row of shiny new locks on the otherwise flimsy door. She shivered, sniffled, then sneezed, and for a brief moment leaned her forehead against the white-painted pine.

It was September in San Francisco, a cold, rainy September that made Ferris long for hot, barren deserts and doors without locks. All her doubts and uncertainties were pressing in on her, culminating in the frustration of the three new locks that she still hadn't managed to make work.

She pushed herself back, shoved her rain-drenched black hair away from her face, and began to search through her tasteful leather purse. She never could find her keys, and after a miserable day like today, starting with no coffee and a broken-down car, then tantrums among the socialites she was busy babysitting, and finally a diabolical cloudburst on the way home, it was clear that her rotten luck would hold.

No keys in her purse. While her apartment was usually a shambles, she kept her purse ruthlessly organized, and there were no keys lurking underneath the slim leather checkbook, the tiny flacon of Obsession, the Estée Lauder lipstick. There was only the piece of paper with the phone number of the garage written in blue ink. The garage where her navy-blue Mercedes was undergoing surgery. The garage that held her car, her car keys and the attached keys to her apartment.

Ferris Byrd, a woman of great self-possession who never cried, promptly burst into tears. She gave in to temptation and pounded on the unyielding door in mute frustration. The only answer was a thin, plaintive mew.

"Blackie," Ferris murmured mournfully to the cat on the other side of her door. "Why can't you be like your namesake and materialize through locked doors?"

Blackie's response was his usual huffy snarl, and through the thin door Ferris could hear thirteen pounds of alley cat stalk away from his mistress's voice.

"Go ahead, be like that," Ferris said bitterly. "Desert me in my hour of need." The unfortunate phrasing came a little too close to the truth of her current situation. Sighing, Ferris faced the unpleasant alternatives. She could either try to find a taxi and make her way to Guido's Imports to fetch her keys, or she could break into her own apartment.

Guido's Imports sounded appealing, but it was almost six o'clock, and Guido kept banker's hours. The big building on Canal Street would be locked up tighter than her apartment.

So breaking and entering it was. Not through the three shiny brass locks adorning her door. She could thank her conscientious fiancé for those. *Trust a retired cat burglar to know the best, most unpickable locks on the market. Of course,* he'd blithely told her that as far as he was concerned no locks were unpickable, but her talents as a cracksman or crackswoman were not as impressive. Besides, she'd mangled Blackheart's picklocks and he'd promised there was no need to replace them. And she'd believed him. Hadn't she?

If she was going to get into the apartment, it would have to be through the second-floor terraced balcony. And while she could always wait a few minutes in the wistful hope that the heavy downpour outside might abate, common sense told her it would be a waste of time. It was getting darker, the rain had been falling steadily for the last hour and a half, and with her luck it might even turn into a thunderstorm. The door wasn't going to open automatically, and she had no choice. It was time to renew her acquaintance with B and E.

She shrugged out of her peach silk raincoat and left it in a sodden pile outside her door. She'd never manage to scramble up the side of the old frame building with that flapping around her, and she was going to get soaked, anyway. She might as well make her attempt at scaling the building in the least encumbered condition.

She considered dumping her purse on top of the raincoat, then thought better of it. Her building wasn't the most secure place in the world; only her apartment was impenetrable. And her purse contained gold credit cards, too much cash and her birth control pills, none of which she cared to replace.

Slinging the thin strap over her head, she headed down the stairs and out into the rain, prepared to assault the fortress.

If anything, the rain had become even more relentless. The weight of it pulled at her loosely knotted hair, and she could feel sopping tendrils drip down her neck and over her high cheekbones like rats' tails. The water was running down her thin silk blouse, pooling in her bra, and her leather high-heeled shoes were squelching noisily as she moved around the outside of the building.

One of San Francisco's steep hilly streets ran along the side of the house, a blessing that Ferris was now heartily grateful for. Approaching her small balcony from the back corner of the building, her apartment was only a story and a half from the street, instead of the two and half that it was from the front.

The rain-swept streets were deserted, a fact that Ferris noticed with mixed feelings. On the one hand, she didn't particularly want an audience as she shinnied up the side of her building. On the other, maybe there would have been a good Samaritan who shared the skills her missing fiancé had in abundance.

Don't think of him, she ordered herself, gritting her teeth as the water poured in sheets down her back. *You'll just get madder. Think of a hot bath, an oversize glass of brandy and ice cream. Double Rainbow coffee, a whole pint of it, while you watch something soothing on TV. Something that has nothing to do with retired cat burglars. Or practicing cat burglars, either.*

The battered trash cans, Blackie's favorite home away from home, were lined up haphazardly in the alley behind Ferris's building, reeking of garbage and heaven only knew what else. Breathing through her mouth, she wrapped her arms around one smelly container and half carried, half dragged it around the corner, stopping under her second-floor balcony. She was cursing beneath her breath, sweating, her hands cold and slippery on the metal, her feet sliding around inside her wet shoes, so intent on her misery that she didn't notice the car parked opposite, didn't feel the gaze boring into her back.

She climbed up onto the rickety garbage can, scraping her knees on the dented lid. She got to her feet, bracing herself against the rain-slick siding, her ankles tottery in the slippery high heels as she stared down at her long, wet legs and shredded stockings.

"Wouldn't you just know it?" she demanded of the rain-dark skies. "The first time in fifteen years I dare to wear a miniskirt, and I end up climbing up a building in it. Hell and damnation."

The sky responded with an ominous rumble of thunder, and the lid of the can collapsed, sending Ferris into the pile of stinking refuse.

She practically catapulted out, beyond recriminations, beyond tears, beyond cursing. Upending the garbage can and scattering the ripped plastic bags of trash over the sidewalk, she kicked off her useless high heels and climbed back up, balancing on the upside-down can as she set one wet stockinged foot on her neighbor's windowsill. Clinging to the framework, she reached for the tendrils of ivy that cascaded down from her balcony, yanking hard.

A few wet leaves came off in her hands, but the vine held. Wrapping her arm in the thick, wet greenery, she hauled herself upward, her body swinging slightly, her purse slapping against her breasts, the ropelike vines cutting into her soft hands. She reached blindly with her feet, stubbing her toes against the wet wood, and pushed her way upward, slowly, painfully, the vine's support slipping slightly, the rain pouring down mercilessly all the while. The rim of her balcony was less than a foot beyond her reach, a tantalizing ten inches or so. If she could just manage one more boost up the clinging tendrils, she'd be home free.

She yanked, the vine pulled away from the wall, and for a moment she was swinging out over the garbage-littered sidewalk. She shut her eyes, uttering a little moan of terror. She hated heights, hated them with a passion bordering on mindless panic. Why in heaven's name hadn't she done the sensible thing and gone to a hotel for the night? Blackie would have survived without her.

She allowed herself a brief glance downward through slitted eyes. It seemed like an endless drop, and the garbage bags didn't look as if they'd provide too soft a landing, even assuming she was lucky enough to hit them. She couldn't go down; her only choice was to keep trying to go up.

She pulled again at the vines, pushing with her feet, and managed to gain another few inches, almost back to within a foot of safety. The miniskirt was tight, too tight, impeding her movements, and for half a moment she considered pulling it up to her waist and climbing the rest of the way in her shredded panty hose. But even with no witnesses she couldn't bring herself to climb around on the streets of San Francisco in her underwear, so she had to content herself with gritting her teeth, hiking the narrow skirt higher up her long thighs and continuing upward.

Her pale, manicured fingernails were just inches below the edge of the balcony. She gave herself one last push, holding her breath as she released the vine and clawed for the edge of the terrace, determined to make it or die trying. Her hands caught the rim, slid for a second and then held, and with more panic than grace Ferris hauled her scantily clad body up and over, sprawling onto the wet slate surface, panting in fear and exhaustion, her eyes shut as the rain poured over her fine-boned face and her wet curtain of hair.

She opened them a moment later and glared at her terrace door. She usually left it ajar, giving her erstwhile alley cat his freedom. But it had been a cold, nasty morning and Blackie didn't like the rain, so like a fool she'd closed and locked it.

She considered taking off her shoe and smashing one of the panes of glass near the locked door handle. But her shoes were down on the sidewalk in a welter of garbage, and she had nothing that would break glass but her own fist. And she wasn't quite desperate enough. Yet.

She could do it, of course, she thought, pulling herself to her feet and yanking her purse from around her neck. She could, for example, picture John Patrick Blackheart's enigmatic face in the glass, a face she hadn't seen in more than three weeks and of whose whereabouts at the moment she didn't have the faintest idea, and she could take her fist and drive it right into his teeth.

But that would hurt her far more than it would him. She didn't need a bloody fist and stitches, simply because she needed to take out on someone else the frustration and confusion of the last three weeks, the last few months, the last few hours and minutes.

She'd used a credit card on a terrace door before and succeeded, so she could do it again. Her bruised knees protested slightly as she knelt in front of the lock, her American Express card in hand, but she merely bit her lip, shoved her sopping hair out of her face, and applied herself. The American Express card bit the dust and was soon joined by her gold Visa card, her Macy's card, and the one from I. Magnin.

Ferris looked longingly up at the glass, wondering if a karate kick might do the trick. She could limp for a while without greatly impairing her efficiency, if she wasn't called upon to climb any more buildings and break into any more apartments. And there was something very appealing about the notion of kicking Blackheart in the teeth.

She pulled out her Daughters of the Pacific membership card. The plastic was sturdier than the others, and it was the symbol of her successful transformation, from

Francesca Berdahofski, daughter of immigrants, always on the outside looking in, to Ferris Byrd, self-made, elegant and self-assured, as if born to privilege. Membership in the Daughters of the Pacific was hard to come by—one had to be proposed by three members, one's lineage had to pass muster, and one had to be voted on by the bluest blood of San Francisco. Even though Ferris knew how hollow such a victory, such a transformation of her life really was, she'd still secretly cherished the card and everything it stood for.

She slid it between the terrace doors, gently, coaxingly, as Blackheart had once taught her to do. The latch clicked, the door swung open, and thirteen pounds of smoky-gray, outraged tomcat raced out into the dusk, disappearing over the balcony without a backward glance.

"Glad to see you, too," she muttered, pushing the door open, letting the heat and light envelope her shivering body. She stepped inside, sneezed, and shut the door behind her.

Her apartment, never known for its neatness, was in a worse shambles than usual. Consisting of six rooms and three short flights of stairs, it was a rambling rabbit warren of a place that she would sorely miss if and when she moved out. She shouldn't be thinking *if*, not with piles of boxes stacked in every available space, waiting for their removal to Blackheart's less colorful, more spacious quarters. But when one's fiancé took to disappearing at odd times during the six months of their engagement, returning without a word of explanation, when he'd gone off again three weeks ago and hadn't been heard from since, when there'd been a string of robberies in Europe that had reminded suspicious authorities of the heyday of the Blackheart family, then she too could only begin to wonder, to fall victim to the kind of doubts no engaged woman should have to harbor.

There was a light burning in the living room. She didn't remember having left it on, but then she'd been in a foul mood that morning, having spent one too many lonely nights in her big bed, and she might not have noticed. She moved down the three steps, through the practically impassible dining room and up two steps into the living room. And stopped dead as her outraged green eyes fell on John Patrick Blackheart lounging casually on her sofa, a glass of brandy in one hand, her discarded raincoat folded neatly on the glass-topped coffee table in front of him.

"What the hell are you doing here?" she demanded, breathless with rage, surprise, and something else that was curiously, infuriatingly close to joy.

"How many times have you asked me that?" Blackheart replied lazily, not moving. "I suppose as many times as I've broken in to your apartment. At this point I've lost count. On the other hand, this was your first attempt, wasn't it? What took you so long on the balcony? That lock should have been a piece of cake."

Ferris dumped her purse onto the floor, ignoring the stray shiver that crept across her body. "You knew I was out there? Of course you did," she answered her own question bitterly. "Why didn't you let me in?"

At this point Blackheart did rise, his lithe, elegant body graceful as always in black denim, a black turtleneck and an ancient tweed jacket. He shed his jacket, dropping it onto the small couch, and advanced toward her. "I thought since you'd gotten that far, I shouldn't deprive you of the triumph of breaking in. After that scramble through the ivy like Tarzan's Jane, you deserved some sort of reward."

"You saw me climbing up the building?" she asked in a carefully restrained tone of voice.

No one had ever thought Blackheart imperceptive. He kept advancing, but his eyes were wary, as if he knew just how dangerous Ferris Byrd was at that moment. "It was very impressive," he said softly. "I think my favorite moment was when you pulled that ridiculous excuse for a skirt halfway up to your waist. Though your descent into the garbage bin had to run a close second."

"You just stood there and watched?" She wanted to make absolutely certain she was understanding him correctly.

"Actually I sat there and watched from my car. It was pouring rain, you know."

"Blackheart," she said through gritted teeth. "I am going to stab you."

"No, you're not, dear heart," he said, moving almost within range of her decidedly murderous rage. "You're going to let me get you out of those wet clothes and ply you with brandy and coffee, and then you're going to let me warm you up properly, and by the time we're finished you'll realize how pleased you are at having broken into your apartment without breaking any laws."

"Don't touch me, Blackheart," she warned, backing away.

"It's been too long since I've touched you, Francesca," he murmured, his voice low and beguiling and completely irresistible. He kept on coming.

"Whose fault is that?" She tried to summon up her earlier outrage, her anger and confusion, but all she managed was a plaintive little cry.

"Mine," he said, reaching for her, his body now within inches of her wet, shivering one.

She batted at him, but his hands were strong, too strong, catching her shoulders and bringing her, willingly enough, to rest against his lean muscled warmth. He didn't kiss her, simply held her against him, held her until the shivering stopped and her tight muscles loosened, held her until her arms slid around his waist and she tilted her wet face upward.

And then a sigh left his body, as if he'd been holding his breath, and his mouth dropped onto hers, lightly, teasingly, arousing her with such immediacy that she was once more lost, lost—and resentful of that fact.

But right then her mind wasn't working too well. He'd already managed to unfasten the buttons on her silk shirt, and now he was pushing the wet material off her shoulders and down her arms, letting it drop in a sodden heap to the floor. He found the zipper of her skirt, and with one deft move had managed both to unzip and slide it along with her shredded panty hose down her long, wet legs. She stepped free of her clothing, clad only in peach silk bikini briefs and a lacy scrap of bra, and was shivering again, this time with something other than cold.

Blackheart slipped his deft, beautiful hands up her sides, cupping the generous breasts that spilled from the inadequate bra, and his tawny-brown eyes were hooded, his breathing was rapid, and his lips were thin with longing. "I missed you, Francesca," he whispered. "I missed you damnably."

In response she moved her trembling hands under the fine cotton knit of his turtleneck and began to draw it upward, her knees weak, ready to pull him down onto the floor and make love to him then and there, when a sudden pounding on her flimsy door broke into her consciousness, wiping away any desire and replacing it with fear.

She jumped away from him as if burned, her green eyes looking up into his in a sudden panic she couldn't hide. His own expression was rueful. "Don't look like that," he said gently. "As far as I know, no one's after me. Go get your robe on, and I'll answer the door."

Ferris ran, slamming her bedroom door behind her as she heard Blackheart head for the front door. She was shaking all over, both with frustration and a sudden, incomprehensible reaction that had nothing to do with the moment, that simply brought back another time, six months ago, when a peremptory rapping at her door had shattered the tenuous relationship she and Blackheart had just managed to build up.

He was right, of course. No one was after him just now. No one should have been after him back then, either, but he'd still ended up in jail. When a man spent half his adult life committing crimes, he was more than likely to spend the other half paying for them, in little ways or big ones.

It was something she had to learn to accept; she knew that. It was just at certain moments, moments like these, that all her good intentions vanished, and she felt vulnerable. And after thirty years of trying to protect herself, she didn't like feeling vulnerable one tiny bit.

She didn't pull on her robe. Now that Blackheart's hands were back where they belonged, she no longer felt so trusting. Before she went to bed with her long-lost fiancé, she wanted to find out exactly where he'd been for the last three weeks and for that matter, where he'd been disappearing to for the last several months. Somehow she needed to pry that information out of him without displaying an unflattering amount of distrust.

She pulled on a faded pair of jeans and another silk shirt over her slightly damp underwear, ran a brush through her wet tangle of brown-black hair, and headed for the doorway. She was foolish to be so paranoid, she told herself. Whoever had come pounding at her door could only be a nosy neighbor or an importunate salesperson.

She opened the bedroom door and moved lightly toward the sound of voices that was coming from the living room. "Who is it, Patrick?" she murmured, then stopped short. She knew, she just knew that all color had drained from her face and her heart had skidded to a stop, just as her body had.

"How can I help you, officer?" she managed in a deceptively calm voice, noting with distant relief that Blackheart's beautiful wrists were free of handcuffs. He was glaring at her, however, his narrow, clever face suddenly cold and distant, and she wondered if he'd been able to read her mind, read her sudden dread and distrust.

"He's come about the littering, Ferris," Blackheart said in a gentle voice. If she'd had any doubts about his anger, they had now vanished. He never called her Ferris unless he was very mad indeed.

"Littering?" she echoed, giving the uniformed officer her full attention. He was tall, bland and beefy, towering over Blackheart's five feet eleven inches by a sizable margin, and he looked both stern and embarrassed.

"Yes, ma'am. Someone dumped some garbage cans onto the street outside, someone answering your description. I wondered if you had anything to say about the matter."

"Give it up, Ferris," Blackheart drawled. "Clearly there's been an informer on the job."

"Probably Mrs. Melton from down the hallway," Ferris said bitterly. "She always sees what she's not supposed to see."

"She was probably having as good a time as I was watching you break in," Blackheart murmured.

"Break in?" the policeman questioned.

"To my own apartment," Ferris hastened to explain, returning Blackheart's glare. "That's how the garbage got spilled. I had to use the empty garbage can to climb up onto my balcony. I'll go down and clean up the mess."

"The city would appreciate that, miss," the cop said stolidly. "I'll let you off with a warning this time, but I wouldn't want it to happen again."

"Neither would I," Ferris said wholeheartedly.

The officer turned to leave, then paused, peering at Blackheart's shuttered face. "You look familiar to me," he said.

"Do I?" Blackheart's own tone was unpromising. "I guess I have that kind of looks."

"You sound foreign, too. English?"

Blackheart wasn't liking this one tiny bit. "Half-English," he said briefly. "I'm not the one who dumped the garbage can, officer."

"Such a gentleman," Ferris said sweetly.

But the policeman wouldn't be distracted. "I never forget a face. I must have seen you somewhere, and it's going to bug me until I remember where and when."

"Then for your sake I hope you'll remember soon," Blackheart said icily. "Was there anything else?"

"I'd better go down," Ferris said hurriedly, eager to break up what might turn into a nasty confrontation. She grabbed her coat from the couch and headed toward the door. "I'll be right back. Why don't you make me some coffee, Black—darling?"

Blackheart's face darkened even more. "Why don't you remember to wear shoes, if you're going out among the garbage again?" he countered.

Ferris stared down at her bare feet, then back at the glowering cop. "I left a pair down there," she said, taking the policeman's burly arm and pushing him, gently but forcibly, through the open door. "I'll be right back."

"Take your time," Blackheart said softly. "I'll be waiting."

THE SLENDER YOUNG WOMAN stood off to one side, leaning against the elegant seating that would soon be folded and packed in readiness for shipping across the Atlantic Ocean, through the Panama Canal to the west coast of the United States. She knew she was in the shadows; no one could see her expression as she watched the act in the center ring of the small, elite circus.

The Porcini Family Circus had been in existence for more than a hundred years. The current owner and latest to bear the name Porcini was high overhead, involved in his act. Marco Porcini was only an adequate aerialist, but he always managed to get the crowd to their feet, if not for his grace, then for his sheer arrogance. He would try anything, and the woman watching knew that if he ever fell, his reaction would be nothing more than astonishment.

She could hear the crowd ooh in anticipation. She looked up, way up, at the man who called himself her husband. She watched him as he edged his way across the narrow wire, digging her fingers into her palms, her heart pounding, her pale face beaded with sweat.

"Pretty dangerous tonight, eh?" Rocco, the old clown, had come up beside her and was following her gaze. "No net. Marco shouldn't count on having a charmed life."

"No," she said in a shaky voice. "He shouldn't."

"Don't worry, *cara*," Rocco said, patting her affectionately on the shoulder. "He'll be all right."

And Dany Bunce, better known as Danielle Porcini, looked up at the man high overhead, and prayed that he might fall.

Chapter Two

Suspicion
(MGM 1947)

The rain was pouring steadily, sliding down the neck of Ferris's raincoat. Her high-heeled pumps were even more uncomfortable on wet, bare feet, and several of the garbage bags had split when she'd tossed them indiscriminately onto the sidewalk. Gritting her teeth, she struggled and shoved and pushed the unwieldy bags back into the battered garbage can, rolling it back into the alley with a furious clang, all under the watchful, unhelpful eye of her disapproving patrolman. Through it all she cursed Blackheart under her breath.

The temperature had dropped with the setting sun, and it took all Ferris's determination to keep from shaking with cold as she stomped back into her building, up the narrow flight of stairs, the simmering heat of her anger the only thing warming her chilled body.

Blackheart was gone. "I'll be waiting," he'd told her. A lie. How many other lies had he told her?

At least he'd left the front door unlocked. If she'd come back to a locked apartment, it would have been the final straw. She slammed the door, snarling with rage as she surveyed the empty living room, then slowly, carefully secured all three locks. Not that it would stop Blackheart if he decided to show up again, but it would slow him down long enough for her to hear him and be waiting with a cast-iron frying pan or something equally daunting.

Stripping off her sodden clothes as she went, she headed straight for the bathroom and a long hot shower, determined to wash away the chill of the early-evening rain and the stink of the garbage from her skin. There was no way she could wash away the tension and anger that were eating into her heart.

The phone rang, but she ignored it as she pulled on a soft yellow sweat suit and braided her wet hair. If it was Blackheart calling with explanations or apologies, she wasn't ready to hear them.

"Who am I kidding?" she demanded of her reflection in the ornate gilt mirror she'd found at a flea market. "Blackheart never apologizes and he never explains. It's up to you to see if you can live with that."

The reflection looked skeptical. She stared back at her alter ego. Francesca's green eyes were shimmering with anger, while Ferris usually managed to keep a cool distant expression in hers. Francesca's generous mouth was soft and pale and vulnerable, while Ferris kept hers carefully lipsticked and slightly compressed. Francesca's high cheekbones and thick dark hair made her look like a passionate gypsy; Ferris's beautiful bones and carefully arranged hair made her look elegant and cared for.

Ferris sighed, staring back at the woman in the mirror. "Who the hell are you?" she demanded wearily. "And what is it you want in life?"

But her reflection had no answers for her. She turned away, ignoring the renewed ringing of the telephone, and went in search of dinner. If Blackheart wanted to talk to her, he'd have to come back. No one in Ferris's large family could hold a candle to her when it came to stubbornness, and if Blackheart thought he could outlast her determination, then he was mistaken.

Curse him, he'd almost finished her brandy. And she simply wasn't in the mood for frozen gourmet dinners. There was no ice cream to speak of in the freezer, only three nearly empty Double Rainbow containers with frosty teaspoons of refrozen ice cream slimed into the bottom.

She settled for Rice Chex, carrying a huge bowl and her brandy snifter into the living room and sinking onto the love seat. She wasn't in the mood for the evening news, half afraid of what she might hear, and she hadn't bought a VCR, despite her love of old movies. It simply didn't make sense when she was about to move in with and marry a man who owned the Cadillac of VCRs. But right then and there she would have given a great deal to snuggle down in her oversize bed with Alfred Hitchcock.

She looked down at the ring on her hand. She'd flatly refused to wear emeralds—they had too many unhappy memories. Blackheart had insisted that diamonds were too cold for her, but he'd settled for a large canary diamond in a beautiful, old-fashioned setting. She seldom took it off, but every now and then she wondered where he'd obtained it, and if it was left over from his ill-gotten gains.

She finished the mixing bowl of cereal, shoving the empty dish under the couch, then heard the footsteps approaching her door. *Not Blackheart,* she thought, listening, ignoring the sinking feeling of disappointment. He was so light on his feet that no one could ever hear him coming. He'd already taken years off her life by sneaking up on her. If he was coming back he wouldn't approach her door with that even measured tread; he'd simply materialize like the Cheshire cat.

She considered ignoring the polite knocking, but like another kind of cat, she was intensely curious. The brandy and cereal had gone some way toward soothing her temper, and the knowledge that Blackheart was back in town, albeit not with her, was an added relief. At least if he was in San Francisco, he couldn't be in the great cities of Europe and couldn't be involved in the sudden, inexplicable rash of jewel thefts that were reminding the authorities of the heyday of the notorious Blackheart and son. Slowly, languidly she pulled herself from the couch and headed for the door.

The middle-aged man standing there looked like a jockey. He came up to her collarbone and not much farther, and he was slightly bowlegged. Instead of jockey's silks, however, he was wearing what looked like a chauffeur's uniform.

"Ms. Berdahofski?" he inquired politely in a voice tinged with the rich, meaty sound of a cockney accent.

No one but Blackheart could have sent him, she decided then and there, ignoring the rush of relief that swept through her. Everyone else still called her by her acquired name, and while she'd been trying to change it back, she was still too diffident to push it. "Yes," she agreed warily.

"I'm Simmons, ma'am. I have a car waiting for you. Compliments of Mr. Blackheart."

"What kind of car?" A ridiculous question, but she was stalling for time. She was also curious to find out how far Blackheart was willing to go to woo her.

"A Bentley, ma'am. The Rolls is being worked on."

She'd never ridden in either of England's fabled limousines. Even in her heyday, when she'd been engaged to State Senator Phillip Merriam, of the very moneyed California Merriams, she'd only managed Cadillacs and Lincolns. Phillip might have preferred British luxury or German engineering, but he knew where his constituency lay, and buying American was almost a second religion with him.

"All right," she said, throwing caution and hurt feelings to the wind. "Let me get my coat."

"I'll wait in the hall while you change, miss."

It was a gentle hint, but Ferris was having none of it. "He'll take me as I am," she said sweetly, "or he can do without."

The chauffeur allowed himself a small grin. "Blackheart's never been a fool, and I've known him for a long time. I'm ready when you are, miss."

The Bentley was a definite treat. Simmons settled her into the upholstered leather seat, handed her a sheaf of creamy-white roses, and began to open a bottle of champagne that had been left chilling in an ice bucket. He was oblivious to the rain pouring off his peaked cap, removing the cork with such efficiency that the quiet pop was barely audible. The champagne was Moët, the fluted glass he poured it into was Waterford, the woven lap robe he tucked around her legs was cashmere.

The engine purred softly when Simmons turned the key, the minor noise quickly overridden by the lilting strains of Mozart as he deftly pulled into traffic. Ferris sat back and laughed out loud, taking a sip of the deliciously chilly Moët. "Is this a package deal, Simmons?" she inquired in her most caustic voice. "Or did Blackheart have time to arrange all this in just the last hour or so?"

"Blackheart wouldn't use a package deal, miss," he said, deeply offended. "He's been planning this for a long time. Just had to wait till the moment was ripe, he told me."

"You mean he wanted to wait until I was so mad he had to use extraordinary measures to placate me. I'm not placated, Simmons. You can tell him so."

"Yes, ma'am." Simmons grinned at her reflection in the rearview mirror. "You like that champagne?"

Ferris noticed she'd drained her glass. "Love it," she said, reaching for the bottle and pouring herself another.

"Can't stand the stuff meself," said Simmons. "Give me a good dark ale any day, that's the ticket. None of the frenchified stuff. I never could understand how a decent lad like Blackheart could abide it."

"How long have you known Blackheart?" she inquired lazily, ignoring the streets of San Francisco speeding by beyond the smoked glass windows.

"Since he was a lad. His father used to bring him out to the racetrack when I was still a jockey. Blackheart senior used to like to play the ponies, and young Blackheart had a real gift for it. He's always been lucky, miss."

"Not always," she said, breathing in the rich, delicious scent of the white roses. "He spent six months in jail after he fell."

"Some would say it could have been a lot worse. They weren't able to pin a whole lot on him. There are people who think he got off too easy by half. But then, there's a lot of judgmental people around. I just likes to let things be. Live and let live, that's my motto."

"What was Blackheart like as a child?" she asked, unable to restrain her curiosity. "Did you know what his father did for a living?"

"Everyone knew. It was sort of a gentleman's agreement—no one ever mentioned it, but everyone knew. Not the toffs, I don't think. I can't believe they'd have kept on inviting him into their homes if they'd known he was going to rob them, but then, I can't be certain. The British upper classes are a strange lot, take my word for it. Blackheart was a good lad. A little wild, a little old for his age.

He loved his old man, he loved his baby sister, and there it ended.''

Ferris sat bolt upright, slopping some of the precious Moët onto the cashmere lap robe. "Sister? I didn't know he had any sisters."

Simmons's face darkened, and he ducked his head. "Just the one, miss. I don't remember what happened to her. Don't tell Blackheart I mentioned her. I don't think it's a very happy memory for him."

"Sorry, Simmons. I'm in a bad mood—I'm not going to make promises to anyone," she said firmly, draining the champagne.

"I understand, miss. But don't be too hard on Blackheart. He's going through a difficult time, if you know what I mean."

"No," she said. "I don't know what you mean. Explain."

Simmons had pulled the huge limousine to a halt outside Blackheart's apartment building. "We're here, miss," he announced, his cockney voice thick with relief.

"I could refuse to budge until you tell me more. There's most of the bottle of champagne back here, and I'm very comfortable."

"Please, miss," Simmons said, sweat standing out on his lined forehead. "Give me a break. If you have questions, ask Blackheart."

There lay the answer, she thought, and the problem. She didn't want to ask Blackheart; she wanted him to volunteer the information. The few times she'd tried to elicit information from him, he'd slithered away from her questions like an eel, and it hadn't been until hours later that she realized he'd never told her a thing.

That would have to change tonight. He could ply her with champagne and white roses and Bentleys, he could

put those beautiful hands on her, and she would remain
adamant. No matter what he said or did, she wasn't going
to give in to the almost obsessive longing that assailed her
whenever she was near him, whenever she even thought
about him. If there was to be any hope for their future, she
was going to need some answers.

Simmons had opened the door and was standing there
patiently, holding a huge black umbrella to keep off the
pouring rain. She half expected him to whip off his jacket
and lay it in the puddled gutter, but he contented himself
with holding out a small-boned hand to help her out of the
car.

Blackheart's building wavered and drifted behind the
curtain of rain. Ferris looked up at the brightly lighted
windows, wondering for the thousandth time whether she
could ever feel at home there.

That was the least of her worries right now, she reminded herself as she slipped out of the car, the white roses
still clutched in her hands, a twisting, nervous feeling in the
pit of her stomach. She had to get through the next few
hours first. After that, she could worry about the rest of
her life.

DANIELLE LAY VERY STILL in the narrow bunk, clutching
her stomach, breathing through her mouth as her body
tried to adjust itself to the rolls and dips of the ocean far
beneath her. She hated the sea, hated tiny dinghies, small
sailboats, large yachts and massive ocean liners. Most of
all she hated smelly diesel freighters that crawled across the
vast, almost endless Atlantic Ocean, crammed with the
contents of the Porcini Family Circus. There were elephants, tigers and lions in the hold of the ship, horses and
monkeys and even seals. The smell on a hot day near the
equator didn't bear thinking about.

There were acrobats and jugglers and clowns, aerialists and sword swallowers and bareback riders, all vying for space on the crowded freighter. Marco Porcini didn't believe in pampering anyone but himself, and Star of Hoboken had clearly seen better days.

The ship rolled to the left, and Danielle emitted a small groan. They were nearing the Panama Canal on their interminable voyage from Madrid to the west coast of the United States.

She heard the door open, but didn't bother to look up. It could only be Marco—no one else would dare enter the one decent cabin the Star of Hoboken boasted without knocking.

"Get up, Danielle."

She didn't bother to open her eyes. "If I get up I'll die."

"I don't care. We want to use the bed."

At that point simple curiosity made Dany open her eyes. Marco Porcini was standing there, luxuriant black hair slicked down, bedroom eyes cold and assessing, thick-lipped mouth tightly compressed. Lurking behind him, looking both nervous and excited, was the new girl he'd hired to repair costumes.

Dany sat up, still clutching her roiling stomach. "Don't you think this will put the lie to our little farce of a happy marriage?" she inquired in her sweetest voice.

Marco smiled. "Of course not. Only if you were foolish enough to say something. And you are seldom stupid, little one."

If there was anything Dany hated it was to be called "Little one." But if Marco could smile, so could she. "What about her?" She gestured toward the nervous-looking girl.

"She wouldn't dare. Would you, darling?" he inquired over his shoulder. The girl shook her head, biting her lip.

Dany swung her legs over the bunk, pausing for a moment as the room spun around her. For a brief moment she prayed that she would throw up all over Marco's shiny black shoes, but she'd thrown up so much in the last few days that there was nothing left in her stomach. She climbed off the bunk, gave the happy couple a weak smile, and headed out the door.

"And Danielle—" Marco called after her.

Dany paused. The girl had already gone into the cabin and was methodically, unemotionally stripping off her clothes. She was out of earshot, but even so Marco lowered his rather high-pitched voice. "If you behave yourself in San Francisco," he murmured, "if all goes as I've planned it, I just might let you go."

She stared up at him, for a brief moment allowing her hatred to fill her eyes. "You promised me," she whispered.

Marco shrugged. "We'll see how you behave."

She didn't move. "This is my last job for you, Marco. If you don't let me go," she said quite calmly, "I'll kill you."

"You could always try. Maybe you'll have better luck next time."

"Next time," Dany said, her voice fierce, "I won't miss."

BLACKHEART STOOD in the doorway of his kitchen, waiting. He'd seen her arguing with Alf Simmons, seen her hold her ground in the Bentley, and he could feel himself smiling ruefully. He should have known it wouldn't be that easy. Francesca wasn't the type to be dazzled into submission by limousines and champagne and roses. The candlelight dinner he'd planned probably wouldn't do the trick, either. He could tell by the defiant tilt of her head, even from the distance of his fifth-floor apartment, that she was looking for trouble.

Looking for answers would be the way she viewed it. Unfortunately this time the two were synonymous. And he was faced with the choice between two evils: having her furious and distrustful, suspecting the worst, or having her know, and thereby endangering any chance he had for success.

No. He'd made his decision, and he'd abide by it. Even if he had to put up with fury, sulks and a constant barrage of questions, he wasn't going to tell her until he was ready. The worst aspect of it all was her lack of trust, but that was always there, whether she had any reason for it or not.

It would have been wonderful, he thought, leaning against the doorjamb, if she'd simply trust him, took him at his word.... *No.* She didn't even have to get to that point, if she just knew he wouldn't do anything wrong and never felt the need to question.

But life wasn't that neat and comfortable. And in fact, he'd been doing a great many illegal things in the weeks he'd been away from her. She'd have too hard a time living with that, so instead she was going to have to live with her own damned lack of trust. He wasn't going to lie to her, he wasn't going to tell her the truth. So they were stuck in a stalemate.

That night, however, he had no intention of giving her a chance to ask those unanswerable questions. If it hadn't been for that damned cop, he would be sound asleep in her arms right now, instead of worrying about placating her. Tonight he needed her, needed her with something bordering on desperation. He needed her lush, sweet body, her warm arms wrapped around him, he needed forgetfulness and comfort and that almost unbelievable release that only she could offer. In bed they communicated perfectly, in

bed she trusted him completely. And that was where he had
every intention of taking her, as soon as he possibly could.

The damp weather was making his leg ache, reminding
him of a bad fall and too many operations. He rubbed it
absently, listening for the sound of the elevator, listening
for the sound of her footsteps in the hallway. For a moment the brief, delicious vision of her scrambling up the
side of her building in a miniskirt assailed him. And then
he pushed himself away from the wall and headed for the
door. If she was still waiting in the Bentley, he'd throw her
over his shoulder and carry her upstairs. Three weeks was
too damned long.

Chapter Three

Shadow of a Doubt
(Universal 1943)

"It's nice to see you dressed for the occasion." Blackheart's faintly British voice was a low drawl from across the candlelit room. Ferris held her ground just inside the doorway, feeling both vulnerable and faintly absurd, still clutching the bouquet of white roses like a Miss America contestant, wearing her pale yellow sweat suit and running shoes instead of a strapless evening gown and high heels.

She could see a table for two, set with crystal and china and silver candlesticks. She could smell the delicious scent of broiled chicken and could see the rain lashing against the windows outside, while inside all was warmth and comfort. She steeled herself against the insidious effect John Patrick Blackheart always had on her, but all she had to do was look at him to know she was fighting a losing battle.

Blackheart wasn't spectacularly tall, nor spectacularly handsome, nor even spectacularly kind. But he had a wiry, catlike grace that enabled him to leap tall buildings in a single bound, insinuate himself into the oddest of places, and sneak up on his fiancée when she least expected it. He wore his dark brown hair too long, the humor that twisted his sensual mouth was occasionally at someone's else's expense, and his tawny-brown eyes were distant, cool and assessing—except when they looked at her, as they were doing now, and then they warmed to an almost blazing heat.

"I didn't realize this was a formal occasion," she said, stepping into the room and closing the door behind her.

"It's whatever you want it to be," he murmured, his voice sliding down her backbone like a hawk's feather. "What happened to Alf?"

"I sent him home with the rest of the champagne, even though he said he'd rather have Guinness than Moët. We had an interesting talk about your childhood on the way over."

He didn't like that, not one tiny bit, she realized, but was making every effort to control his annoyance. "I expect it was very boring. Why don't you set those flowers down and come here?"

"Because I don't trust myself within touching distance of you," she said frankly, setting down the roses anyway.

"Don't trust yourself?" he said softly. "Or me?"

The room was very quiet. He'd started a fire in his fireplace, and the soft hiss and crackle of dry wood blended with the tap-tap of the rain against the windows. Ferris opened her mouth to speak, then shut it again. The moment of truth was at hand. It was a perfect opening for all the questions, all the doubts. All she had to do was ask.

"I trust you, Blackheart," she said.

He moved toward her then, his face in shadow, unreadable, his body taut with a tension she couldn't begin to understand. "No, you don't," he said, putting his hands on her, his devilish, wonderful hands. "But right now I don't care."

All her sanity and good intentions flew out the window at the touch of his hands on her shoulders. The heat burned through the fleece of her sweat suit, the scent of roses mingled with the wood smoke and coffee and dinner, and Blackheart was so close to her that she could feel the heat, the tension thrumming through him. *Neither do I,* she thought, half believing it. But she couldn't say the words out loud, couldn't give him that much solace.

Instead she slipped her arms around his neck and kissed him, her mouth soft and full of promise. He groaned deep in his throat, and then there was no longer any room for doubt, trust or conscious thought. He pushed her gently back against the wall, and in one swift movement he'd stripped the sweatshirt from her willing body. She kicked off her sneakers, the loose pants followed, and she stood there in a lavender silk teddy and nothing else.

"You dressed for the occasion, after all," Blackheart murmured in her ear, his hands possessive and dangerous on her suddenly heated skin.

She wanted to deny it. She made one last attempt, catching his long, clever hands at her waist and stopping their errant path along her sensitized body. "No, Blackheart," she whispered, her voice a raw thread of sound. "Please don't."

He was suddenly very still, his hands hard and motionless within hers. "No?" he echoed, his voice quizzical. "I've never forced a woman in my life, Francesca, and I'm certainly not about to start with you." Still his hands didn't move; he stayed where he was, inches, millimeters from her, his body a promise. And a threat.

She recognized the threat for what it was—a threat of mindless, almost frightening pleasure. The threat of losing herself, when she'd only just found herself. The threat of becoming so caught up in John Patrick Blackheart that she'd cease to exist.

"No?" he murmured, his voice like silk.

At the that moment she hated him, hated the power he had over her. But most of all she hated herself for giving in to that power. "Yes," she said, closing her eyes and leaning against him, her slender body trembling. "Yes, Blackheart. Anything."

He hesitated for only a moment, and a distant part of her wanted to open her eyes to see his expression. Would it be triumphant or troubled? Or both? And then he scooped her up in his strong arms, lifting her high against his chest. "Not anything, Francesca." His voice was rough with promise. "Everything."

He reached behind her and flicked off the lights, so that the living room was bathed in the fitful glow of firelight and candlelight. He set her on the big, comfortable sofa, following her down, his mouth catching, teasing hers, so that she could ask no more questions, make no more promises of a trust she couldn't deliver, voice no more doubts. Quickly, efficiently he stripped off his clothes, then his body covered hers.

She ran her hands up his arms, her fingers caressing the taut muscles, and she shifted beneath him, her body instinctively ready to accommodate his, her long legs ready to wrap themselves around him, her hips ready to rise in mute supplication. She kept her eyes tightly shut, but her hands were growing more and more fevered, clutching at him as she kissed him back with a kind of desperate frenzy that had only something to do with love.

He pulled his mouth away, and she could feel his breath on her upturned face, warm and sweet and tasting of brandy and coffee and Blackheart. "Slow down," he whispered. "This isn't a race. We can take our time...."

But that was just what Ferris was afraid of. "No," she murmured. "I want you. Now." She tugged at him, trying to pull him on top of her, but he caught her hands in his, shifting to the side, holding her still.

"Open your eyes, Francesca." His voice was low, his tone inexorable. She tried to turn away, to hide her face against the rough cotton of the sofa, but his hand beneath her chin wouldn't let her. "Open your eyes."

She had no choice but to obey. She had no doubt he'd see the tears swimming in her eyes—the dim glow of the firelight would only make them shine. She had no doubt he'd see the fear and distrust there. Blackheart had always seen her far too clearly for her own peace of mind.

"Oh, Francesca," he whispered, his face in shadow, his voice weary and very, very sad. "What have I done to you? What have I done to yourself?"

She tried to summon up a smile, but it was a miserable failure. "We need to talk."

"Yes," said Blackheart. "But not now."

She could feel her heart beating at a rapid, headlong pace that matched his. His skin was a white gold in the firelight, shadow and light and dancing shadows gilding his flesh. "Not now," she agreed, her voice a mere thread of sound.

He reached down and unsnapped the teddy, pulling it away and sending it sailing across the room. His body covered hers, shutting out the light, and he entered her, driving deep with a swift, sure stroke that left her breathless.

She made a small, whimpering noise in the back of her throat, but she was ready, desperate for him. Her hands clutched at him, fingers digging in, and her mouth met his in a sudden, frenzied seeking.

His hands framed her face, pushing the cloud of hair away from her tear-streaked cheeks as his mouth caressed, aroused and promised.

It had been too long. She convulsed around him almost immediately, her heart beating in spasms, her body rigid, and he held her, waiting, his hands impossibly tender, until she was past the first peak and ready for more.

He knew her body so well. He knew when to go slowly, to give her time to accustom herself to his alien presence. He knew when to go fast, to build up the tempo until she was ready to scream. He knew when to be gentle, when the softest of touches was exquisite pleasure. And he knew when to be rough, when gentle pressure wasn't what she needed at all.

There were times when she resented his control, but just then she was beyond rational thought. As he began to move again and began the inexorable buildup, she simply wrapped her arms and legs around him and held on, lost, as always, in the wonder and mystery of making love with John Patrick Blackheart.

But even Blackheart's control wasn't absolute. She could feel him tremble in her arms, feel the sweat that covered his back as he struggled to keep the pace of his driving thrusts steady. But it had been three long weeks for him, too, of that she had no doubt, and when the second peak hit her Blackheart was with her, rigid in her arms, his voice rasping in her ear, whispering something she couldn't hear as she found herself in that now-familiar darkness that was both haven and menace.

She would have fallen asleep if he'd let her. But when his heartbeat slowed to a semblance of normalcy, when his breathing was no longer labored, he pulled away, ignoring her clinging arms.

The lamp beside the couch glared as he switched it on. He sat at her feet, calmly ignoring his nudity, and stared at her, his eyes dark and shadowed. "All right, Francesca," he said, resigned. "Let's have it."

She lay there for a moment, wanting to postpone the inevitable. Finally she pulled herself into a sitting position, grabbing his discarded chambray shirt from the floor and wrapping it around her. Maybe he could have a discussion like this in the nude, but she was feeling vulnerable after the last half hour. She needed all the defenses she could muster. Even if her only defense was a soft cotton shirt that smelled all too enticingly of Blackheart.

"Where were you?" The question came out accusingly, but she couldn't help it. "Why didn't you tell me where you were going? Why didn't you call me?"

He shut his eyes, leaning his head back against the sofa with a pained expression. And then he turned to look at her, his face remote and guileless. "I had business."

"Business."

He must have known her reaction wasn't promising. "In Europe," he added. "It came up suddenly, and there was too much involved for me to be in touch. Kate was supposed to let you know what was happening."

"Your secretary has never liked me and she never will," Ferris said flatly. "Where in Europe?"

"London."

"That's all?"

"I can show you my passport if you need proof," he snapped.

Ferris flinched. "I'm sorry. I didn't mean to cross-examine you."

"Didn't you?" His voice was cool. "What else did you want to know? I'm not going to tell you about the case. It's private information, and if you can't live with that . . ."

"I can live with that," she said in a low voice. "As long as it has nothing to do with me."

"It has nothing to do with you."

"Are you going to make a habit of that? Of just disappearing with no warning, no explanation?" She huddled deeper into the sofa, waiting for him to destroy her future.

He hesitated. "No," he said finally. "This was unusual. I wish I could tell you what was going on, but this time you're just going to have to trust me."

A simple enough request of a woman in love, Ferris thought miserably, hating herself. "Of course," she said, lying.

"You can tell me one thing," he drawled, and she knew enough to hate that tone of voice. "Exactly what did you think I was doing the last three weeks?"

"I hadn't the faintest idea."

"I don't suppose you were aware of the fact that there has been a rash of burglaries in Lisbon and Madrid during that time."

He couldn't see the guilty color stain her face—the bright pool of light beside him cast it into shadow. Didn't it? "I hadn't realized that," she lied easily. And then the question slipped out when she least expected it. "Did you have anything to do with them?"

She couldn't believe she'd actually asked him that. She sat motionless, waiting for the ax to fall.

Blackheart's reaction was surprisingly sanguine. "Such trust," he murmured. "No, Francesca. I didn't."

At least he still called her Francesca. If he were really angry with her he would have called her Ferris. He was looking at her quite calmly, expectantly.

"I'm sorry. I shouldn't have asked that."

"No, you shouldn't have."

She looked at him, guilt and something else twisting inside her, something she didn't want to examine too closely. She looked at him and didn't believe him.

"Is that all?"

"Yes," she said.

"Then let's go to bed."

She could think of a million reasons not to, but not one rose to her lips. She just sat there, waiting, and he leaned over, brushing the wetness of tears from her cheeks. "Come to bed with me, Francesca," he said again, his voice low and loving. "We can work this out tomorrow."

"Tomorrow," she agreed, ignoring her better judgment. He held out his hand, and she placed her smaller one in his, noting its whiteness against his, his long, clever fingers, flat palm, strong wrist. She lifted his hand against her face, holding it there as she let out a pent-up breath. "Tomorrow," she said.

MARCO WAS LYING, Dany thought, shivering beneath the light raincoat as she leaned over the railing. He couldn't tell the truth if his life depended on it. But whether he intended it or not, this was going to be the last time she helped him. She'd been a miserable, sniveling coward for too long. This endless time on the ocean had done more than make her horribly sick. It had given her the chance to think, to realize that she didn't have to be a victim. After this last job was over, she was going to walk away. America was a very big country—it should be a simple enough matter to lose one small female in its vastness. Particularly if that one small female had enough money.

She'd help him on this last job, for several reasons. The most important was that she needed enough money to escape. She wouldn't get very far on the pesetas she had rattling around in her pocket. America was big but it was expensive, and she needed her share, whether Marco gave it willingly or not.

She also had an old score to settle. A lifelong grievance that she'd finally be able to settle added to the allure of this last, dangerous enterprise, and she intended to take full advantage of that fact. When it was over she'd be gone, her purse full of American dollars, Marco Porcini would be richer but missing his helpful patsy, and her nemesis would be ruined. Her only regret was that she wouldn't be able to wait around and watch as John Patrick Blackheart got what he deserved.

But then, life was never that convenient. All that mattered was that life finally evened things out a bit. Blackheart would rot in jail, and Dany Bunce, better known as Danielle Porcini, would finally have revenge. It was enough to make her smile for one brief moment before the ocean shifted and her stomach shifted with it. Soon it would all be over. It couldn't be soon enough.

FERRIS SLOWLY OPENED HER EYES. The rain had stopped, the bedroom was shrouded in darkness, and only the faint light of approaching dawn was to be seen over the city rooftops. Ferris looked at those rooftops and shuddered in memory.

She squinted at the bedside clock. Blackheart hated digital clocks, but the round dial with the small gilt hands was too difficult to see in the predawn light. She shifted slightly in the navy-blue sheets, turning to look at the man sleeping beside her.

He was lying on his stomach, his arms over his head, his long brown hair rumpled. Like all men he looked innocent and boyish in sleep, years younger than the thirty-eight that he admitted to. At some point during the endless, too-brief night she'd scratched his back, and a blush rose to her cheeks as she looked at the shallow red marks. She tried to remember when she'd done it, but the whole night had dissolved into a mindless blur of pleasure. But done it she had, during the second, or maybe it was the third time they'd made love. Probably the third, she thought. The second had been slow, gentle, languorous, reminding each of them that they were in love. The third had been full of resurfacing anger and doubt, and they'd taken it out on each other, ending spent and lonely in the big bed.

She put out a hand and ran it ever so softly along the smooth warm skin of his back. He barely stirred. She leaned down, resting her cheek against one shoulder blade, and he murmured something approving in his sleep, shifting to take her into his arms.

Instead she scuttled away, not without deep regret, and he settled once more into a sound sleep, barely aware of her absence as she slipped from the bed and padded silently into the bathroom.

The long hot shower did wonders to improve her equilibrium. As she surveyed her damp reflection in Blackheart's steamed-up mirror, she could almost convince herself that she was immune to her fiancé's charm, that the last few questions could be dealt with over coffee and something, anything to eat.

She suddenly realized she was famished. She could only hope Blackheart had something better than moldy bread and beer in his refrigerator. She knew for a fact that he'd left the chicken out all night, making it a dangerous possibility for breakfast, but if there was nothing else she'd risk salmonella for the sake of her empty stomach.

She grabbed Blackheart's navy-blue terry bathrobe and wrapped it around her, then searched for a comb.

He'd left his leather shaving kit on the back of the toilet. Without even a moment's hesitation she dived into it, searching for something to tame her thick wet hair.

At first glance she didn't notice anything unusual. Inside the large leather bag were the usual toiletries. Blackheart favored a single-edged razor, a shaving brush and soap, a British shampoo and an organic toothpaste. For some reason he'd left his passport in the bottom of the leather bag, and she stared it for a long moment, considering the value of trust versus the comfort of certainty.

She knew she shouldn't do it. She knew she was going to do it, anyway. She started to move a small zippered case out of the way of the passport, then stopped, staring at the thing in her hand as if it were a dead slug.

It looked like a manicure kit. When she unzipped it that was what she'd find, she told herself. When it came right down to it, she didn't need to unzip it to prove that he had never replaced the picklocks he'd sworn he wouldn't need again. She didn't need to check his passport to know he'd been to England and only England and nowhere near Madrid or Lisbon and the recent rash of jewel robberies. She could put everything back, walk out of the bathroom and take him on blind faith.

She unzipped the small leather pouch. She knew picklocks when she saw them—she'd broken half his previous set in an amateurish attempt at breaking and entering.

And it was with a curious deadness in her heart and no surprise whatsoever that she opened his navy-blue passport and read the entry stamp from Madrid, Spain, dated two weeks ago.

"Learn anything interesting?" Blackheart inquired from the open door, his face an unreadable mask.

"Enough," said Ferris. "How many people have you robbed?"

He'd pulled on a pair of jeans but hadn't bothered with a shirt. She'd scratched his chest as well as his back, she noticed absently, and there were love bites on his neck. He opened the door wider, and there was no expression on his face at all. "I lost count years ago, Ferris. Why do you ask?"

"Thief."

"You already knew that."

"Liar," she added, some of the ice cracking around her heart.

"That should come as no surprise either," he said coolly. "You want to tell me some more about how much you trust me?"

"Do you want to tell me you haven't robbed anyone these last few weeks?"

"You wouldn't believe anything I told you. You've made up your mind. Hell, I've faced more impartial judges in my time."

"I'm sure you have. You're so good at manipulating people."

"But not you."

"No," said Ferris. She took off the canary diamond ring and set it on the sink. "Not me. Goodbye, Blackheart."

He could have said something sarcastic, considering she was standing in his bathroom wearing his bathrobe and nothing else. But he didn't. "Goodbye, Ferris," he said, the phony name saying everything. And shut the bathroom door.

Chapter Four

The Man Who Knew Too Much
(Paramount 1956)

For five days Ferris Byrd did nothing but drink coffee, pick at her food when she remembered she was supposed to eat, and brood. Everywhere she turned in her apartment she could see the piles of boxes, a nasty reminder of her shattered plans. Even Blackie seemed to think she'd made a terrible mistake. Not even Brie at the perfect stage of ripeness could tempt his finicky appetite. He showed up just long enough to hunch his shoulders at his mistress with a perfect display of contempt before taking off into the streets once more. And Ferris had nothing to cry into but her pillow.

At least she wasn't due in to work. In one of her more stupid moves, right up there with falling in love with John Patrick Blackheart, Ferris had taken a job as director of the Committee for Saving the Bay. *Babysitting socialites,* Blackheart had called it, and he wasn't far off the mark. But with the termination of her engagement to Phillip Merriam had come the end of her job as his administrative assistant, and the ensuing publicity of the whole Von Emmerling affair had made her profile a little too high for the discreet sort of employment she fancied. So she'd taken what she could get, herding a bunch of good-hearted but basically inefficient women through their charitable duties, fund-raising events such as balls, theater benefits and auctions. While this raft of unpaid assistants managed to arrange dinner parties for twenty-four and direct the running of mansions and their childrens' lives, most of them had never held a paying job and they were unused to some of the practicalities of life as most people lived it.

It was Ferris's job, as the only salaried employee, to herd her ladies through these shark-infested waters, and to do so with tact and diplomacy.

Right then she didn't feel terribly tactful or diplomatic. Fortunately the committee closed its offices at the drop of a hat, and September offered horse racing in Santa Barbara, yacht racing in Santa Cruz, and changing leaves any place one cared to look for them. So Ferris could spend five days holed up in her apartment, coming to terms with the shambles of her life, and no one would even miss her.

By the time Monday rolled around and Ferris, her social armor fully in place, made it in to work, she'd moved from despair and anorexia to something far more satisfying: anger and gluttony. Everyone had heard, of course. And everyone was very kind, very tactful, though Regina Merriam, Ferris's favorite person in the world and the major reason she'd once considered marrying her son, State Senator Phillip Merriam, had taken her to task about it.

Regina strode into Ferris's uncharacteristically neat office, her faded blue eyes blazing, her Calvin Klein suit hanging on her somewhat bony frame. "What's this I hear about you and Patrick?"

Ferris swallowed the jelly doughnut she'd shoved into her mouth and managed a disinterested smile as she wiped the powdered sugar from her face. "Word gets around fast," she said.

"Of course it does. Patrick's a particular friend of mine. As are you. Anything that concerns the two of you would be bound to reach my ears sooner or later."

"Sooner," Ferris grumbled. "It's only been five days."

"Ferris, are you certain you aren't making a very great mistake?" Regina said earnestly. "I can't believe there could be an insurmountable problem between you and Blackheart. You two are made for each other."

"No, we're not." Ferris's voice was very firm.

Regina didn't bother to hide her skepticism. "I'm assuming this breakup was your idea? I have too high an opinion of Blackheart's intelligence to think him capable of such a mistake."

"Thanks a lot."

"Blackheart's a man who recognizes true love when he sees it. He wouldn't let pride or misunderstanding get in his way."

"Neither would I."

"Then why...?"

Ferris pressed a hand to her temple, leaving a trail of powdered sugar in her dark hair. There was no way she was going to tell Regina that Blackheart was on the prowl again. "I'm not going to offer any justification or explanation, Regina. We simply decided it wasn't going to work. Blackheart's free to pursue his own interests." *Cat burgling,* she added mentally. "As am I." She stared morosely at her jelly doughnuts.

Regina shook her head, clearly unconvinced. "I hope it doesn't take you too long to see reason. You're not getting any younger, darling, and fertility decreases after you're thirty."

"Regina!"

"Though I did have Phillip when I was thirty-seven. And look how he turned out," she added gloomily, twirling her perfectly matched string of pearls.

"Regina, Phillip is charming."

"I know. Charming, handsome, kindly, manipulative and shallow. The perfect politician. It's a good thing he never had to work for a living. Though I suppose he could always be a salesman."

"What would he say if he heard you talk like this?" Ferris was both amused and appalled by Regina's customary plain speaking.

"But he has. Many times. And he thinks I'm a meddling, hard-hearted old woman who ought to support him with the mindless adoration of his constituents. We still adore each other. I just wish he'd find someone like you to marry and give me grandchildren."

"He did," Ferris pointed out. "He found me."

"But you weren't in love with him. He needs someone with your combination of brains, ambition and warmth, but he needs it tempered by love. Someone to keep from taking the easy way out."

Ferris added guilt to all the negative emotions assailing her. "Regina, I thought I loved him."

"Of course you did. He's really very lovable. But he wasn't right for you. John Patrick Blackheart is. And nothing you say can convince me otherwise."

"I won't even try." Ferris reached for another doughnut and stuffed half of it into her mouth. "Did you have anything else you wanted to tell me, or were you just here to chastise me about my love life?"

Regina grinned. "I suppose I'll have to leave it to you to come to your senses. Or to Patrick. He can be very persuasive."

"Not this time." In fact he hadn't even tried. No phone calls, no notes, no sudden appearances in her apartment when she least expected it. Blackheart had taken the severing of their relationship with perfect equanimity, and she told herself that was relief burning in the pit of her stomach and at the back of her eyes. Regina was right, he was very persuasive indeed. And if he'd had any interest in persuading her, she might have a very hard time resisting.

"As a matter of fact I did have something for you. I wanted to make sure the permits are all in order for our next fund-raising extravaganza. It's only eight days away."

"They're in order," Ferris replied. "My love life might be a mess, but at least I'm efficient. Why do you ask?"

"Efficient, yes, but you're getting forgetful in your old age," the ageless Regina said with a smirk. "Who do you think is arriving today?"

"I haven't the faintest—" Ferris smacked her forehead in disgust. "Of course. The Porcini Family Circus."

"All set for Circus Night for the Bay. We were lucky to get them, you know."

"I know we were. I still can't imagine why they offered. Not that it matters. Do you need any help on the reception?"

"All under control. Just show up tonight and smile." Regina reached out and snatched the final jelly doughnut from Ferris's grasp. "Circuses are supposed to be fun."

DANY SURVEYED her motel room with profound distaste. She'd never been in America before, and what she saw she didn't like. Everything was very new, very clean, very plastic. She'd take a tacky hotel room in Paris any day— paint peeling, water-stained walls, lumpy mattress—rather than this soulless perfection.

She listened to Marco moving around in the room next door. The connecting door was closed, and she wished she dared lock it. It would have been an absurd gesture— Marco could get through the most challenging of locks with effortless ease. Hadn't she taught him everything she knew? The one-cylinder lock on this motel door would be child's play.

At least she didn't have to put up with his so-called conjugal rights. To the curious eyes of the circus performers the adjoining rooms put up a perfect front. If most of them were also aware of Marco's interest in the voluptuous but cowed-looking wardrobe assistant, they turned a blind eye to it. Circuses were like one big family, but the family members learned discretion from the cradle.

Eight days. She had eight days left, and then she'd be free. One last hit, one last big score, then she would never have to answer to anyone again. All she had to do was play it cool, do her part, and it would be over.

At least Marco no longer touched her. It had been almost two years since she'd had to put up with his particularly nasty form of lovemaking, and God willing, she would never have to again. *Eight more days.*

THE QUEEN-SIZE BED in Ferris's bedroom took up almost all the floor space. She lay on her stomach on the tiny section of rug, fishing under the bed for her other black shoe, fighting her way through discarded panty hose, old magazines, empty tissue boxes and crumpled-up bags of Mrs. Field's Cookies, when her hand caught what felt like a high heel. She pulled it out, and then promptly threw it back under the bed. Instead of her black sandal she'd found a sparkly red shoe, reminiscent of Dorothy's ruby slippers, a gift from Blackheart in better days.

She pulled herself into a sitting position, crossing her legs, and let out a shuddering sigh. She shouldn't have left the shoe under there; she should have taken it and hurled it off her tiny balcony. With her luck that huge, humorless policeman would have caught her doing it, and she would have ended up in prison. The place where Blackheart belonged.

To hell with the red shoes. She wouldn't even remember it was under there. *And to hell with the black shoes, too.* She wasn't going to wrestle around in dark places looking for it anymore. Heaven only knew what nasty thing she'd come up with.

Back to the closet. She was already late for Regina's welcoming reception for the Porcini Family Circus, and she was feeling edgy, guilty and hungry. She'd have to find something else to wear, something that would go with the one matching pair of shoes she could find, and then get the hell out of there.

She was pawing through her closet when she heard the doorbell ring. Her immediate reaction was panic, a reaction she quickly squashed. "Don't be ridiculous," she muttered to herself, grabbing the first thing she could reach and pulling it down over her ice-blue camisole and tap pants. "No one's after you. If anyone's done anything wrong it's Blackheart, and you don't have anything to do with him."

She padded barefoot to the front door, shifting the clinging silk dress around her curves, curves that were getting a little curvier after two days of nonstop eating. She didn't even take the elementary precaution of asking who was there. With the impatient doorbell buzzing in her brain once more, she fiddled with the three stiff locks and flung open the door.

She'd been expecting Blackheart, she realized with a sudden wary disappointment. She should have known better, but deep in her heart she'd hoped he might show up and try to cajole her.

The man standing in her doorway was about as far removed from John Patrick Blackheart as a human being could possibly be. He was good-looking, as was Blackheart, in a sort of rumpled, world-weary fashion. He was somewhere in his mid- to late thirties, as was Blackheart, with sandy-colored hair and steely gray eyes. He was also holding police identification and a badge, something the most famous retired cat burglar in the world would never come close to possessing.

Ferris swallowed, her throat suddenly dry. "Can I help you?"

"I'm Police Detective Stephen McNab," he said, his voice raspy from the memory of too many cigarettes. "I wondered if I might talk to you for a few minutes."

"About what?"

"About whom," he said. "The man who was in your apartment last week when you were involved in an episode of littering. It took Officer Sweeney a few days to place him, but when he did he came straight to me."

"Why?"

McNab's mouth twisted in a grim smile. "He knew of my particular interest in John Patrick Blackheart, alias Edwin Bunce." He looked pointedly over her shoulder. "May I come in?"

"No."

"Ms. Byrd, I've done some checking." He had the patience of a saint, it seemed. Or the tenacity of a bulldog. "You were engaged to Blackheart for a period of six months, an engagement that came to an abrupt end when he returned from Madrid last week. I might mention that there was a spectacular jewel robbery in Madrid around the time Blackheart was in Spain. I don't suppose you know anything about that?''

Her blood had frozen in her veins, an odd sensation, when her heart and stomach were burning and churning in panic. ''Not a thing.'' Her voice was wintry.

''And it had nothing to do with the termination of your engagement?''

''Do I have to answer these questions?''

McNab smiled again, but his light gray eyes were chilling. ''Certainly not. Not now. When I bring you in for questioning that might be a different matter.''

''When?''

''If,'' he amended. ''It would be a lot easier on both of us if you were helpful. May I come in?''

She couldn't help it. She felt like a lioness whose cub was being threatened. It didn't matter that she'd severed her ties with Blackheart, it didn't matter that he'd accepted his dismissal with too damned much grace. She wasn't going to stand by and let this rumpled, deceptively mild detective hound him. ''You,'' she said, ''may go to hell.''

It was a mistake, she knew that from the broadening of his smile, the very real pleasure lighting his eyes. ''You've been very helpful,'' he murmured. ''If I had any doubts about Blackheart's involvement in the Madrid case, you've set them to rest. I don't suppose you care to comment on the Vasquez robbery in Lisbon? Or the Phelps Museum in Paris?''

She slammed the door in his face, her hands shaking as she secured the row of locks. She started toward the kitchen, in search of the comfort only ice cream could provide, when she heard McNab's raspy voice through a thin pine door. ''Loyalty's a fine thing, Ms. Byrd. When it's justified. I'll be seeing you.''

It took her half a pint of coffee fudge ripple before she felt up to facing the rest of the evening. The dress she'd pulled on in a rush would do—it was blue silk and the small spot of ice cream near the waist wouldn't show if she was careful. She wouldn't have to stay long, just spend enough time there to make sure the ladies of the committee and their husbands were enjoying themselves, and to make sure the Porcini Circus was set for the benefit performance next week.

They'd been a stroke of luck she was still thankful for. The committee had already made arrangements with another small European circus, when those plans had fallen through. The owner and star performer of the Mendoses *Cirque du Lyon* had been the victim of a vicious mugging that had left him laid up for at least three months. It was no time for them to start their first American tour.

But Marco Porcini had heard of his old friend Henri Mendoses's troubles and offered his own small circus instead through his agent, who also happened to be his wife. It would be no trouble—the Porcini Family Circus had been planning an American tour for years. They wouldn't mind the rush in the slightest. And the location of the proposed benefit should be no problem. The spacious grounds surrounding Regina Merriam's mansion should be fine, and no one would be bothered by the noise of the animals but the staid patrons of the adjoining Museum of Decorative Arts. Since Regina's family had built and endowed the huge, sprawling museum and given the land in the first place, not to mention the fact that both she and her son still sat on the board of directors, there should be no objections whatsoever.

It must have been her worries about Blackheart that had caused her groundless fears concerning the Porcinis. It had been luck, wonderful luck that had brought the Commit-

tee for Saving the Bay together with the Porcini Family
Circus, just as it had been bad luck that Henri Mendoses
had been set on by a pair of thugs. But she couldn't rid
herself of the feeling that things had been a little too convenient.

She was getting neurotic as well as forgetful in her old
age. She needed to go to the party, to flirt with handsome
lion tamers, if the Porcini circus came equipped with such
things, and drink too much champagne. Maybe the handsome lion tamer would have to drive her home, and maybe
she'd invite him in and have him make her forget all about
Blackheart.

Whom was she kidding? She didn't want anyone else
showing her anything. She was planning to enjoy a nice
healthy bout of celibacy, maybe for a year or two before
she made the mistake of blindly trusting a convicted felon
with her hand and heart. She'd even tossed her birth control pills in her certainty that she wouldn't be needing
them. She couldn't afford to change her mind at this point.

She took one last, critical look at her reflection in the
bathroom mirror. *Not bad,* she thought as she wiped the
ice cream mustache from her upper lip. She'd left her dark
hair loose around her elegantly boned face, her bright red
lipstick had faded a bit from the ice cream, but her green
eyes were as cold as the famous Von Emmerling emeralds
she had once held so briefly. No one would ever guess
she'd just broken her engagement to a man she loved with
such passion that it frightened her.

Had loved, she corrected herself. *No.* Still loved. But it
would fade, it would disappear, with time and his palpa-
ble lack of interest it would vanish. *You can't love a man
you don't trust,* she told herself. And the brightness of her
eyes was simply the reflection of the lights, not the brilliance of unshed tears.

In fact, the lion tamer was in his late fifties, a roly-poly Armenian with an equally roly-poly wife. No one even to tempt her, she thought as she glided through the crowds filling Regina's spaciously appointed downstairs rooms. She could drink as much champagne as she wanted, smile brilliantly, and take a taxi home. For tonight she didn't even need to remember her heart was broken, didn't have to think about Stephen McNab and his unsettling questions, didn't have to think about anything but the exotic, brightly dressed circus people mingling with the richest blood on the upper west coast of California. Just for tonight she didn't have to think about anything.

She'd drained her first glass of champagne and was standing there looking for a refill, when a hand reached out from behind her, deftly removing the empty glass and replacing it with a full one. She turned with a smile of gratitude, a smile that died on her lips as she looked into Blackheart's fathomless dark eyes.

"Cat got your tongue?" he murmured, his expression wickedly amused and completely unrepentant.

She considered throwing her champagne in his face, but it would have been a waste of good Moët. She opened her mouth to blister him with her anger and contempt, then shut it again. Over his shoulder, back by the doorway, stood two familiar figures deep in conversation. If she'd thought the person she least wanted to see was Blackheart, she knew now that she was wrong.

She didn't want to see Phillip Merriam, her ex-fiancé and Regina's only son, now that she was once more unattached. And she certainly didn't want to see S.F.P.D. Detective Stephen McNab's clear gray eyes boring into Blackheart's elegant back with an expression that could only be called determined.

She turned back to Blackheart with a despairing sigh. "If I were you I'd get the hell out of here," she said under her breath, giving him a completely false smile.

He was more fascinated than fooled by her affable expression. He could probably hear her grinding her teeth. "Why?"

"Because that man wants you," she replied grimly.

He turned and followed her gaze, looking into McNab's eyes with no expression whatsoever. "As long as someone does," he said sweetly. And without another word he walked away.

Chapter Five

Family Plot
(Universal 1976)

I can't take this, Ferris thought, draining her champagne and looking in desperation for a quick escape route. There were some things too difficult for even the strongest of humans, and being in a crowded, noisy room with Blackheart, Phillip and a burglar-hungry police detective was one of them. Not to mention the fact that it seemed as if half of San Francisco was watching her, watching her reaction to the presence of her two ex-fiancés.

The main exit was blocked by a surge of latecomers, and the French doors leading to the terraces were similarly inaccessible. That left sneaking through the kitchens. Not an unattractive alternative, since she'd already managed to finish the shrimp puffs within reach and she knew Mrs. Maguire, Regina's cook, would have another five dozen stashed out back. She set down her glass and began to slither through the crowd, doing her best to blend in with the other chattering magpies. She'd almost made it, the swinging door was just within reach, when Phillip's mellifluous, politician's tones reached her.

The curse under her breath was short and succinct, then she turned, giving him a brilliant smile that never faltered even as she realized he was still accompanied by McNab, and that fully half the occupants of the crowded room were avidly observing their little encounter.

"Hello, Phillip," she replied dutifully, reaching up to kiss his smoothly shaven cheek.

"You're looking radiant as ever. Breaking engagements must agree with you." There was just the faintest edge beneath Phillip's voice, an edge that surprised Ferris. It was unlike Phillip to let anything ruffle his carefully guarded emotions. He'd never shown any hint that she might have hurt him six months ago when she, or rather Blackheart, had severed their engagement. Apparently she'd been wrong.

"I've decided I'm not the marrying kind," she said with a light laugh. "Clearly I'm the love them and leave them type."

"I wouldn't say that. I think you just made a mistake."

Oh, no, she thought miserably, still keeping her smile firmly planted on her stiff face. *Don't tell me he's going to try to get me back.*

Leaning forward, Phillip slipped a smooth, perfectly manicured hand beneath her elbow, turning her in his companion's direction. "Let me introduce you to Lieutenant McNab."

"We've already met," McNab said brusquely.

Phillip's smile was surprisingly cheerful. "Then you know why he's here."

"It's not really any of my concern." She tried to pull her arm out of Phillip's grasp, but his fingers tightened their grip.

"He doesn't think Blackheart's retired."

"How interesting." She began edging toward the kitchen door, but the shifting crowds had blocked her one and only exit, and she was trapped. She didn't know how completely trapped she was until she saw Blackheart within hearing distance, flirting with a newly-divorced redhead with seeming rapt attention. She knew by the tension in his shoulders that he was listening to every word of their conversation, even as he flirted. *Damn him*.

"You don't think he's retired, either," Phillip said with sudden acumen. "You've been so besotted with him that it could only take something of that nature to break you up."

"Phillip, I find this tiresome." In desperation she reached for another glass of champagne as it whizzed by on a silver tray. "Blackheart and I had several differences, none of them concerning his former line of work. Why should it matter to you?"

"Perhaps my hurt pride?"

"I wouldn't think Lieutenant McNab would find the bruised ego of a politician to be of much help in an impartial investigation."

McNab was as fully aware of Blackheart's proximity as was Ferris. "I never said I was impartial, Ms. Byrd. I have every intention of putting John Patrick Blackheart exactly where he belongs. Which is behind bars for a good long time."

Even the eavesdropping Blackheart had his limits. Excusing himself from the redhead with his usual grace, he sauntered over to the threesome by the kitchen door. "It'll be a cold day in hell, McNab," he remarked pleasantly. "I've done nothing."

"Maybe not within my jurisdiction," McNab allowed. "But I know you, Blackheart, I know you better than you know yourself. Sooner or later you're going to slip up. You can't keep flying off to Europe, pulling a heist, and then coming back here expecting to be welcomed with open arms. It's a sickness with people like you, and sooner or later the craving will come over you and you'll try it again in your own backyard. In my city. And this time I'll get you."

Blackheart's yawn was perfection. "Have you always had such a well-rounded fantasy life, McNab? Or is it just part of a mid-life crisis?"

His casual pose might have fooled the others. But Ferris knew him too well, knew his body too well. She could sense the tension radiating from the corners of his dark brown eyes, could see the faint tightness in his thin-lipped mouth, could feel the anger and something else emanating from him, going straight to her heart with that inexplicable emotional telepathy that lovers sometimes had.

But they were no longer lovers. And he was lying, lying to everyone. Lying through that sexy mouth of his, lying with his eyes.

"Gentlemen," Phillip said smoothly, his fingers still clutching Ferris's arm. "Let's not have a quarrel in my mother's living room."

Blackheart's expression was no longer affable, it was downright dangerous. "Good idea, Phillip. If you just take your hands off Ferris there'll be no need to flatten you."

Phillip was an inch or two taller than Blackheart and much broader. "Try it," Phillip said, digging his fingers in harder.

"I should warn you, Phillip, that I don't fight fair, and I don't like people manhandling my ex-fiancée."

"She happens to be my ex-fiancée, too."

"For heaven's sake, let go of me, Phillip," Ferris snapped, yanking her arm out of his grasp. This time he let her go, but the tightness of his earlier grip had left red marks she could only hope Blackheart wouldn't notice. "I'm not an old bone to be fought over by a pair of pit bulls."

Blackheart laughed, some of the tension vanishing. "Hardly a pit bull. Phillip's more of an overbred Afghan. Big on looks and short on brain."

"What about you?" she couldn't keep from asking.

For a moment his hard brown eyes softened, and they were alone in the crowded room. "Nothing but an old alley cat, darling. Not worth the bother."

"There you are!" Regina's sonorous voice cut through the sudden hush, and Ferris greeted her intrusion with real relief. "I wanted to introduce you all to the Porcinis. We wouldn't be here tonight without their gracious offer, and I know you'll want to welcome them."

Danielle and Marco Porcini were more what Ferris had had in mind when she envisioned circus performers, she thought as Regina made her usual effortless introductions. Marco was tall, dark and handsome, the epitome of European allure. He practically glistened in the soft light, from his shiny black mustache, his perfect mane of hair to his small, white teeth and bulging biceps. If he'd been an unmarried lion tamer and Ferris even dumber than she was, she would have gone off with him in a flash.

But he came equipped with a small-boned, delicate English wife. Danielle Porcini had blue eyes and blond hair, a pale rose complexion, and no expression on her face whatsoever as she smiled and said all the right things. *Strange,* Ferris thought, momentarily distracted from her own troubles.

None of them, with the possible exception of McNab, had any illusion as to why Regina felt it necessary to introduce the Porcinis to the hostile little group by the kitchen door. As usual Phillip was suddenly all charm, and Ferris was tempted to remind him that Mr. and Mrs. Porcini couldn't vote. She bit her tongue, stealing a look at Blackheart.

She didn't like what she saw, didn't like it one tiny bit. He was staring at Danielle Porcini and pretending not to. He was pale beneath his tan, and for Blackheart the rest of the crowd, herself included, failed to exist.

Madame Porcini seemed unmoved by his covert attention. Her eyes were on her husband, her delicate hand tucked into his burly arm. She treated the three men, McNab included, with impartial politeness, but it was as if part of her simply wasn't there.

Ferris felt such a sweeping of unfathomable jealousy wash over her that she was more than willing to hope the woman was a mental incompetent rather than a rational human being who might possibly succumb to Blackheart's wiles. As any rational human being would, she thought morosely.

And then Danielle Porcini's eyes briefly met hers, before moving back to her husband, and Ferris realized that far from being slow-witted, the circus owner's wife was one smart cookie indeed. Dangerously so.

"Ferris, I was just going to show Danielle the powder room. Would you do so for me?" Regina requested in the tone she occasionally used for royal decrees. Clearly she wanted to break up the unpleasant little scene in the corner, and she did so with her customary dispatch.

While part of Ferris was amused at Regina's high-handed disposition, another part was grateful. "Of course. Mrs. Porcini?"

As they made their way through the crowded room toward the hallway and the curving staircase, Ferris could feel any number of eyes boring into her back. It was an unnerving feeling, since she didn't for a moment suppose any of those interested gazes were particularly friendly.

The crowds thinned out as the two women slowly climbed the flight of stairs. Mrs. Porcini seemed unnaturally composed for someone so young, and without meaning to Ferris blurted out the first thing that came to mind.

"How old are you?"

The self-contained woman beside her smiled briefly. "Twenty-four. How old are you?"

"Thirty. I'm sorry, that was a very rude question. It's just that you seem older."

"I am," Danielle Porcini said briefly.

There was no response she could make to that. As she preceded the younger woman into the bathroom that was larger than half her apartment, she cursed the convention that women should accompany each other to the powder room. Mrs. Porcini made her acutely uncomfortable for many reasons, not the least of which had been the expression on Blackheart's face when he saw her. The young Englishwoman had appeared not to notice, but Ferris's misery and guilt hadn't blunted her powers of observation. Mrs. Porcini might never have seen Blackheart before, but she knew who he was.

Ferris sank onto a tufted velvet stool in front of the wall-size mirror and disconsolately surveyed her reflection. Her hair was still in place, but she'd managed to chew off the rest of her lipstick, and despite the artful application of foundation and blusher she looked pale, wan and depressed.

Would Blackheart regret what he'd thrown away? For all that she knew him so well, she couldn't read the emotions in his carefully shuttered eyes. He was still very angry with her, that much was certain.

Danielle sat down beside her, running a brush through her silvery-blond mane, her face perfectly composed. "An interesting group of men," she murmured in an indifferent tone of voice. "Tell me about them."

Ferris's instincts, already on edge, swung into over-drive. For a moment she considered telling the girl to mind her own business, then decided otherwise. She wouldn't tell her anything Danielle couldn't find out from anyone at the party. If *she* told her, she could control the information.

"They were an interesting bunch," Ferris conceded, tossing back her hair and admiring her own casual response. If Danielle Porcini could act, so could she. "Phillip is a politician, looking for more power than he's got. McNab is a cop, and that's about all I know."

"And the other man?"

You know as well as I do his name is Blackheart, sweetie, Ferris thought. "He's the most interesting one of all. His name is John Patrick Blackheart, and he's a retired jewel thief. You've never heard of him?"

"As a matter of fact, I haven't," Danielle said, and Ferris didn't believe her for a moment. "And is he friends with this McNab?"

"Sworn enemies, more likely."

Danielle Porcini smiled, a small, vengeful cat's smile that vanished as quickly as it appeared. But not so quickly that Ferris missed it. And her unease about the self-contained Madame Porcini increased tenfold.

BLACKHEART was in a foul mood, one of the foulest moods he'd ever suffered through in his entire life. Every time he turned around there was a new stumbling block, a new disaster or complication looming on the horizon.

And there was no way out. He couldn't walk away from the incredible mess his life had become, for the simple reason that he hadn't made the mess. *Sure,* he might have contributed a bit in the past, but right now someone was diabolically intent on framing him for the recent rash of robberies plaguing the major cities of Europe. And he was damned if he was going to sit back and play the patsy anymore.

Of course Ferris immediately condemned him. A hanging judge if ever there was one, dear Ferris-Francesca. He was going to enjoy making her eat her words, having her crawling in abject apology when he was finally able to flush out the real thief.

But he was going to have to watch his step. He'd almost got caught last week when he broke into the Vendades town house to see if the thief had left anything incriminating that the police and Interpol might have missed. He couldn't really blame the police. When confronted with the exact modus operandi with which he'd operated for a good fifteen years, it was no wonder they weren't looking too far for another culprit. For a while he'd had very real doubts as to his ability to get back out of Spain.

But his passport was incontrovertible evidence. He hadn't been in Spain at the time of the robbery, any more than he'd been in Lisbon during the Vasquez robbery or anywhere near the Phelps Museum in Paris. *Granted,* he'd appeared on the scene as soon as he'd heard about it. And he hadn't been particularly cooperative toward the police. He couldn't change a lifetime of habit, and he never could, never would trust the police.

The final straw, the last insulting touch, had been the tarot card left behind at each scene. Very few people knew about that obscure part of the Blackheart family past. His father and uncle had started their careers in the late twenties, when interest in the occult had been high among the British upper classes. It had been their particular conceit to leave behind a Knight of Pentacles at each scene, and Blackheart had done the same until the romance of the business had gone stale and he'd been more interested in simply doing the job and getting out safely.

Very few people knew about that telltale signature. The police had always been very circumspect about mentioning it, for fear they'd end up with copycat crimes. So whoever was patterning crimes after the Blackheart family tradition had inside information.

Blackheart stared out over Regina Merriam's perfectly manicured grounds, across the wide expanse that would hold a circus tent, over to the impressive roofline of the Museum of Decorative Arts, the domed and angled roofs a perfect foil against the night sky. There'd been one link between all the recent robberies that had been plaguing Europe for the last couple of years, and Blackheart didn't know if anyone but himself was aware of it. Each time a robbery occurred, somewhere within an hour's journey of the crime the Porcini Family Circus was in residence.

He hadn't been sure it wasn't a simple coincidence until he'd heard of their benefit performance in his hometown. A benefit performance for a very moneyed charity. Most of the women volunteering for the Committee for Saving the Bay wouldn't go swimming without their diamonds. They wouldn't know how to dress down to attend a circus. And somewhere in that crowd of fifty or so employed by the Porcini Family Circus was someone who knew far too much about the Blackhearts and had much too great an interest in jewels.

He'd expected to have to cajole Regina into letting him take care of the security for the benefit. *After all,* it wasn't as if priceless jewels were involved in the performance. But he'd reckoned without Regina's romantic streak. If Blackheart and Co. were in charge of the security then they, he, would have no choice but to deal with Ferris.

He wasn't sure if that was an advantage or a drawback. On the one hand, he had every intention of enticing the skittish, distrustful Ms. Byrd-Berdahofski back into his arms, his bed, his life. On the other hand, things would be a lot easier if he could concentrate on one thing at a time and didn't have to worry about being framed for a succession of jewel robberies—not to mention the distinctly unpleasant sensation of having Stephen McNab breathing down his neck.

McNab hadn't liked it when Blackheart and Co. had received its license. He hadn't liked it when the company had prospered, and particularly hadn't liked it when he'd had Blackheart safely in custody over the theft of the Von Emmerling emeralds, then been forced to let him go when the real thieves turned up. He hadn't gotten it through his thick cop's brain that Blackheart had been completely innocent, and he probably never would.

Sooner or later it would all come together, Blackheart thought, more in devout hope than in certainty. He was already one step ahead of the game. He'd thought it would take days to find out who'd been following in his family's footsteps, and in the end it had been shockingly simple. He'd taken one look at Danielle Porcini's bland, distant face and seen his long-lost sister staring back. And if he was still shaken by the fact, maybe even Dany herself didn't realize it. No one did. With the possible exception of his maddening, gorgeous ex- and future fiancée. He was going to have to watch his step.

THE FIRST THING Ferris wanted to do was to get the hell out of Regina's overcrowded house. Regina was in the front hall, and she'd have too many uncomfortable questions. McNab and Phillip were where Danielle and herself had left them, by the kitchen, and Danielle Porcini was threading her way back toward them with the effortless grace of an athlete.

That left the terrace. It was a little cool for it to be a popular place, and unless she was mistaken a light rain was about to fall. Her silk dress would be ruined, but that was a minor price to pay for a quick getaway. She'd sneak out on the porch, climb over the railing and make her way across the grounds before anyone even realized she was gone.

In theory it was a wonderful idea; in practice she hadn't taken fate into account. No sooner had she slipped out the door, pulling it shut behind her, when a too-familiar voice purred in her ear. "Pussycat, pussycat, where have you been?"

"Damn you, Blackheart," she said with surprisingly little rancor. "I was trying to escape."

He was leaning against the stone railing, oblivious to the lightly falling mist, and it was too dark to read his expression. Not that she would have been able to guess what he was thinking, even in broad daylight. Blackheart was adept at keeping hidden what he wished to keep hidden.

"With the family jewels?" he countered, still not moving from his indolent pose.

"That's more your style, isn't it?"

"Not with my friends."

"That's right, you have your standards." She wanted to keep her voice lightly mocking, but an edge had crept into it. An edge of anger, but also of hurt and confusion. Why hadn't he fought for her?

"Indeed. By the way, I hate that dress. You look like you used to look before we . . . before. All elegant and refined and half alive. If it weren't for that blot of ice cream, I would have been afraid the real Francesca had gone for good."

"Only you would notice the ice cream," she mourned, staring down at the practically invisible stain. The light mist had soaked into the material, making it cling to her well-rounded figure, cling to the lavender silk underwear and the skin beneath.

"Only I would have been paying close enough attention," he agreed. "As I am now. Maybe I don't hate that dress, after all." He moved as he usually did, with speed and a kind of lethal grace that she was too bemused to fight. At one moment she was standing in the rain, in the next she'd been pulled quite firmly into his arms, the wet silk dress a thin barrier between his body and her own.

She was too surprised to fight him, too surprised to do anything but stand perfectly still in the circle of his arms, absorbing his quite remarkable body heat. He didn't kiss her; he just looked down into her rain-damp face, and his eyes were shadowed.

"What are you doing to us, Francesca?" he murmured, his mouth close to hers.

For a moment she wanted to dissolve in his arms, but she fought it, fought herself, fought him. "If you don't let go of me, John Patrick Blackheart, I will toss you through the French doors, and you'll lose another one of your nine lives."

To her surprise he grinned. "Right now I don't have them to spare, lady." And he released her, stepping back.

It was so cold without his arms around her. So cold and lonely. "Thanks," she said politely, and without another word she hiked her trailing skirts up to her thighs and scrambled over the wide stone railing, dropping lightly to the ground some five feet below. By then the rain had begun in earnest, and slipping off her high heels, she took off across the cold wet grass, running, telling herself she was running from the rain. But she was running from the man who stayed behind, watching her through the heavy curtain of rain.

Chapter Six

The Wrong Man
(Warner Brothers 1957)

Ferris's late model Mercedes SL coughed, sputtered, and limped its way back to her apartment in the marina section of San Francisco. Her forty-thousand-dollar automobile didn't like the rain, the fog, or damp weather of any sort, and she was a fool to hold on to it in rainy, damp, foggy San Francisco. But by that time the car was so fully integrated with her invented self-image that she couldn't imagine herself without it, inefficient engine and all. Besides, it gave her something to curse, something to think about besides Blackheart as she drove home through the rain-slick streets.

It stalled two blocks from her apartment and refused to start again, but for once fate had the kindness to provide a nearby parking space on a downhill slope. She climbed out of the car and pushed, her feet squishing around in her wet high-heeled sandals, her hair hanging like a limp curtain around her face, her silk dress ruined. The parking spot was directly in front of a fire hydrant, but Ferris was beyond caring. She left the car at an angle, its elegant tail pointing out into the street, and she slammed the door with all her strength. She didn't bother to lock it. With luck someone would steal it, preferably before she got a park-

ing ticket, and her worries would be over. At least one of
them.

She would have left her keys, just to make sure any
would-be thief didn't give up at the first little setback, but
she didn't fancy shinnying up her building again. If someone wanted her Mercedes, they'd simply have to work for
it.

The rain turned into a downpour as she hiked the two
blocks to her apartment, cursing and muttering under her
breath. She was too physically miserable to think about
Blackheart, to think about the strange undercurrents in
Regina's odd assortment of guests. She still hadn't figured out how McNab had managed to show up. The *A* list
of the Committee for Saving the Bay didn't include cops,
even if retired and semiretired cat burglars figured high on
the list of desirables. He was awfully chummy with Phillip Merriam, but then, a politician on the stump was
everyone's friend.

Still, it seemed as if there was more to it than that. She
might almost have suspected Phillip of bringing him, but
then her former fiancé had no motive. Unless he was
holding a grudge.

Her three locks gave easily enough, a small consolation
on a miserable night. Slamming the door behind her, she
stood in the middle of her living room and yanked off her
clothes, dropping her sodden dress into a wastebasket,
kicking her muddy shoes across the room, stripping off her
lavender underwear and walking naked through the twisty
little apartment, past the piles of boxes into her bedroom.

Blackie had gone out on his nightly rounds. Ferris shut
the terrace door, shivering in the chilly night air, grabbed
her flannel nightshirt and had started back toward the
kitchen when something caught her eye.

If she hadn't been so miserable, both physically and emotionally, she would have realized someone had been in her apartment. She had only a moment of uneasiness before irritation and a reluctant amusement washed over. Blackheart hadn't let go as easily as she'd thought.

She'd left her bed a rumpled mess. It was now neatly made, the pretty pastel sheets smooth. And sitting in the middle of the bed was a familiar-looking bag. Mrs. Field's Cookies. She didn't even have to open the bag to find out they were the coconut kind.

She and Blackheart had shared half a dozen of them on their walk around San Francisco after he'd initiated her into the art of cat burglary, centuries ago. They'd eaten them on picnics, on drives, in movies and for breakfast. Most of all they'd eaten them in bed.

She should take the bag and hurl them off the terrace. But then McNab would probably show up and bust her for littering again. She'd had too many sweets that day—she should throw them out. Run them under water first, to blunt temptation.

But then she hadn't eaten much at Regina's. And after almost a week of not eating, surely she could afford to eat a cookie or two. She'd throw the rest out, of course she would.

By the time the ten o'clock news was over she'd finished the bag. Her pastel sheets were littered with crumbs, her stomach was complaining at the sudden influx of sugar, and she was very close to tears. The taste of those damned cookies was forever linked in her brain with the taste of Blackheart. He couldn't have chosen a more insidious punishment. Or was it a bribe?

Crumpling up the bag, she tossed it under the bed, flipped off the light, and nestled down among the sheets, ignoring the crumbs as they dug into her skin. *Six cook-*

ies. Wasn't there an old legend about that? Someone had gone down into hell, eaten six pomegranate seeds, and ended up having to spend six months of every year in bed with the devil.

She'd already done her six months with Blackheart, a six months that had felt uncomfortably akin to demonic possession. Had she just committed herself to another six months? Was it worth fighting?

With a moan she rolled over, burying her face in her pillow. It was too late and she was too tired. Tomorrow she'd recognize what she'd done, pigged out on too many cookies and Blackheart's fiendish sense of humor. Maybe tomorrow she'd send him a pint of Double Rainbow ice cream.

Maybe, if she had any sense at all, she'd forget it. Ignore the cookies, ignore Blackheart. The caloric gift was probably just his way of saying goodbye. If it wasn't, she certainly couldn't be won over by a sugar buzz. Answers were what she needed, and answers were just what he wasn't going to give.

At least she had no reason to see him again. Regina might have invited him to her party, but there'd be no reason to run into him from then on. Why, with any luck she wouldn't even see him for months and months and months. With any luck she'd have enough time to get over him.

Because it had only taken one look at him, one touch of his hands on her body, and she'd known she was just as in love, just as obsessed as she'd always been. And God only knew how long it was going to take her to forget him.

"WHO WAS HE?"

Dany stared at the pale face in the mirror, ignoring the reflection of the blustering man behind her. Marco had

had too much to drink, and he'd been further stimulated by the obvious, idiotic admiration of all the fawning females at the big house tonight. She could see by the glitter in his eyes that he was in a dangerous mood, and if she had any sense at all she'd watch what she said.

But when had she ever had any sense? "Who was who?" she countered, taking off her crystal earrings and dropping them onto the plastic counter in front of her.

He moved swiftly, the drink scarcely slowing him down at all, but she'd been watching, and she was able to tense herself when he grabbed her, his thick arm going around her neck, snapping her head back. His breath smelled of whiskey and garlic, his body was sweaty and muscular, but she controlled the shiver of fear that had started deep within her.

"You know who. The man who was looking down your dress and trying not to."

"My brother?"

The arm tightened for a moment, and she choked before he lessened the pressure. "Don't be too brave, little one. As you may remember, I have a temper."

"Not my brother, then. He didn't know who I was," she added smugly.

"No," Marco agreed. "The great Blackheart has been overrated. But we're not talking about your obtuse half brother, are we? We're talking about the other man."

"The cop."

For a moment she wondered whether he'd snap her neck. It might almost be a relief. There wasn't an ounce of joy or pleasure in her life, and hadn't been for years. Maybe it would be better to end it here than to carry through her intricate revenge and then hope to find some better sort of life.

Marco released her, stepping back. "A cop," he echoed flatly. "What did he want? What did you tell him?"

"Nothing, I told him nothing. I'm in this just as deeply as you are."

"Don't forget it," Marco snarled, sobering up. "That still doesn't explain what he wanted."

Dany smiled. "To look down my dress."

Then he hit her. Not as hard as he could; it was an openhanded blow that knocked her back against the bed. She knew how to fall, how to relax her muscles and roll with it. She lay on the bed, staring up at him, veiling the contempt and hatred that threatened to consume her. She knew from bitter experience that hatred only managed to excite him.

It was a close thing. Marco stood there, weaving slightly, his eyes hooded, contemplating his alternatives. There was a dead silence in the room, broken only by the sound of her breathing. "Don't push your luck, *cara*," he murmured finally. "I get tired of your smart mouth. Did the cop have any suspicions?"

Her face tingled from the blow. She'd been hit so often that she'd developed a second sense about how much damage he'd done. This one wouldn't even leave a bruise. Just a little stiffness around the jaw. "The cop was interested in Blackheart," she replied, keeping her hatred banked and out of her carefully neutral voice. "He wanted to know if I knew anything about him, and I think he was attracted to me. But as far as I could tell he didn't have any suspicions about either of us."

Marco nodded, apparently satisfied. "Attracted to you, eh? No accounting for tastes. Maybe American men like flat-chested little man-eaters."

Dany sat up, careful not to make any sudden moves that might ignite Marco's temper. "Somehow I don't think there's a future in it."

Marco laughed, his good humor restored. "True enough. I can't see an American cop and a thief having a good time together. Unless it's in the police car on the way to jail."

"If I go to jail, Marco, you go too." She was pushing it, she knew, but she had her limits.

Fortunately Marco's temper had vanished. "No one's going to jail, Danielle. No one but your long-lost brother. Think of that when you get sullen, little one. You're about to get your fondest hope. Revenge."

"Yes," she said, wishing she could feel better about it, wishing she could forget the little tendrils of doubt that were curling inside her, wishing she could simply have looked up into Stephen McNab's eyes and believed what she saw reflected there.

"You're not having second thoughts, are you?" Marco was headed toward the connecting door. Dany could hear the muffled sound of someone moving around behind that closed door, and she knew that for now she was safe.

"Not when I'm so close," she said.

"Cheer up. In a few days you'll be rich, you'll have your revenge, and you'll be rid of me."

"A lovely thought," she said, pushing her hair out of her face. "Your friend is waiting."

For a moment he hesitated, his dark eyes running over her body with an expression she'd learned to dread. "I might send her away."

"No, Marco."

It was a mistake. He liked a fight. His mouth widened in a smile, and his hand left the doorknob. "No?" he echoed.

It took all her self-possession to shrug lightly. "As you wish."

He frowned, and she knew from bitter experience that her capitulation was like a bucket of ice water on the coals of his desire. "Not this time, *cara*. But soon."

Over my dead body, she thought, smiling faintly at him. "As you wish," she said again. And her smile broadened as he slammed the door behind him.

Until she remembered McNab. She'd been left alone with him in the crowded room while Phillip Merriam had been enticed into showing Marco the layout of the mansion. She'd already been uneasy—she wasn't used to casual conversation with a policeman, nor was she used to the undisguised admiration in his chilly gray eyes. Most of the men she met knew she was Marco's property, and they knew of Marco's temper. McNab had known, and he hadn't said a word that was less than proper. But she'd seen the look in his eyes.

A stray shiver washed over her body, and for the first time she wished she'd taken some whiskey herself. Now wasn't the time to lose her nerve, and the blank expression on Blackheart's face when he'd met her had only strengthened her resolve. Not only had he forgotten her very existence, he hadn't even recognized her when she turned up.

He'd remember her eight days from now, when she'd be very rich and long gone. And maybe McNab would remember her, if he wasn't too busy reveling in his triumph at finally having nailed Blackheart to the wall.

She should be happier about the whole thing. She should be delighted that things were happening at last. She looked across the room at her reflection in the mirror, the imprint of Marco's hand red across her pale face, her blond hair hanging down, her mouth trembling. She summoned forth her coolest, most controlled expression. And then watched in horror as her reflection burst into silent, ugly tears.

FERRIS BREEZED into her office, a wide smile on her carefully lipsticked mouth. The rain and despair of the last few days had lifted, almost as if by magic. When she woke the next morning the sun was out, a crisp breeze had blown the last of the clouds away, and with it all the doubts and depression that had tormented her. Suddenly anything was possible.

She'd washed the crumbs from her skin, dressed in a green silk suit that matched her eyes, and stepped out into the morning air with nothing short of a swagger.

Her car was where she'd left it, and no one had given her a ticket. It started right up, running smoothly as she drove across town to the office. Life was suddenly back under her control, something that hadn't happened since she first set eyes on John Patrick Blackheart. Her life was once more her own, and she had no reason to see Blackheart and fall under his spell again. A new life spread out before her, and she was ready to greet it with open arms.

She was halfway through her second cup of coffee, completely preoccupied with the papers she was leafing through, when something landed on her desk with a disrupting thump. She looked up, only mildly irritated, to find Blackheart's partner, Trace Walker, staring down at her with gloomy disapproval.

"Trace," Ferris said politely, leaning back and setting down her coffee mug—next to the bag of Mrs. Field's Cookies Trace had delivered. "What can I do for you?"

"Now isn't the time to go into it," he growled. "I told Patrick I'd drop these off on my way to the Merriams' place."

The moment she'd set eyes on Trace, she'd felt her ebullient mood begin to ebb. It now vanished with a crashing thud. "Merriams?" she echoed very cautiously. "Why would you go to the Merriams'?"

"Preliminary security check. Patrick's going to meet me there."

"Why do we need security for a damned circus?" It came out in a shriek that rattled the windows and sent several indolent volunteers scuttling past her office.

Trace drew himself up to his full six feet three or four, and his beefy, handsome face was forbidding. "I expect you'll have to ask Regina about that. She and Patrick made all the arrangements."

"You can bet I'll ask Regina," Ferris snarled. "We don't need Blackheart and Company's specialized services and you know it as well as I do. We certainly don't need to waste the committee's hard-earned money on expensive security when simple security guards will do just as well."

"If you can find simple security guards," Patrick's smooth voice broke through her rage. "Most of the ones I know are reasonably intelligent."

Trace's imposing bulk had shielded Blackheart's characteristically silent approach, but then, Ferris had been in such a towering, noisy rage that she might not have noticed, anyway.

She picked up the bag of cookies and hurled it at his head. "Get out of here, Blackheart!" she shouted, all her newly-won self-control vanishing.

Blackheart caught them deftly, snaked around his partner and pushed him out the door, then closed it behind him, sealing himself in the spacious office with his furious ex-fiancée. "Tsk-tsk," he said reprovingly. "Such a temper, Ferris. One would think you cared."

She just glared at him. No one in the world could strip away her calm, her defenses, as John Patrick Blackheart could. She was overreacting as always, but she couldn't help it. Just moments ago she'd thought her life was back in her control and that she was beyond caring. All he had to do was appear, his lean, black-clad figure lounging in her best chair, and she knew she was a long way from being over him.

"I don't care," she said. "I just don't see the need to waste our limited resources on your very substantial fees."

"We're donating them."

"Don't be absurd. Half of your work is for charity functions. You can't afford to work for free."

"All in a good cause." Blackheart's smile was bland. She might almost have believed him, if it weren't for the shadows lingering in his cool brown eyes, the cynical twist of his mouth—and the fact that she desperately wanted to believe otherwise.

"All right," she said. "We never turn down donations."

"Good." He tossed the cookies back onto the desk in front of her.

"The committee doesn't turn down donations." She picked up the battered bag and dropped it into her trash basket. Turning back to Blackheart, she gave him her most professional smile. "I'll arrange for one of my assistants to accompany you out to Regina's. I'm certain it won't take much of your time...."

"Guess again."

"I beg your pardon?"

"This is a bigger job than it appears. And I don't believe in working with assistants."

Ferris controlled the urge to scream again. "Black-heart, it's a circus, for heaven's sake. Not some priceless collection of diamonds."

"Or emeralds," he reminded her softly. "Nevertheless, there are still substantial jewels involved. Not to mention Regina's collection of artwork."

For a moment she forgot they were enemies, forgot that he'd betrayed her and broken her heart. "Have you ever stolen works of art?" she asked with nothing but simple curiosity.

"Never. Jewels were the family tradition, and besides, they were far more portable."

"So at least Regina's collection is safe from you." She'd pushed him too far, she knew it the moment the words were out of her mouth, but her anger was still too fresh.

He just stared at her for a long moment. "Nothing is safe from me," he said. "And no one. Remember that." He rose, his indolent grace deceptive. She knew the fury that was vibrating through his body. "I'll meet you at Regina's in an hour."

"I don't think I can make it...."

"Be there." His voice was a silken threat, one she didn't quite dare to fight.

She half expected him to slam her door as he left, but he closed it very, very quietly. She stared after him, prey, as always, to conflicting emotions. On the one hand she regretted making him so angry. She didn't for a moment believe he would rip off Regina or any of their friends.

On the other hand, the angrier she made him, the farther away she'd drive him. And if she was to have any hope of recovery, she needed to drive him very far away indeed.

She'd go out to Regina's and accompany him over the grounds, if that was what he insisted on. She'd prove to him that he couldn't goad her into a fury. Then maybe he'd leave her alone.

In the meantime she was suddenly, astonishingly hungry. With one furtive glance at the now-empty hallway beyond her glass-doored office, she reached into the wastebasket and retrieved the now-mangled bag of cookies. And leaning back, she began to munch.

MCNAB WAS IN A VERY BAD MOOD. Not only was John Patrick Blackheart being an exemplary citizen, but his ex-fiancée had proved a complete washout. So far, at least. The only one interested in helping him was State Senator Phillip Merriam, and when it got to the point where a cop had to trust a politician, then things were in pretty bad shape. Particularly since this politician had an ax to grind.

On top of that there was Danielle Porcini. Married to that walking sweat gland, barely meeting his eye, moving through the noisy crowds at Mrs. Merriam's with a self-possessed calm that he didn't quite believe. As a cop he counted on his instincts, and they were telling him something wasn't right about the young Mrs. Porcini.

That wasn't his only reaction to the circus owner's wife. While she hadn't been the prettiest woman in the room, the richest or the friendliest, there was something about her that spoke to him on a very elemental level. Which was incredibly stupid on his part. It had been three years since his civilized divorce, and if he'd had any doubts as to whether a sane woman could survive being married to a cop he'd found out otherwise. No woman could put up with the hours he put in, the obsessions that ruled his life when he was on a hot case. The smartest thing he could do would be to put her out of his mind, considering that she came equipped with a very large husband. If he could just get rid of the feeling that there was more to her than met the eye.

First things first. The first thing on his agenda was catching John Patrick Blackheart in the act of robbery and putting him behind bars for a long, long time. And the second was to figure out exactly what the Porcinis, Danielle in particular, were doing. If those two goals happened to coincide, so much the better. But he knew what his first priority was, and he was getting so close that he could taste it. He was going to nail Blackheart to the wall. Then he could think about his love life.

Chapter Seven

Notorious
(RKO 1946)

In the clear, beautiful sunlight Regina Merriam's acres and acres of manicured lawns looked more like a battle zone. The Porcini Family Circus came equipped with a huge tent, several smaller ones, trailers, motor homes, trucks and cars, and a brightly arrayed sea of humanity swarmed over the grass. Ferris parked her car up by the house, brushed the last cookie crumb from her mouth and carefully reapplied her pale lip gloss. Blackheart hated pale lips. She smiled smugly at her reflection, her joy in the perfect day returning. If her pleasure was augmented by the upcoming battle with Blackheart, she didn't have to admit it, even to herself. But as she crossed the graveled drive to the front door she was humming tunelessly to herself, and even the distant roar of what had to be some sort of caged jungle cat couldn't dent her cheerfulness.

Regina greeted her arrival with uncustomary relief. Her silvery hair was falling in wisps around her shoulders, her faded blue eyes were edged with cheerful desperation, and her silk blouse was coming untucked. "Thank goodness you're here," she said. "They're driving me crazy."

Ferris did her best to sound callous even as she gave Regina a reassuring hug. "It's your fault. We don't need

Blackheart and Company for something as straightforward as a circus."

"Who said anything about Blackheart and Company? They're the least of my worries. It's Nelbert Securities that's giving me a migraine headache."

Ferris let out a soundless whistle. "What in the world are you doing with the two biggest security companies crawling all over your house? I don't imagine Blackheart was too pleased to run into one of Jeff Nelbert's minions roaming your hallways."

"It's Jeff himself. And it's not my fault—Phillip arranged for them without consulting me."

"Fire them."

"I can't. It's *The Hyacinths*."

"You've lost me."

"That damned little painting Henry bought a few years before he died. It happens to be a Van Gogh," Regina said in a mournful tone. "You must remember what happened to his painting of irises a year or two ago?"

"Vaguely."

"It sold for somewhere around forty million dollars, and it was painted during the same period. I don't want to be sitting in a house with what might conceivably be one of the world's most valuable paintings. Ever since the iris sale I've been making arrangements to get rid of it. I'm donating it to the museum—that way I can simply walk down the hill and see it, if I have a mind to. Nelbert's in charge of museum security, and he's busy taking measurements, making plans. So I have to suffer."

"You're giving it away?"

Regina shrugged. "I don't need the money—I have more than enough to keep me comfortably, and Phillip has his own substantial income. Besides, think of the publicity if I put it onto the auction block. People, nasty criminal types, might start wondering what other treasures I had tucked away here, and then there'd be no peace.''

Blackheart had appeared beyond Regina's shoulder, his expression guarded. "So instead you have to put up with nasty criminal types crawling all over the place, trying to keep your treasures intact," he murmured.

"Patrick, don't even think such a thing!" Regina protested.

"I thought I'd better say it before Ferris could open her mouth. At this point I can read her mind."

You always could, she thought. "He's already assured me he wouldn't touch works of art. Too bulky, right?"

"Right. Of course, *The Hyacinths* is actually quite small. I could tuck it into a briefcase and walk right out with it and no one would be the wiser." He smiled faintly at Ferris. "It's worth considering."

"He's teasing you, my dear," Regina said kindly.

"He's wasting my time." Ferris glared at him. "I'm going back to the office." She turned to head out the door, but his hand had already caught her arm, his long, clever fingers digging in with just a trace too much force.

"I want to show you my security precautions first, dear heart." The edge in his voice was so subtle that only Ferris noticed it. "Then you can run back and hide in your office."

"Go along, darling." Regina waved her away, much cheerier than when Ferris had first arrived. "I'm sure I can manage to withstand Jeff Nelbert's overwhelming personality, if you can manage to withstand Blackheart. Can you?"

"Ferris has a will of iron," Blackheart drawled, tugging her toward the stairs. "She can withstand anything."

I only wish that were true, Ferris thought mournfully. Even the impersonal, vaguely hostile touch of his hand on her arm was melting her brain at an alarming rate. "Why are we going upstairs?" she inquired in her calmest voice, once they were out of sight of Regina's fond eyes.

Blackheart grinned at her, momentarily lighthearted. "I have several suggestions."

"I'm sure you do."

"I wouldn't jump to any conclusions if I were you. Distrust is not an aphrodisiac. Regina was thinking of having a dinner before the circus, with a guest list of some one hundred and fifty people. The only criterion for an invitation is money, something like two hundred dollars a plate, which leaves us in a bind. Anyone with the price can get in, and two hundred dollars is a small enough investment when you think of what someone could get away with. So I thought I'd use your considerable expertise to go over the house and see where the problems lie."

"My considerable expertise?"

"You have a natural talent for breaking and entering, darling. You're a born thief. I'm counting on you to be able to figure out how an amateur burglar would think. I tend to be too convoluted in my planning. No one is as good as I am, and I might expect something too complex in the way of a heist."

"As good as you are?" she echoed. "Or were?"

They were at the top of the curving staircase. The upper hall was deserted, the morning sunlight streaming through a vast, multipaned skylight and sending shadows spearing around them. "Don't push it, Francesca," he said. "Or I'll think you have a reason for wanting to goad me."

"I'm not about to make off with Regina's jewelry collection, if that's what you're thinking. You'll have to look elsewhere for a suspect. Like in a mirror."

For a minute his hand tightened on her arm, then he released her, forcing a laugh. "You have a definite talent for making me crazy. No, I don't think you're going to rob anybody. I think you're unable to leave me alone, so you taunt me to get a reaction.''

The truth was like a slap in the face, robbing her of her defenses. ''I can leave you alone,'' she said. ''There's no reason for me to be here. For that matter there's no real reason for you to be here, either. It's not as if you're guarding some specific, priceless object. Why don't you leave me alone?''

''You might find this difficult to believe, but I didn't con my way into this job simply to be near you.''

She ignored the shaft of pain that shot through her. ''I believe you. You know as well as I do that what was between us is over.''

''Goading me again, Francesca,'' he murmured.

She ignored it. ''But what I don't understand is why you talked Regina into letting you do it.''

''And the reason you don't understand is that you jump to conclusions, you don't consider alternatives, and you're so damned quick to judge.'' His voice was bitter. ''Come along, Ferris. We'll look at *The Hyacinths*, we'll be charming to Nelbert, and we'll go over the kind of locks and alarm systems Regina has in place. And then you can run away.''

''How about if I run away now?'' Her voice was low, almost pleading. But if she was hoping for pity from Blackheart, it was a waste of time.

''I'll catch you and bring you back. I'm not going to let you go, Francesca.''

''You won't have any say in the matter.''

''You don't think so?''

It was enough. She pulled free of him, shoving him back against the banister, and took off down the stairs, never looking back. She could feel him watching in the silent hallway, but right then her defenses had gone. One minute more and she would either have thrown him over the balcony or ended up kissing his knees. She hadn't had time to build up a protective layer yet, and the only thing she could do was run like the coward she'd never considered herself to be.

BLACKHEART LEANED against the railing, watching her race away from him. The streaks of sun from the skylight made patches of light and shadow that she ran through, graceful as an elfin creature, never looking back. He rubbed his knees with a surreptitious touch. He'd twisted it, keeping his balance when she'd shoved him, and after three operations and years of physical therapy it still wasn't perfect, and never would be again. All because of another woman scorned, he thought, remembering Prudence Hornsby's red-faced rage when she'd locked him in the basement after catching him stealing her ugly but quite valuable jewels.

It was just as well Francesca had run. She was too distracting. He hadn't needed her there that day—it would have been better all around if he let her immure herself in her office until this whole mess was sorted out.

But he never did have much sense, particularly where Francesca was concerned. It was bad enough sleeping alone, not having her grumbling over his coffee, his apartment and his peripatetic existence. He could survive a few weeks, even months of celibacy if he knew Francesca would be there at the end of the wait. But doing without her entirely, even her distrust and baiting, was a little more difficult. He'd take an insult from Francesca over a dozen sweet words from anyone else, and she probably knew it.

At least he had no doubt at all that she was still just as much in love with him as she'd always been. She was fighting it, fighting it with all her strength, and he couldn't get rid of the nagging fear that if he did leave her alone and concentrate on his myriad problems, she might just manage to get over him. He wasn't romantic enough to think that true love would conquer all and last forever. True love needed to be nourished and encouraged.

"Is she worth the trouble?" Jeff Nelbert had crept up on him. Blackheart betrayed no surprise, but inwardly he cursed. The day that a cigar-smoking, two-hundred-and-forty-pound Jeff Nelbert could sneak up on a retired cat burglar of Blackheart's talents was a sad day, indeed.

He turned to face his greatest rival, his expression bland. "None of your damned business." Nelbert was a paunchy, aggressive, not very ethical individual, but he was a born salesman, and that arcane talent had brought him too far in the security business for Blackheart's peace of mind. Blackheart disliked and distrusted the man, but right then he didn't have the energy to waste on a minor irritant like Jeff Nelbert.

"Heard you two had a falling-out." Nelbert licked his thick, pink lips. "I thought I might have a crack at her. She has the cutest little..."

Blackheart found the energy. "You'll keep your sweaty hands off her," he said with his friendliest smile, "or I'll tie your tongue in knots and dump you into the bay. She's mine."

"I don't know if she agrees with you on that. Word has it she dumped you, and no one can figure out why. If two people ever looked like they were in love it was you two. The only thing I can guess is that she must have caught you doing something you shouldn't have. And I'm betting it was something our friend McNab would want to hear about. Am I right?"

"You're an idiot, Nelbert."

Nelbert's grin widened. "That answers my question. But don't worry, Blackheart. I know when to keep my mouth shut. When someone makes it worth my while, that is."

He could toss him over the railing without much difficulty, Blackheart mused. The splat he'd make on the marble floor beneath was too nasty to contemplate, however, so he merely shrugged. "You're swamp algae, Nelbert. Go protect *The Hyacinths* and leave us poor working stiffs alone."

"Sorry, old boy. *The Hyacinths* are your responsibility as long as they're here. They don't become my problem until they hit the museum next week. And you can be sure I've got an alarm system designed that not even you could break through."

"Is that a challenge?"

"Let's just call it a friendly warning. You've got problems enough in this life, Blackheart. Keep away from *The Hyacinths*."

FERRIS WANTED nothing more than to run to her car and drive like crazy straight back to her office, or even better to her apartment, and shut herself away from the disparate emotions that were assailing her. *Damn Blackheart!* Did he want her, or didn't he? Was he still stealing, or a victim of circumstance? Had he lied to her, or was there some reason for his mysteriousness?

No reason was good enough. If he'd ever really loved her, wanted to marry her, then there was nothing he couldn't tell her. She was wasting her time trying to drum up excuses, when her emotional energies could be much better spent turning her life in new directions.

And she had no doubt whatsoever what her first move should be. The Committee for Saving the Bay would do very well without her—half the volunteer help had exceptional organizational skills. Anything they didn't know how to do, they could hire someone to take care of.

Her second move would be away from San Francisco. Maybe up to Seattle, though she wasn't sure if she could stand all that rain. Or the mountains—Colorado, maybe northern New Mexico. Away from the bay and the fog that came in on little cat's feet or however that cursed poem went.

Seven days. Seven days until the circus, their next big fund-raising event. She'd give Regina her notice and make her plans. And in seven days she'd be gone.

So why didn't she feel the weight of the world lifting from her shoulders? In seven days she'd never have to see John Patrick Blackheart again.

"Because you're still in love with him, you stupid fool," she muttered. "And you have exactly seven days to get him out of your system." She squared her shoulders, that small physical gesture telling her, reminding her that she wasn't powerless. "In the meantime, you have a job to do." She could see Danielle Porcini's lithe figure down by one of the Winnebagos. The least she could do was make sure the Porcinis had everything they needed. The committee expected to make a great deal of money from the benefit, and Ferris was both puzzled about and grateful for the Porcinis' generous offer. Besides, she was also curious about the mysterious Mrs. Porcini.

She threaded her way through the preoccupied crowds of circus people, local electricians, circus-struck socialites and yuppies on their lunch hour, her attention centered on Danielle's disappearing back, when a strong, thick-fingered hand caught her arm, pulling her up short.

"Ms. Byrd." Marco Porcini displayed an enviable set of teeth in a grin that reminded Ferris of the big bad wolf. "Or may I call you Ferris?"

"Certainly." She tugged surreptitiously at her arm, but Marco didn't seem to notice. She was getting tired of being manhandled, she thought wearily. If anyone was going to clamp onto her arm she'd just as soon it were Blackheart. "How may I help you?"

He lifted his moist eyes for a moment, staring in the direction Danielle had taken, and then all his attention was centered on Ferris. "You were looking for my wife?"

If Marco was adept at phony smiles, Ferris was no amateur. She curled her lips obligingly. "I wanted to see if you had everything you needed."

"Why not ask me?" He lowered his voice an octave, the breath hissing out of him as if he were a snake. A garlic-laden snake at that, Ferris thought, controlling the urge to wrinkle her nose. He'd been working out—he was wearing a mesh tank top despite the cool, damp weather, and his bronzed muscles were glistening with sweat.

"All right," Ferris said gamely. "Do you have everything you need?"

"There's a problem in the caravan."

"Caravan?"

"This thing." Porcini slapped the side of the Winnebago. "If I could just show you . . . ?"

At thirty years of age Ferris was old enough to know better. In retrospect it was just one more thing she could blame on Blackheart. If she hadn't still been so addled by her encounter with him up at the mansion, she would never have walked blindly into the Winnebago with an over-sexed aerialist at her back.

The closing of the door behind them blocked out the bright daylight. Ferris reached out for a light switch, and found Porcini instead.

In a matter of seconds he'd wrapped his sweaty arms around her and maneuvered her onto a convenient bunk, his well-muscled body covering hers.

Her first thought was sheer annoyance. She would have to pick today of all days to wear linen. It was going to end up rumpled and sweat-stained. Her second thought was the beginning of concern. Marco Porcini was very strong indeed.

"Would you like to let me up?" she inquired politely as his mouth nibbled, *no*, gobbled at her neck.

He wrapped his meaty hand in her hair, pulling it free from its pins. "You've been begging for this, *cara*," he muttered. "I've seen you watching me."

Ferris laughed. She couldn't help it, even though she knew it wasn't the most promising defense. "I've been watching your wife, Marco. Not you."

"Why?" He lifted his head, staring down at her in disbelief.

"Your wife reminds me of someone." The moment she came up with that, she realized it was true. In addition to Danielle Porcini's unnatural calm, there was a curiously familiar air about her, one she couldn't place.

With a suddenness that was as welcome as it was unflattering, Porcini lost interest. He climbed off her, headed for the door and flung it open, letting in the daylight. Ferris pulled herself upright, brushed back her hair and tried to straighten her pale green jacket around her. "You're mistaken," Marco said, not bothering to look at her, the impressive muscles in his shoulders noticeably tense. "My wife doesn't look like anyone but herself. You couldn't have seen her before. She's lived in Europe all her life."

"But I must have seen her...."

"She's spent the last year in Lisbon, Paris and Madrid," he growled. "If you were there, if you saw the circus, then perhaps you might have seen her perform."

Lisbon, Paris, Madrid. Why did those cities sound familiar? "I've never been to Europe."

"And she's never been to the States before. That answers your question. She's a stranger." He started down the three short steps of the vehicle. "Close the door behind you," he ordered, disappearing into the crowd.

Ferris stared after him. "Curiouser and curiouser," she said aloud. She looked around the tiny, shipshape little RV, but it was still spotless, no sign of habitation marring its plasticity. What had managed to discourage Marco so quickly, when he'd been so intent on a conquest? And why did those three cities sound so familiar?

It wasn't her problem, she reminded herself, deliberately leaving the Winnebago's door open as she stepped out onto the grass. She only had a week to go, and then she wouldn't have to think about circuses, benefits or semiretired cat burglars. *Seven more days.*

SEVEN MORE DAYS, Dany thought. Surely she could make it that long. The unnatural hush of the Museum of Decorative Arts crowded in on her, adding to her uneasiness. After the ceaseless noise of the circus, coupled with Marco's constant litany of self-praise and abuse, she should have welcomed the thick silence. It just went to prove that anyone could get used to anything. As her leather-shod feet moved silently through the marble halls, she found herself longing for noise, for a chattering family of tourists, a noisy security guard, anything.

But the Museum of Decorative Arts wasn't a major tourist attraction in San Francisco, and there was scarcely a security guard to be seen. Something was going on in the west wing, something to do with a new painting, but that was the least of Dany's worries. Paintings held no interest for her, not even a priceless Van Gogh. She paused for a moment, wondering what the silly Americans were doing putting a Van Gogh into a museum devoted to decorative arts, then dismissed the question. Understanding the natives of her new home would take time, a commodity she would have in abundance in seven days.

In the meantime, the rest of the world could worry about Van Gogh. Directly ahead of her was something far more inspiring, and a great deal more portable.

They sat there on their marble and gold bases, four jewel-studded, ridiculously ornate eggs. For a moment Dany had the fancy that they had been laid there by a fantastic jewel-encrusted bird, some mythical beastie committing its last act before vanishing into the mists of time.

Absurd, of course, Dany thought with a sniff. The eggs hadn't been laid by some extinct creature. Unless you could call Peter Carl Gustavovitch Fabergé extinct, which, since he died sometime after the Russian Revolution, you probably could. But he left behind these eggs, four of some twenty or thirty.

Dany stared at them, her palms damp, her mouth dry, her heart racing in anticipation. She might not want to steal them, but since she had no choice in the matter, her instincts were clicking into place, and that old, dangerous excitement was taking over. No wonder Blackheart had done it for so long.

The exhibit was in a small room, one of many sectioned out of a huge hallway. She looked overhead, assessing the security system. It was basic, no frills, tricky enough to be a challenge, predictable enough to ensure eventual success. Timing was everything. Once the Van Gogh was in place and the security beefed up, then they might remember that the Fabergé eggs were worth a tidy bit on their own.

Of course, they'd be long gone by then. Gone by the time the Van Gogh made its stately trek from the mansion up the hill. And she'd be gone with them.

Seven days, she thought again, rubbing her damp hands on her khaki pants. *And no one even suspects.*

"Lovely, aren't they?" a voice murmured in her ear. "It makes one understand why some people are thieves and some are cops. Make your fingers itch just to look at them, don't they?"

Slowly Dany turned, expecting Blackheart, preparing herself for a confrontation she both anticipated and dreaded. Instead she found herself looking up into Police Detective Stephen McNab's cool gray eyes. And for the first time in years, she was lost.

Chapter Eight

Stage Fright
(Elstree Studios 1950)

It was a very strange emotion, Dany thought, still silent, looking up into the face of a man she could fall in love with. A man who was the sworn enemy of everything she'd worked for, everything her energies were directed toward at that very moment. The question was, did he suspect?

She glanced back at the Fabergé eggs with a careful nonchalance that betrayed nothing more than curiosity. "They certainly don't incite any latent criminal tendencies on my part," she said with great truthfulness. Her criminal tendencies were nothing if not overt. "I mean, what could you do with them? Sit and gloat, I suppose. They're a little too fat to sit on a mantel, assuming one even has a mantel in one's flat. Chances are the kids would knock them over and they'd smash, and then where would you be? A few hundred thousand dollars in the red. Do you have any children?"

The question came out before she even realized it had been in her mind. McNab didn't seem the slightest bit surprised. "Approximately three hundred and fifty thousand dollars in the red, per egg, according to the last price paid at auction. No."

"No?"

"No, I don't have any children. Do you?"

"I'm not even...planning to have any," she amended quickly, about to betray the speciousness of her married state.

"Why not?"

"Too much responsibility. You can't help but let them down, and then where are you? Better not to take a chance of ruining some young kid's life."

"Did someone ruin your life?"

Dany tossed back her silvery-blond mane and laughed. Only a very observant man would know that laugh was hollow, but McNab had struck her as very observant. "Do all Americans have such intimate conversations with strangers?" she countered.

"We do tend to be an outspoken race. Why are you here? Don't you have work to do with the circus?"

"Is this a professional inquiry, Lieutenant? Do you think I'm planning to pop the eggs into my handbag and walk out with them?" She could feel the adrenaline buzzing through her veins. This was what she would miss, the excitement of taking absurd risks and getting away with it.

"Stephen," he corrected. "And no, it's not a professional inquiry. I might be more concerned if you were watching them set up the new security system for Mrs. Merriam's Van Gogh, but I don't think anyone's going to bother with the eggs."

"Just out of curiosity, why?"

"Too hard to fence. And as you said, if you don't have a mantel you're just plain out of luck." There was a glint in his wintry-gray eyes, but his expression was suitably grave. He was laughing, secretly amused, but Dany wasn't threatened. As long as there was that light in his eyes, he couldn't suspect her of any worse crime than that of a married woman flirting with a police detective.

"Wouldn't the Van Gogh be even harder to sell?"

"Indeed. But one would go to a lot more trouble for something worth forty million than for a Fabergé egg."

"Well then," Dany said, smiling easily, "I'll be certain to steal the Van Gogh if I feel a sudden larcenous streak coming on."

"You do that," Stephen said cheerfully. "In the meantime, can I buy you a cup of coffee?"

"I don't think my husband would like that." Her eyes were demurely lowered, her tone chaste. "I'd better get back to him and tell him about the Van Gogh. Who knows, he might decide thievery is a better profession than owning a circus."

Stephen laughed. "He might, at that. It certainly pays better than police work. Well, if you won't join me, I suppose I'd better get back to work, too."

"What are you doing here, for that matter? Just taking in the works of art, or were you planning to pull off a heist on your own?"

"You know, I never thought of that. Police pensions being what they are, I certainly ought to keep all possibilities in mind. But I don't think *The Hyacinths* is the answer. So there's nothing left for me to do but make sure the security system conforms to city regulations."

"Isn't that some minor bureaucrat's job?"

"I hate to tell you this, Mrs. Porcini, but I am a minor bureaucrat."

"Call me Dany," she said suddenly, impulsively. No one had called her Dany for more than fifteen years.

"Dany," he agreed. "Besides, if anything gets taken from this museum, it's my butt on the line. So it behooves me to make sure security is everything it should be, particularly when it comes to the Van Gogh. But I wish she'd left it to some other city, one not in my jurisdiction."

"Cheer up. Maybe someone will steal it when you're not on duty."

"Somehow that doesn't make me feel better." Beneath the lightly spoken banter something else was shifting, stirring, something incredibly enticing and too dangerous to bear. "Have coffee with me," he said again, his voice deep and warm, like no voice she had ever heard before. He held out his hand, a good hand, with long, well-shaped fingers, a narrow palm, and strength that wouldn't fail her.

She wanted to put her hand into his. She wanted to turn her back on the Fabergé eggs, once and for all. But there had been too many years, too many lies, and there could be no future at all for a cop and a thief. "Marco would rip your head off," she said with a laugh. "He's a very jealous husband. I'll see you around." And she took off, her high heels clicking lightly on the floor in her haste to get away from him.

"Yes." McNab's voice followed her, just reaching her ears as she made her precipitous escape. "You will."

It was after seven when Ferris let herself into her apartment. The sun had already set, and shadows filled the twisting line of rooms that made up her apartment. Blackie was still in residence, waiting with regal feline disdain to be fed and released from bondage. Ferris kicked off her shoes and headed for the kitchen, dumping her bag of Mrs. Field's Cookies and the *pasta primavera* from Willey's Deli onto her spotless counter.

She held herself very still. Nothing in her apartment was ever spotless—it went against the very grain of her nature. And Blackie had gone out that morning, refusing her enticements to return inside, and the early-morning chill had precluded leaving the terrace door open even a crack.

She knew all the rules—any single woman living alone in a city knew them. *If you suspect your apartment has been broken into, you don't wait around looking to see what has been taken. The perpetrator might still be lurking inside a closet. You run, and call the police from the nearest public phone.*

Of course, those rules applied to single women unacquainted with John Patrick Blackheart's peripatetic ways. Besides, he had already gone, and the apartment was empty. She knew that as well as she knew her own name—whichever one she happened to be using—and if she felt a wrenching regret, she told herself it was only because she wanted to scream at him.

"I bet you welcomed him with open arms," she accused her haughty alley cat, dishing him up a generous portion of herring in sour cream that hadn't been in her refrigerator that morning. She peered into its barren depths, wondering if Patrick had left her any other tokens of esteem, but nothing but Diet Coke, yogurt and Sara Lee Cheesecake, her usual staples, met her eyes.

There must be something else. Fond as Blackheart was of his namesake, he wouldn't have broken into her apartment and left nothing but herring and clean counters.

He'd made the bed, too. Not with the pastel flowered sheets she'd been using; he'd managed to unearth the maroon ones that reminded her far too clearly of him. "Damn him," she muttered under her breath. There was no way she'd be able to get a decent night's sleep in those sheets. She should have thrown them out, not hidden them under a pile of towels.

Of course, she thought, dropping onto the bed and folding her arms under her head, in the normal course of events those sheets would have stayed hidden. It wasn't her fault that she'd fallen in love with a cat burglar who made himself at home in her apartment, rummaging through her linens to his heart's content....

She sat bolt upright, staring ahead of her. The one thing her tiny bedroom held, beside the queen-size bed, was an oversize television set, its top usually cluttered with empty ice-cream dishes, old magazines, discarded panty hose, single earrings, and anything else that a normal person would throw out. All that had been ruthlessly removed, and Ferris had no doubt she'd find everything in the trash. In its place was a sleek, black, beautiful VCR, a twin to the one she'd coveted in Blackheart's apartment.

Two tapes sat on top of the black metal. She was almost afraid to look, but curiosity overruled caution. The first was obvious. *To Catch a Thief*. It would be a cold day in hell before she watched that one, she thought, dropping it into her overflowing wastebasket, knowing perfectly well she'd retrieve it before she took the trash out. Still, the gesture was satisfying.

She picked up the other box. *Spanish Dancing*, it read. The woman on the cover was wearing red shoes just like the ones Blackheart had given her, the ones that were hiding somewhere under her bed. Holding the tape in her hands, she sat back and burst into tears.

No one knew he was there. The house was empty, with only the servants sound asleep in their beds. He looked at *The Hyacinths*, reveling in the wash of sheer color and beauty that had somehow sprung from a madman's mind. He could see the tiny pinpricks of red light from the security system; a system only three people could legally circumvent. It didn't matter who took the blame when the painting disappeared. The only issue of any importance was that no one would suspect him. If he could pay off an old score or two into the bargain, then so much the better.

If life were only just a tiny bit simpler. Someone was going to take this painting and lock it into a vault, gloating over it in deepest privacy, never allowing anyone else to marvel at its beauty. Decades, generations later it might resurface, after enough time had passed to cloud its dubious passage from the Merriams' San Francisco mansion. He wondered briefly if the painting was insured. Certainly not at forty million. But if Regina Merriam could afford to give forty million away, she could certainly afford a loss on her insurance.

And speaking of her, she'd be back anytime now. He'd have a hard time explaining his presence in her upper halls with nothing but moonlight and the occasional beam of infrared to keep him company. He'd better get out, fast. He'd be back soon enough.

DANY KNEW Marco was watching her, much more closely than he had in recent months. There was no way he could have the faintest idea what she'd planned, but his watchfulness disturbed her. He hadn't seen her meeting with Stephen McNab. He'd sent her over to scout out the museum while he was busy at the circus grounds—otherwise he would have gone himself. Wouldn't he? So it couldn't be misplaced jealousy. Of course, he did have a dog-in-the-manger air about him. Even if, *thank heavens*, he didn't want her, he didn't want anyone else to have her.

But he'd been so busy preening before a crowd of fascinated women that he wouldn't have had time to notice if Stephen McNab had shown a flattering amount of interest. He couldn't possibly have guessed her plans. She'd been very outspoken about her decision that this would be the last job. Marco was the sort who believed only what he wanted to believe, and if her future didn't fit in with what he wanted, then he would ignore them.

But she'd been very careful. There were no plane or train tickets, and her tiny horde of cash was so well hidden even Marco couldn't find it. Not that it would take her very far. She was counting on her share of the money from the eggs to keep her, not in style for a few months, but in modest peace and safety for years. She'd grown up making do on very little. She could survive for years on her ill-gotten gains.

Marco was sitting on the bed in the crowded little caravan, watching her. She had never thought she'd look back on that antiseptic little motel room with nostalgia, but anything was better than these close quarters, closer even than their cabin on the old freighter. This time she had nowhere to run.

"I want to know," he said suddenly, his voice breaking through the silence like a rusty saw blade, "what you told the cop."

Damn, thought Dany. So much for thinking she was safe. "Not a thing. We talked about the Van Gogh."

"I'm going to have to remind you of something, little one," Marco growled, flexing his fingers. Marco had very strong hands. "You belong to me. Until I let you go, whether I want you or not, you're mine."

Her response didn't matter. If she meekly agreed with him, he'd hit her anyway. She had nothing to lose.

She met his gaze with blithe indifference, her chin held high in defiance. "I don't belong to you, I have never belonged to you, and I never will."

She hadn't taken into account the fact that if she angered him, he'd hit her even harder. The force of the blow knocked her backward and she fell against the side of the van.

"Go to hell, Marco," she said, her voice muffled from her split lip.

He was advancing on her, meaty hand upraised, his face contorted in rage, when her calm voice stopped him. "Don't you think my new boyfriend will notice if I'm bruised?" she taunted him.

"You think your handsome cop will come to your rescue? He's more likely to slap you in jail, once I get through talking. And what about your long-lost brother? You think you can count on him for anything? You never could before."

"I can count on myself. And I can count on you to remember the bottom line and not jeopardize your career because you don't like the way a man looks at me. If the cop has the hots for me, so much the better. He's less likely to think I'm up to something if he wants me."

"Maybe," Marco said. "But he's more likely to want me out of the way."

"It's only seven days. Don't you think I can string him along for that short a time?"

"I don't trust you, Danielle."

"That makes us even. I don't trust you. But you should remember that you can't get the eggs without me. You don't have time to train anyone new. And I can't get the eggs without you. So we're just going to have to keep on with this unpleasant partnership for one more week."

He nodded in reluctant agreement. "Just don't push it. I might decide it would be worth the risk to do without you."

She was so close, so very close to everything she'd ever worked for. She'd be a fool to risk it for the sake of taunting Marco, for the sake of McNab's beautiful gray eyes. "You do your part," she said, "and I'll do mine."

Marco nodded. "Now all we have to worry about," he said in a dream voice that sent shivers down her back, "is the very nosy Ms. Ferris Byrd. A small accident, don't you think? Something to incapacitate her for the next seven days?''

"Why?" Dany breathed.

"She's just a little more observant than I like. I prefer women who lie back and keep their eyes and mouths shut."

"I'm sure you do. What has Ms. Byrd said to make you nervous?''

Marco smiled. "I don't think I need burden you with that information. You have too much to worry about already."

Dany was growing more and more distraught. *Damn Marco.* If he couldn't hit her, he still knew other ways to get to her. "What are you going to do to her?"

"Something creative, little one. Something creative."

FERRIS HAD STRANGE DREAMS that night. It was little wonder. She'd spent the evening crying, crying until runnels of mascara streaked her face, crying until her cheeks were bright red and her lashes bleached white from the salt water of her tears. She lay on her back and let the tears race down her face and drip into her ears. She lay on her stomach and cried into the maroon sheets. She wandered through her apartment, hiccuping and sobbing, occasionally flopping onto the love seat to beat against the pillows until she remembered the first night she'd made love with Blackheart, starting on his love seat and ending in her bed. She'd jumped up, bawling anew, and sobbed her way into the kitchen, into half the Sara Lee Cheesecake, which wasn't improved by the added salt, and then on into her oversize bathroom. But her bedraggled reflection wasn't the sort of thing to cheer her up, either.

Blackie offered no comfort at all, demanding to be let out and away from his howling mistress. That was the difference between dogs and cats, Ferris thought morosely. A dog would cuddle up to you, licking your face and sharing your distress. A cat simply shrugged his elegant feline shoulders and stalked away. Maybe she should trade in this model Blackheart, too, for something affectionate and malleable. Maybe a Peek-a-poo, one those peculiar crosses between a Pekingese and a toy poodle.

Once the tears subsided, she considered resorting to brandy to induce a decent night's sleep. But she didn't want to get into the habit of it—Blackheart had already had far too devastating an effect on her. He wasn't going to turn her into a secret tippler besides.

So she drowned her sorrows in Diet Coke and ice cream. She took as long and as hot a shower as she could stand, pulled on her softest, oldest flannel nightgown, and climbed into bed. And fell asleep watching *To Catch a Thief*.

When she awoke in the drizzly gray light of a rainy predawn, she had a smile on her face and a warm, delicious feeling in her body. It took her only a moment to remember she had nothing to smile about. She sat up, pushing the hair out of her face, grimacing at the rain falling on her slate terrace. The television screen was black. That was odd. She thought she'd fallen asleep just as Cary Grant went swimming in the Mediterranean. She must have gotten up sometime during the night and turned the set off.

It was a shame she'd had to wake up. Whatever she'd been dreaming had been both comforting and definitely erotic. Maybe it hadn't even been about Blackheart, she thought hopefully. Anything was possible in this world. Though not very likely.

Ferris suddenly sniffed the air. It smelled like roses. She'd bought flowers a few days ago in a vain effort to cheer herself up, but they'd been scentless daisies, and they were sitting, brown and dried out, in a vase in the living room. Slowly she turned her head. There on the pillow next to her lay a single white rose.

She reached out for it, her hand trembling slightly. And on her finger was the canary-yellow diamond engagement ring she'd thrust back at Blackheart days ago.

She stared at it for a long moment, considering whether she should once more bathe herself in tears. But she'd cried enough to last for a good long time. Looking down at her replaced engagement ring, she began to laugh.

MARCO WAS ACCUSTOMED to getting up early. If he slept too much, his body grew slow and sluggish, and he couldn't afford to have anything happen to his body. His talent was a gift, and he had to treat it with the respect it deserved.

He started with a hundred push-ups, then moved into the weights. This was the time he could think and plan the best, when his body was being pushed to its limits and no one was around to disturb him with their idle chatter. He stood there in the early-morning drizzle, curling two hundred pounds of metal weights against his bulging chest, and thought about the future. And of how he was going to kill Ms. Ferris Byrd.

Chapter Nine

Spellbound
(Selznick International 1945)

John Patrick Blackheart, né Edwin Bunce, was sitting on Regina Merriam's flagstone terrace overlooking the early-morning bustle on the circus grounds, waiting for his Francesca. She might be having a little trouble recognizing that she was, in fact, his, but sooner or later he'd be able to convince her.

Leaving her this morning had been one of the hardest things he'd ever done. She'd been lying there in the maroon sheets, the blank television screen bathing the pre-dawn room in an unearthly light, and he could see dried tears on her elegant cheekbones. The flannel nightgown was endearingly sexy, more so than one of her silk and lace confections, and he'd wanted to strip off his clothes, crawl into bed with her and just hold her in his arms.

She would have woken up screeching. *Maybe.* He couldn't take the chance. Even worse, she might have cried some more, and then his resolve would have vanished. And he couldn't tell her what was going on. He couldn't incriminate his own sister, but that was the only way he could exonerate himself. If McNab proved to be as tenacious and tricky as Blackheart suspected he was, it was going to be a close-run thing. And if he told Francesca what was going

on, she'd have no familial qualms. She'd sacrifice Danielle Porcini without a second thought in order to keep him
out of jail, and he couldn't let her do that.

Besides, he knew better than anyone alive that Dany
couldn't have pulled the Madrid job herself. She wasn't tall
enough for some of the reaches, even if she used the best
of equipment. He had no doubt at all that she'd been in-
strumental in planning—there was simply too much
Blackheart brilliance in the three recent robberies that had
been placed on his doorstep. *And who knows how many
before?* he thought wearily, shivering in the chilly morning air. His sweet little long-lost sister might have been active for years.

But she hadn't been active alone. With any luck at all he
could pin everything on her accomplice, and get her out of
reach of McNab's long arm. Now he just had to figure if
the identity of her accomplice was as obvious as it appeared to be.

If he was going to save his sister's neck without putting
his own onto the chopping block, he was going to have to
be very busy. As long as no one knew of his relationship
with Danielle Porcini, they'd have no reason to suspect
anyone involved in the circus. Blackheart and Company's
considerable reputation was behind the Porcini Family
Circus, guaranteeing their trustworthiness. If he blew it,
he'd blow it for Trace and Kate as well as himself. His
partner and his wife were as dependent on the well-being
of Blackheart and Company as he was. Not to mention any
future with Francesca.

"Damn," he said out loud, his voice soft and bitter
above the distant sounds of wild animals. "What did I do
to deserve such a mess?"

"You tell me."

It wasn't Francesca. If he knew his slothful darling, she was probably still buried under the covers, unaware of the ring back on her finger.

Instead Dany Bunce stood there, dressed in black chinos and a black turtleneck, her blond hair tied back, her blue eyes cool and mocking.

He hadn't seen her since she was three years old. He'd been seventeen, their father had just died in a fall from a slippery copper roof, and he was embarking on a career in the family business. He couldn't take care of his three-year-old half sister. Both their mothers were dead—his of cancer when he was a child, hers in a car crash in Nice. The only solution was his aunt and uncle in the Lake District. The Eustace Bunces were stoutly disapproving of the family business. Uncle Eustace was a farmer, Aunt Prunella a dedicated farm wife who'd already raised three docile children. They were the best able to cope with a half-wild toddler. If they weren't adept at showing affection, at least they'd instill conventional, comfortable values. And the farm was beautiful.

He'd just about forgotten her existence. And now here she was, a defiant expression in eyes that weren't much different from that angry three-year-old's. Clearly the Bunces' conventional values hadn't taken hold.

He'd been sitting in a tipped-back wrought iron deck chair and didn't bother to change his position or his expression. He also chose to ignore her provocative statement. "Can I help you? Mrs. Porcini, isn't it?"

His sister smiled, showing very straight, very white teeth, either the result of orthodontia or the good Bunce genes. "Call me Dany," she said affably, and her blue eyes were waiting, daring him to react.

If she thought she could fence with him and win, she would soon find she was way out of her league, Blackheart thought, keeping his face smooth. "Dany," he agreed.

She moved over and perched on the wide stone wall, very lithe, very graceful. She would have been good, Blackheart, very good indeed. Who had she been working with?

"I was interested in the Van Gogh. Lieutenant McNab said there was a painting here worth millions of dollars. I wondered if I might see it."

"Why ask me?"

"Aren't you in charge of security? I'd think you'd be very wary of anyone messing with a priceless painting that's your responsibility."

"I thought you wanted to look at it, not mess with it," he drawled.

"I expected you to be a bit paranoid. Anyone in your position might be."

"Oh, I'm never paranoid. Extremely distrustful, but never paranoid. Certainly you can see the Van Gogh, if you so desire. But not right now."

"Why not? Do you want to check out my background first and make sure I'm a decent security risk?" Her cool blue eyes were assessing.

Feisty little creature, isn't she? thought Blackheart, half amused, half irritated. He could still see traces of that three-year-old glaring at him. "We ran standard security checks on everyone connected with the circus before you even arrived in the States." Which went to prove how worthless those security checks had been. They'd turned up nothing more exciting than one of the knife throwers having spent time in jail for spearing a rival. No mention of Madame Porcini's clouded past, or anything that might point to her accomplice.

She absolutely grinned at that point, and he resisted the urge to throttle her. "And you discovered we have spotless reputations?"

"Something like that. You'll still have to wait. Regina sleeps later than the working classes, and I don't think she'd care to have people traipsing through her third-floor hallway."

"Is that where she keeps it?"

He was getting tired of this, mortally tired. Dany Bunce had no more interest in the Van Gogh, no matter what its vaunted worth, than he did. The question was, what did she want? She wasn't here for a family reunion. Unless he was greatly mistaken, she was out for blood. His. Those robberies in Lisbon, Paris and Madrid hadn't pointed to John Patrick Blackheart's famous modus operandi by accident. She'd framed him then, and she probably had every intention of framing him again. But how? And how was he going to protect himself, Francesca and his self-destructive half sister?

"Come back in a couple of hours, and I'll have someone show you exactly where she keeps it. We'll even acquaint you with the security system, in case you're interested."

"I'm not."

"Oh, you never can tell when a knowledge of heat sensors and infrared lighting can come in handy. Life is full of possibilities. In the meantime, don't you think you ought to be getting back to the business at hand?" He nodded toward the organized chaos of activity out on the south lawn. "Don't you need to practice, warm up, something like that?"

"I'm no longer a performer. I used to be an aerialist, but now I work strictly in a business capacity."

"Why? Did you fall?" He didn't like that idea one tiny bit. A fall had killed their father, a fall had nearly crippled him. He didn't want to think of his larcenous baby sister tumbling down, down....

She smiled sweetly. "I'm scared of heights." She slid off the wide stone wall, dusted her black chinos, and moved toward him. "What about you, Mr. Blackheart? Are you scared of heights?"

"Nope. I love them. It runs in my family."

She blinked, her only reaction to his veiled taunt. But she was persevering and game. "I heard you were once a famous cat burglar. Is that true?"

He reached up, caught her cheek between his thumb and forefinger and pinched, just hard enough to leave a red mark. "That runs in my family, too."

She jerked away from him, startled, her mouth open to say something, anything. Even the truth might have been a remote possibility. And then saw something over his shoulder, and her mouth curved in a smug, engaging grin that was a twin to his father's, and her eyes lighted with malicious amusement. "What a happy childhood you must have had, surrounded by such a colorful family. Let me know when I can see the Van Gogh." And she sauntered away, down the wide expanse of slate terrace.

He watched her go for a brief moment. If he'd had any doubt why she hated him, she'd just put that to rest. Her life with the Eustace Bunces must have been hell. And she was determined to pay him back for that.

He sighed, leaning back and shutting his eyes for a moment. And then he remembered that something had caught her eye and stopped her from incriminating herself. And that something, someone, had opened the French doors and stepped out onto the terrace behind him.

He didn't turn to look. The faint whiff of perfume was new, unfamiliar, a spicy, defiant scent unlike Ferris's usual Cabochard. But he knew it was his beloved Ferris-Francesca behind him, knew it even before she dropped the big canary-yellow diamond ring into his lap.

"I hope I wasn't interrupting anything," she said in a voice that was even chillier than the autumn morning. "But you misplaced this, and I thought it should be back where it belonged as soon as possible."

"So did I," he said calmly. "That's where I left it."

"Stay out of my apartment, Blackheart. No secret visits, no gifts or bribes, for me or my cat. Leave me alone. Concentrate on your little circus girl."

At that he turned and looked up at her, a wide smile of genuine delight on his face. "You're jealous," he said, amazed. Ferris was never jealous.

She was looking particularly gorgeous that morning, he thought with a resigned sigh, knowing that he shouldn't touch her. She must have raced after him without bothering to put on her yuppie armament. Her thick black hair hung loose and wavy around her unmade-up face. The faded jeans she was wearing had seen years of service, and they hugged her long legs and wonderful hips as he longed to. She'd taken time to wear a bra under the cotton sweater, but if he pulled her into his lap and slid his hands up under that sweater he could probably unfasten it in record time. With another resigned sigh he closed his eyes again, shutting out the enticing picture she made, resting his folded hands strategically over his lap.

"Blackheart," she said in a weary voice that a less intelligent man might almost have believed, "I wish you every happiness in the world. Run away with Mrs. Porcini, pray that her husband with the bulging biceps doesn't catch up with you, and live happily ever after. Just leave me alone.''

Blackheart's eyes flew open, her words triggering a sudden memory. ''They're not really married,'' he said abruptly. That was one thing the security check had picked up, something he'd disregarded as of no importance until he'd seen the face that went with the name Danielle Porcini. There was no record of any marriage ceremony, legal or religious, between the two circus members.

''Then I hope you'll be very happy.'' Her footsteps made angry, clicking noises as she walked away from him and the French door slammed behind her.

He caught up with her in Regina's deserted living room. There was no one in sight, the lights were still off, and the spacious, empty room was filled with shadows.

When he put his hands on her shoulders she didn't fight him. She had enough sense not to. Any resistance and he would have pulled her into his arms against his taut needful body. As long as she stood, quiescent and watchful beneath his hands, he couldn't do anything more than hold her there.

''How did you get in here? Are any of the servants up?'' *Stupid question,* he mocked himself. He was just wasting time, prolonging the brief contact his body and soul were crying out for.

''What if I told you I broke in?'' Her voice was hushed, solemn.

''I'd be charmed.''

''Too bad. Regina gave me a key years ago.''

''Back when you were on your first fiancé,'' he countered. If he made her mad enough, she might struggle.

''Second,'' she corrected him. ''I was engaged to my high school sweetheart. You ran a distant third, Blackheart.''

"Then how come I was the only one able to get you into bed?"

"Is that how you viewed it, Blackheart? 'Getting me into bed'? Well, now that you've accomplished such a remarkable feat, I would think the challenge would be gone. Time to move on to greener pastures. Maybe you can find another twenty-nine-year-old virgin to seduce."

She was getting very angry indeed. *Good,* he thought, sliding one hand up her shoulder to cup her neck. He could feel the pulse pounding beneath her delicate skin, and he wanted to feel that pulse beneath his lips. "I didn't seduce you, Francesca," he whispered. "I fell in love with you."

"Don't." The word was a quiet, helpless moan. But she wasn't pulling away from him, she was swaying toward him, and the muscles in her shoulders had gone from tense and stiff to soft and warm and weak, and he slid up his other hand, cupping her face, his thumbs gently brushing her pale, lipstickless mouth. Her green eyes were lost and pleading, and he knew he could drown in those eyes, drown in her body, lose himself forever in the sweet tangle of her smooth flesh.

She was the one to bring their mouths together. In the lonely hours and days that followed he would remind himself of that, cherishing that small, temporary act of trust. Her soft, warm lips touched his, for no more than a brief instant. And then his self-control vanished, he slanted his mouth across her, forcing her lips open, and held her there, kissing her with all the longing and despair that were ripping through his shaking body.

For a moment she struggled, and he knew he should let her go, when her arms escaped the prison of his body and slipped around his neck, pulling him closer. He could feel the softness of her breasts through the sweater, the hardness of her nipples, the sweet warmth of her hips pressed up against his, and he groaned deep in his throat. Surely this was worth more than honor, family, safety, anything at all?

He'd gotten his hands under her sweater, just as he'd wanted to since the moment he'd seen her, and he'd just managed to unfasten her bra when a bright light flooded the living room, streaking through their temporary insanity like a lightning bolt from an angry god.

She tore out of his arms, as he knew she would, and he turned to rage at the intruder, frustration and fury wiping out the last tiny bit of common sense he possessed.

The sight of Regina Merriam, her thick white hair in a plait down her back, her designer silk dressing gown reaching the floor, her usually kind, serene face creased with worry, brought back a measure of sanity.

He looked at Francesca. She was out of reach, halfway across the room, surreptitiously fumbling with her bra clasp. He wanted to go to her, to brush her awkward hands away and take care of it, but he knew his touch wouldn't be welcome. He stayed where he was, watched her flushed, miserable face, and cursed his sister with all his heart.

"I don't suppose this is a reconciliation?" Regina asked in a sorrowing voice.

For some stupid, romantic reason Blackheart held his breath. But Francesca shook her head, her long dark hair hiding her face. "Just another mistake. I seem to be making a lot of them nowadays. I hope we didn't disturb you, Regina?"

"Not at all. I was just coming down to share coffee with Blackheart when I heard the two of you. I'm sorry I interrupted."

"I'm glad you did."

Damn her, if she could be cool and unconcerned, so could he. "Yes, it was probably just as well," he drawled, taking a small, perverse pleasure in her sudden start.

Regina looked from one to the other, her sorrow now shadowing her face. "Why don't you both join me for coffee? Surely we can at least share some decent morning conversation?"

"Could I have a rain check?" Ferris pleaded, pushing her hair back and looking calm and very determined. "There's something I want to find out."

Blackheart was a man who'd lived on his instincts for far too long not to listen to them when they were shrieking at him. "What's that?" he demanded.

"Mrs. Porcini," she said. "I can't get over the feeling I've met her before. I wanted to discover if that's possible. I thought I'd ask her where she'd been for the last five years."

If Regina hadn't been there listening, he would have let out a string of curses that would have turned the air blue. If Regina hadn't been there he would have threatened, yelled, coerced, kidnapped her before he let her literally go down among the lions, with her jealousy blinding her to far more dangerous possibilities.

As it was, he had to make do with a veiled warning. He knew his Francesca. Anything more overt would only fuel her determination. "Circus people are a funny breed, dear heart," he murmured. "I don't think they like answering personal questions about their pasts."

He should have known it would be a waste of time. "Oh, I can be discreet, Blackheart. I just want to warn her about you."

"She doesn't need a warning. She already knows."

Wrong again. His ex-fiancée's smile was bitter indeed. "I'm so glad to hear you confide in someone. I still intend to talk to her. See you."

She left without a backward glance. He watched her go, then turned to meet Regina's stern gaze. "Patrick, my boy," she said, "you blew it."

"Regina, my girl," he responded wearily, "I'm afraid you're right."

FERRIS DIDN'T KNOW who told her Danielle Porcini was looking for her. A clown passed a message from an acrobat who'd gotten it from an elephant handler who'd gotten it from a seamstress. But Mrs. Porcini was down near the cages that held the big cats, waiting for her.

If Ferris hadn't been still shaken by her encounter with Blackheart, she would have been more observant. If her mouth weren't still tingling from the feel of his kiss, if her knees weren't weak, if her bra weren't hooked awry... If only her brains didn't fly out the window the moment that man touched her—the moment that man even looked at her.

If onlys were a waste of time. And she wasn't jealous of Danielle Porcini, truly she wasn't. If the lady was unencumbered, she'd be only too happy to hand Blackheart over to her. But the lady came equipped not only with a large husband type—even if Blackheart said they weren't really married—but that police detective, McNab, had been far too interested in her. He already had reason enough to want to nail Blackheart. It certainly wouldn't be too smart to add sexual jealousy to the potent mix.

The early-morning sun had just hit the lions' cages, and the stench, even in the vast green outdoors of Regina Merriam's south lawn, was almost overpowering. She wasn't too happy with the noise, either. It seemed as if all the circus people were busy someplace else. She could clearly hear cute little kittylike purrs, nasty little kittylike growls, and the ominous sound of claws clicking on a metal floor.

"Mrs. Porcini?" she called. Her voice came out with just the tiniest bit of a tremor. "Danielle?"

The Porcini Family Circus has too many big cats, she thought nervously, edging around one of the cages. She could see at least six lions, two tigers and a couple of pure white cats she couldn't even begin to identify. They were watching her just as she was watching them, and they all looked very hungry.

"Danielle?" she called again, her voice now absolutely wobbly. Her shoes were silent on the soft, squishy ground as she turned another corner, but her heart was beating loudly enough to alert even the sleepiest tiger. It was a lucky thing the cages were locked. There was no one close enough to come running if she called for help, and the huge white cat in front of her looked as if he was positively clamoring for a taste of Ferris Byrd.

She heard a noise behind her and whirled, but there was nothing, just the back of another cage. "Danielle?" she tried once more, her voice a plaintive whisper this time.

Then she froze. Slowly Ferris turned to her right, telling herself that it could only be Danielle Porcini.

She was wrong. Standing there, its evil, colorless eyes trained on her defenseless throat, was the hungry white beast she'd been eyeing warily just moments before. It had made no noise in the wet grass. Huge, clawed paws were just as silent on the damp earth as Ferris's sneakers. It didn't growl. It didn't have to. The cage door was open, and the cat was moving slowly, inexorably, toward its breakfast.

Chapter Ten

Dial M for Murder
(Warner Brothers 1953)

Ferris considered screaming. Considered, then rejected the notion. She had seen no one anywhere near the animal cages. The pure white cat was moving steadily closer, but if she startled it there was no telling what it might do. One shriek, one leap, and Ferris Byrd would never have to worry about John Patrick Blackheart again.

"Nice kitty," she said, surreptitiously taking a step backward. The nice kitty growled low in its throat.

Ferris considered crying. Considered, then rejected the notion. She didn't want to die a coward. When they found her, she wanted her expression noble and unblemished by tears.

The early-morning sun had risen higher in the sky, burning through the cool damp mist and beating down on her head. Ferris shivered, wondering if she dared run for it.

"Don't move." The voice came from directly behind her, and Ferris swiveled her head to look into Danielle Porcini's pale, sweating face. The hungry cat growled again. "I told you not to move!" Danielle snapped.

Ferris turned back to look at the animal that was still moving slowly toward her. "What the hell am I supposed to do?'' she muttered under her breath. ''Stand still and become this lion's Big Mac?''

''Tiger,'' Danielle corrected. ''Albino tiger.''

''Just tell me one thing.'' Ferris's normally husky voice had risen several octaves. ''Is it going to eat me?''

''I don't know.''

''Some help you are.''

''I don't know which tiger it is. We have two albinos, Simba and Tarzan. Tarzan'll tear your throat out as soon as look at you—he's a born killer. Simba is a sweet old pussycat.''

''Don't tell me,'' Ferris begged. ''You don't know which one this is.''

''I don't spend much time around the big cats.''

The albino tiger certainly looked ferocious. It was yawning, displaying a very nasty set of teeth, one that made Jaws seem nothing more threatening than a grouper with an overbite. A few more steps, a very few more steps, and he'd be within touching distance. In chewing distance.

''Big cats?'' Ferris echoed, resigned. ''Unfortunately I have. At least the human variety. I don't mean to sound hysterical or anything, but don't you think you might go for help?'' There was just the trace of an edge in her voice.

''I don't want to make any quick moves, in case it's Tarzan. The wrong move, and it'll be all over.''

''You're so comforting,'' Ferris said feelingly. ''So we're just going to stand here like this?''

''I don't think so. He's getting closer.''

Ferris looked directly into a pair of colorless feral eyes. ''Well, if you aren't going to help me and there's no knight in shining armor nearby, it's up to me.'' Slowly, carefully, she held out a shaking hand. ''Nice kitty,'' she whispered, her voice a raw croak. ''Nice kitty.''

The tiger took another step closer, opening its massive jaws. Ferris shut her eyes, unable to watch as she held out her trembling arm. "Nice kitty," she said hopefully. "Nice Simba."

The untamed jungle cat growled deep in its hairy throat, moved closer and sent his long, wet tongue lapping against Ferris's hand.

"It's Simba," Danielle announced, her voice rough with relief.

"Nice kitty," Ferris said again, this time with real enthusiasm. "Want to go back into your nice cage?"

He was still licking her trembling fingers with the air of a connoisseur, and Ferris thanked heaven she hadn't taken the time to wash her hands after she'd given Blackie his herring in sour cream. If she could just get this oversize alley cat back into his cage, she'd bring him a whole case of the stuff.

Danielle moved into view, and Ferris noted with distant surprise that she looked just as shaken as Ferris felt. "Come on, Simba," she said, giving a huge shoulder a push. "Back into your cage."

The tiger allowed himself a snarl, then ignored the rude interruption as he sought out Ferris's other hand. There was a limit to her self-control, as well as to her ability to keep standing. She wasn't going to be able to remain a salt lick for a jungle cat for much longer, and as innocent as Simba appeared, she wasn't too sure how he'd react if she landed in a dead faint at his feet.

"Simba," she said, pulling her hand away from his voracious tongue and holding it out in front of him like a carrot before a horse. "Into your cage, Simba. Good pussy, come on. Come with mama."

"Ferris—" Danielle interrupted.

"Shut up," Ferris murmured in a low, throaty growl meant to appease the hungry beast in front of her. "Come on, pussy. Come get breakfast." She backed toward the empty cage, and Simba followed, eyeing her fishy hand with feline determination. She had no choice but to back up the ramp, back into the awful-smelling cage herself.

It was a horrifying moment; her back was against the bars as Simba filled the doorway, blocking any chance of escape. In the meantime, though, Danielle had found something foul-smelling and particularly destined to appeal to animal appetites, and was busy dumping it through the bars into his dish. Simba ignored the shaking hand of his captive, and sauntered past her to the dish of rancid red meat, swishing his tail as he went.

In two seconds Ferris was out of the cage, the door locked and barred behind her. She slid down the ramp and collapsed onto the wet grass, forcing herself to take slow, deep breaths as reaction set in. Her skin felt too tight, prickling all over her body, her heart was too big for her chest, and her breath was strangled in her lungs. A small, strong hand reached behind her neck and shoved her head down between her knees. "Calm down," Danielle said briskly. "It's over."

Ferris considered throwing up in the grass. The smell of the animal cages wasn't contributing to her peace of mind or the state of her stomach, but she hadn't the energy to move. She just sat there, her head between her knees, and breathed through her mouth.

It was a long time before she could lift her head. Danielle Porcini was kneeling in the grass beside her, her own face pale. "Feeling better?"

"A little bit. What are you doing here, anyway? Just come to watch the results of your little ambush?"

"My ambush?"

"You set me up. I was told you were waiting for me down by the big cats. Instead, I find I'm about to be first course."

"I didn't even know you were here on the grounds. Why should I want to meet you down here? Why should I want you dead?"

"You tell me. Maybe it has something to do with the fact that I know you from someplace."

If Danielle had seemed wary before, it was nothing compared to her expression now. "I've never seen you before the party two days ago."

"Maybe. And maybe I've never met you before. But there's something about you that's driving me crazy. Maybe I saw your picture in the newspaper. Maybe you remind me of someone. Maybe I saw you someplace where you shouldn't be, and you need to get rid of me before I remember where it was."

Danielle's laugh was cool enough to be believable, if Ferris's instincts hadn't been razor sharp after what she'd just been through. "That's all very interesting. But I didn't know you thought I looked familiar. You hadn't bothered to mention it to me, had you? Even if I had a deep dark secret to hide, there's no reason for me to try to kill you. And if it was me, why didn't I lock the cage behind Simba and leave you two alone? He's a nice cat, but even the nicest ones get hungry."

"Maybe you thought it would take too long."

"You still haven't answered my question. Why would I try to kill you if I didn't know you thought I looked familiar?"

"Because I was stupid enough to tell someone else."

She flinched, an expression so brief Ferris almost thought she'd imagined it. "Well, if I really am an international terrorist or a murderer or something, then it must be my accomplice who tried to kill you. Who did you tell?''

For a moment Ferris thought she might really throw up. Sickness washed over her as she remembered her words to Blackheart, taunting him with having seen Danielle Porcini before. He couldn't have, he wouldn't have. . . .

The sickness vanished. She might have been weak-minded, besotted and foolish on many accounts, but she couldn't have been that far-off. She couldn't have fallen in love with a man who was capable of murder.

And then she remembered the other person. "Actually I did say something to the man pretending to be your husband. And he certainly showed a great deal more distress than you do.''

"Marco wouldn't feed you to the tigers," Danielle scoffed, her blue eyes worried. "He'd be more likely to seduce you into silence."

"That's what he was trying to do. Although seduce might be too polite a word for it. When I mentioned you looked familiar, he let go of me immediately."

"Marco is impetuous. Aren't you going to ask why we pretend to be married? You see, I'm being perfectly honest with you—I won't try to deny it."

"Perfectly honest," Ferris echoed. "I'm sure you have a wonderful reason all ready."

"It makes the red tape easier when going from country to country."

"Does that mean your passport identifies you as Danielle Porcini?"

"Don't be so eager to find trouble where none exists. Women keep their maiden names in Europe as well as the States, Ferris. My passport is legal."

"What is your maiden name?"

"Thatcher."

"And Maggie's your mother?"

"She was a little strict, but very loving."

"I thought you were going to be honest with me," Ferris shot back.

"I will. I'll warn you away from Marco. I don't think anyone let the tiger out of the cage to kill you. If anyone wanted to, they'd have the sense to release Tarzan, not Simba. Maybe someone wanted to have you keep your nose out of things that don't concern you. But for your own sake, keep away from Marco. And if you have any sense of self-preservation at all, I'd keep away from Patrick Blackheart, too, if I were you."

A blinding, jealous rage swept over Ferris, one that left her feeling stupid and shaken. "You want them both."

Danielle smiled. "In a manner of speaking. They're nothing but trouble, but it's trouble I can handle. I gather you broke your engagement to Blackheart. It was the smartest thing you could have done. Keep away from him."

"I was thinking of taking him back," Ferris drawled, her face bland, her eyes filled with rage.

"You're too smart for that. You wouldn't want a man who didn't want you. Don't go looking for any more heartbreak, Ferris. I give you a friendly woman-to-woman warning. Go for that nice politician that hangs around you. But keep away from my men."

Ferris rose, brushing the grass from her jeans. Her hands were still trembling, though this time it was from fury rather than fear. "I'll keep your warning in mind. Thanks for the help with Simba."

Danielle rose also, her smaller, lithe body incomparably graceful. "I was going to say anytime, but I trust there won't be another chance. You strike me as a woman of sense. Use it, and pay attention to my warnings."

"What are you doing down here, Danielle?" A blond, scantily dressed giant with a Teutonic accent strolled into view. Walking beside him, placidly enough, was another albino tiger, a twin to the beast now safely locked in the cage.

Danielle was eyeing the cat warily. "Just talking with a friend, Franz. What's Tarzan doing out without a restraint? You know as well as I do how dangerous he could be."

Ferris stared at the white beast, at the colorless eyes and sleek body. She knew before Franz opened his mouth what he would say.

"I'm not an idiot, Danielle. I wouldn't let out a killer like Tarzan. This is Simba." And he rubbed the friendly tiger behind the ears.

FERRIS SANK into the soft leather seat of her Mercedes, shutting the door behind her. She managed to get the key into the ignition, but that was where her energy failed her. There was no one in the parking area in front of Regina's mansion. In the long walk from the animal cages, with a hundred curious eyes following her calm, measured stride, she had held her head high and her shoulders back. Now, for the first time, she had no audience. With a low, miserable moan she let her head fall onto the steering wheel and shook.

She heard the rattle at the passenger door and looked up—into Blackheart's angry face as he tugged at the locked door. "Go away," she said, loudly enough for him to hear it through the closed windows. And she locked her own door for good measure. She dropped her head back onto the steering wheel, hoping for once he'd do as she asked, but it was a vain hope. She heard the rasp of metal, and looked up again to see him calmly inserting one of his new picklocks into the passenger door lock.

She should turn the ignition and roar away from there, leaving him in the dust. She even managed to reach out her still-shaking hand to do just that, then let it drop onto her knee. She had no energy for a confrontation, but even less for a wild ride home. She wasn't calm enough to drive yet. She had no choice but to put up with Blackheart.

The door opened, and he slid in beside her. It had started to rain again, a steady drizzle that obscured even the house directly in front of them, and his dark hair was beaded with drops of rain. In the murky light she could see the tenderness in his eyes, the gentleness in his demoralizing mouth, so before she could give in to the comfort she so badly needed, she went on the attack.

"It's reassuring to see you carry your burglar's tools wherever you go." She tried for an arch tone, but it was somewhat diminished by the raw shakiness that lingered. "You still want to tell me you're retired?"

"I don't want to tell you a damned thing. Come here." He didn't even give her time for a protest, but simply reached out and hauled her shaking body into his arms, over the gearshift and the emergency brake, over the half-filled can of Diet Coke and the crumpled bag of Mrs. Field's Cookies. He wrapped his long, strong arms around her, shoved her face against his shoulder and held her there, one deft hand stroking her long hair.

She lay in his arms stiffly, without moving for countless seconds. And then, sighing, she sank into him, her bones melting, her body flowing over him as she gave up fighting. At least for the moment.

He was so warm, and she was so very cold. She could hear the steady thudding of his heart beneath her, racing just slightly, as if something had frightened him. His hands were tough but gentle, brushing the hair away from her face, holding her trembling body in the shelter of his arms, and for a short while she allowed herself the luxury of believing that as long as he held her, everything would be all right.

The mindless state, delicious though it was, couldn't last forever. The heavy downpour lessened, her own throbbing heart slowed its tumultuous pace, and sanity, with its evil twin, uncertainty, returned.

She pushed away from him, and he let her go, not moving to stop her as she made her ungainly way back across the gearshift and the emergency brake and junk food trash. Once she was back in the safety of her own bucket seat, her hands firmly on the leather-covered steering wheel for the sole purpose of giving her something to hold on to rather than Blackheart, then she could toss her hair back over her shoulder and meet his gaze directly.

"Better now?"

She could be gracious. "Yes, thank you."

He looked as if he wanted to grab her again, but was controlling the urge. "You want to tell me what happened?"

"Not particularly."

"Let me rephrase that. You are going to tell me what happened."

It would have been useless to argue. Besides, she needed to talk to him. "I went looking for Danielle. Someone told me she was waiting for me down by the animal cages. I went down there to find her, and someone let one of the tigers out."

"Who told you she was there?"

"I don't remember. One of the clowns, I think, but he told me an acrobat had gotten the message from someone else."

"All right. What happened next?"

"Danielle showed up, together we lured the tiger back into the cage and locked the door, and then I came back up here."

"Somehow I think I'm missing something."

She managed a wry smile. "Actually I was wondering where you were. Like a fool, I kept expecting you to show up at the last moment and rescue me."

"Francesca..."

"And actually you did. I still had some of the herring you brought for Blackie on my hands. The tiger licked my fingers and followed me into the cage. So you've done your good deed for the day, and now you can go...."

"Shut up, Francesca." He didn't pull her this time; he climbed across the barrier and put his arms around her, drawing her face close to his. "You're all right now?"

He was too close for her peace of mind. Her equilibrium had been restored, at least to a working level, and she had no excuse to move closer. "I'm fine, Blackheart. I just want to go home and change."

"You should do more than that. You should leave town."

"Sounds like an excellent idea. I'm sure you'd be happy enough to see me go. Unfortunately I can't leave until after the circus benefit."

"To hell with the circus benefit. A dozen women at the committee could do what you're doing."

"Yes, I know just how dispensable I am. Nevertheless, I have a responsibility, and I'm not going to shirk it just so you can chase after Danielle whoever she is without me watching."

He sank back into his own seat with a snort of disgust. "Is there any way you can control your jealousy long enough to see reason?"

"I'm not jealous. Maybe you have no carnal interest in Danielle. But you're interested in something, something that makes you carry your picklocks around with you. And I'm not going to go away, and I'm not going to stand idly by while you give in to your baser urges."

"The only thing my baser urges want is you, Francesca. Go away, dear heart. Somewhere deep in that flintlike heart of yours there must be a spark of feeling left for me. Give in to that spark, just for two weeks. Go away, and when you come back everything will be over and I can explain...."

"Trust is a two-way street, Blackheart. Tell me now."

He looked at her for a long moment. "I can't."

"And I can't go away. So it looks as if we're at an impasse."

"That's what it looks like," he said wearily. "Just do me one favor."

"If I can."

"Keep away from lion cages. I'm not the only person you can't trust."

HE ALREADY HAD A BUYER. A man of untold wealth and spotless reputation would pay anything, anything to own *The Hyacinths*. He didn't care where it came from, he didn't care that no one would ever know he owned it. He didn't care that he was paying possibly more than it would get at current inflated auction prices. He wanted it with an obsessive passion and he would stop at nothing to get it.

Fortunately there was nothing the buyer needed to do but come up with an enormous supply of untraceable bills and bearer bonds—and wait for him to do the dirty work.

And fortunately for him, the dirty work wasn't all that dirty. Taking *The Hyacinths* from its current location in Regina Merriam's third-floor hallway would be child's play. He had a key to circumvent the alarm system, he had an accomplice, and he had not one but two possible scapegoats. The way his luck was going, there was no telling where it might end. Possibly beyond his fondest dreams. Although his dreams were pretty grandiose already.

He almost wished he didn't have to wait. He almost didn't trust the utter simplicity of it. He wanted to get it over with, to make certain it really was as easy as it appeared to be. But his buyer wasn't ready, his accomplice wasn't ready, his alibi wasn't ready, and his scapegoat wasn't quite ready. Eager or not, he'd have to wait. And gloat, in anticipation. Things would only be getting better.

Chapter Eleven

Psycho
(Paramount 1960)

The damned ring was back on her finger. Ferris stared down at it, her eyes still blurred with sleep, and cursed. Last night had been bad enough. She's somehow managed to put in most of a day at work, had crawled home and sat in her huge old bathtub until the water cooled and Blackie drove her crazy with his incessant mewing. She'd fed him herring, shuddering in memory, and had gone to turn on the television.

A video tape of *Mary Poppins* was sitting on top of the VCR. She'd stared at it, mystified. The mind of John Patrick Blackheart worked in mysterious ways, but right then she needed something mindless and soothing. A Walt Disney musical, complete with animated foxes and the like, should hit the spot, and there'd be nothing to remind her of a certain cat burglar.

Wrong. Two thirds of the way through the movie, when she'd been lulled into a comfortable acceptance, the entire cast started dancing over the rooftops of London, leaping from building to building with the expertise of a dozen cat burglars. She watched, throat dry, heart pounding, even the glossiness of a Disney extravaganza unable to calm her fear of the dizzying heights. *Damn Blackheart,* she thought miserably, unable to simply press the button and turn off the machine. *Damn his black heart.*

She sat up, the morning light filtering around her, and peered at her digital clock. Later than she'd thought—after ten. It was a good thing the office was closed—the way things were going she'd be out of even her menial job. Becoming irresponsible wasn't the way to start a new life.

It had never been in her nature to be irresponsible. So why was she still lying in bed, when anyone else would be up and accomplishing things? Maybe she didn't feel like accomplishing anything. Maybe she just wanted to sit in her lonely bed and feel sorry for herself.

She tugged at the ring. It was too tight on her finger—she'd need soap to get it off. How had Patrick managed to slip it on while she still slept? Maybe he'd used Krazy Glue—she wouldn't put anything past him.

She looked around her uneasily, then breathed a sigh of relief. She'd stripped the maroon sheets off the bed and replaced them with pink flowered ones that had never seen Blackheart's irresistible body. With his ability to cloud her mind and walk through walls, she wouldn't have been surprised if he'd managed to change the sheets under her sleeping body, but the pink ones were still in place. Then she smelled the coffee.

"Hell and damnation," she said.

"Is that any way to start a morning?" Patrick's voice floated in from the kitchen. He appeared in her doorway, a cup of steaming coffee in his hand.

Ferris didn't know which vision had the stronger emotional effect on her—Blackheart in his black denims and ancient tweed coat or the cup of perfect coffee that only he could make. She'd been making do on instant, and she missed Blackheart's coffee almost as much as she missed the man himself.

"If that coffee's for me, bring it here," she grumbled, still tugging absently at the ring. "Otherwise go away."

"It's for you." He sank onto the bed beside her with his customary grace, the coffee barely sloshing the sides of the full cup. "And don't tell me to get off the bed. You don't get the coffee unless I sit here."

"I may be an idiot where you're concerned, Blackheart, but my price is a little bit higher than a cup of coffee." She could smell it, the aroma dancing across the air to tease her nostrils and make her mouth water.

"Not the price of my coffee," he countered. "Lighten up, Francesca. I said sit here, not have my wicked way with you. Stop tugging on the ring, drink your coffee, and listen to me."

Certain things weren't worth fighting. She took the coffee, mentally absorbing the caffeine with a contented sigh. "That's where I get into trouble. Listening to you. You're tricky, Blackheart."

"I know you don't trust me, Francesca. You've told me so in as many ways as you can manage. Right now I don't give a damn. Your lack of trust is your problem, not mine."

"Is it?" The coolness in her voice would have chilled a less stalwart soul than Blackheart.

He leaned back on the bed, away from her. "I'll say it just once, Francesca, and then we'll drop it. It's not me you don't trust. It's yourself. You're afraid of being in love with me, afraid of losing yourself. So you manufacture excuses, when deep down inside you know perfectly well that if you listened to your heart, you'd know that you can trust me. You'd know that I love you and that you love me, and if we have that then everything else can be worked out. But as long as you're too much of a coward to listen, it's a waste of time. Besides, I have more important things on my mind right now. Your neuroses can wait.''

She'd gone through a dizzying range of emotions during his short speech, moving from annoyance to melting love to absolute fury. She would have thrown her coffee at him, but at that point the coffee was worth more to her than the man. She drained it, shoving the empty mug under her bed and glaring at him. ''All right. Then let's talk about more important things than my puny little neuroses. You slimy, conniving little—''

''Ah-ah-ah,'' he reproved. ''You don't want to use those nasty words, do you, dear heart? You might have me convinced you really care.''

''You're so egocentric, you'll believe anything you want to believe.'' She was tugging fretfully at the canary diamond again. He reached out and covered her hands with his.

''Stop yanking at it,'' he said. ''If you just stopped eating so many cookies, it would probably fall off.''

''You've been sending me the cookies!'' she snapped, outraged.

''That's because you were getting too skinny. Eating your heart out over me, I suppose. I thought I'd better fatten you up.'' Before she realized what he was doing, he'd levered his body across hers, his hands cupping her rounded hips. ''I don't know, maybe you could do with a few more cookies. I like you with a few extra pounds.''

''Go drown yourself, Blackheart.'' She tried to push him off, but it was a half-hearted effort, and they both knew it. She squirmed, then realized with sudden astonishment that he was completely aroused.

''Yes,'' he said. ''You do have that effect on me.''

''Tough.''

"Yes," he said, lowering his mouth to hers. "Tough." And he kissed her, long and fully, pushing her back into the pillows, kissed her with lips and tongue and teeth and soul until she was feverishly kissing him back, her hands trapped beneath their bodies, her hips reaching up to him, her body straining for his. Once more it was starting, the dark midnight of desire that wiped out thought and will and any lingering trace of sanity, and with the last ounce of effort she yanked out her hands from beneath them, bringing them up to his shoulders to push him away.

For a brief moment her fingers clung to him, to the thick tweed and the tense shoulders beneath, clung and kneaded. And then she shoved, taking him off guard, so that he fell back onto the bed beside her.

He just lay there for a moment, breathing deeply, his chest rising and falling, his eyes closed. And then he opened them, turning to look at her, and there was a wicked gleam in their brown depths. "You can't blame me for trying," he said. "Or maybe you can. You have the ability to blame me for all sorts of things, whether I've done them or not."

"Have you?"

"Have I what?"

"Done them? Did you rob the people in Madrid and the museum in Paris and the people in Lisbon? Have you been breaking into places? Have you been breaking the law and lying to the police?"

He said nothing, looking up at her, his face expressionless, wiped free of desire, irritation or any emotion at all.

"Please answer me." To her inner disgust her voice was cracking. "I can't stand this uncertainty. Tell me the truth."

"The truth, Francesca, wouldn't end your uncertainty," he said briskly, sitting up and withdrawing from her, physically, mentally, emotionally. "You want any more coffee?"

"I want answers."

"You'll have to find your own." His voice was colder than she'd ever heard it, and she knew with sudden despair that she'd gone too far. Past the point of no return.

All right, she thought, drawing her defenses back around her like invisible armor. *I can survive. I can survive anything.* "Did you just come to make me coffee and harass me?" she demanded. "Or was there something you wanted?"

He paused in the doorway, and a blessed glint of humor lit his somber eyes. "Loaded questions again. If you think this is harassment, you ain't seen nothing yet. And I thought I made it clear there was something I wanted."

"Stop it!"

He shrugged. "All right. Yes, there's something I need from you. A little help for old times' sake, and I didn't know who else to ask. Surely you can be noble enough to do me one small favor."

"One small favor? All right, Blackheart. For old times' sake I'll do you one small favor. What is it?"

His face was wreathed in an innocent smile. "Do a little roof-hopping and housebreaking," he replied. "What else?"

DANY WAITED until the door to the Winnebago slammed, waited until she was sure he was well and truly gone. She lay in the narrow bunk, unmoving, not quite daring to believe she was alone at last. He'd been whistling something cheerful and jaunty, and the grating sound of that tuneless little song died away as Marco moved across the grounds.

She'd been such a complete fool. Hadn't she learned anything in the twenty-four hard years she'd been on this planet? Hadn't she learned you don't threaten and provoke a wild beast, no matter how tame it seemed? Hadn't she learned not to hope for happy endings?

She pulled her aching body out of the bunk, her fingers clinging to the edge as dizziness swept over her. She shook her head to try to clear the mists, but the pain was so intolerable that she fell back against the hard mattress with a wordless moan. She lay there, and for the first time in the last long, horrible day, she cried.

The salt tears stung her face, reminding her that she couldn't spend the day in bed feeling sorry for herself. She'd gotten herself into this mess and was simply paying the price for her own stupidity. This time she was able to get to her feet and totter across the narrow aisle to the miniature bathroom, holding on as she went.

She hadn't meant to look into the mirror. She waited until she'd finished her shower, waited until she'd drained the water reservoir and stumbled back into the tiny bathroom. And then she caught sight of her reflection, the swollen jaw, the raw scrapes from Marco's knuckles, the black eye. It was going to take five pounds of makeup to cover it this time, she thought wearily, swallowing three aspirin and praying that they'd work quickly. If only she could cover up what he'd done to her body.

She stared at her reflection in the mirror. Yellow covered the red marks, green toned down the purple bruises, and a heavy matt makeup did an adequate job. She'd have to stay out of bright sunlight and away from curious eyes, particularly those of Stephen McNab. What a fool she was, to think he was comfort and safety! Stephen McNab was the long arm of the law, and if he knew what she'd been doing for most of her adult life, he'd slap her in jail so fast her head would spin. *No.* There was no one she could turn to, no one who could help her. Only her own wits could do that now.

Ferris Byrd was going to have to use her own wits, too. She'd done what she could to protect her, and had probably put her in worse danger. There were times when Dany wasn't sure if Marco was quite sane. But it wasn't a question of sanity. It was a question of a not too bright, not too civilized creature feeling threatened. And when stupid creatures were threatened, they reacted violently.

She was going to have to be very careful, Dany thought, pulling on a turtleneck shirt that covered the bruise at the base of her throat. Five more days and she'd be free. In the meantime she had to go out into the sunny morning and hope that no one looked too closely. And that she didn't run into the eagle-eyed Stephen McNab.

"I DON'T WANT to be doing this," Ferris said.

Blackheart had his back to her. They were standing in a grove of trees on the west side of Regina's stately mansion, and her ex-fiancé was looking upward, way, way upward, to the sharply angled roof four stories above.

"Then why are you here?" he countered, not bothering to turn and look.

He didn't need to. He knew as well as she did that she was dressed in black denims and a turtleneck, with ballet slippers on her feet and her dark hair tied back with a dark bandanna. He knew that panic would lurk in her eyes despite the determination on her lips. And he knew she'd have no argument against the indefensible. He asked, and she was here. It was as simple and as stupid as that.

"Do you expect me to climb up the side of the building like Spider-Man?" she demanded. She could hear the distant noise from the circus on the great lawn on the eastern side of the building, could hear the muffled roar of the big cats.

"I expect you to follow my lead, dear heart. If the two of us can break in, then the place isn't as secure as it should be."

"What do you mean, if the two of us can break in? I thought we'd be a formidable combination."

He glanced back at that, his expression inscrutable. "So did I," he said. "But you're not viewing this from a distance. We've got one experienced cat burglar, but one who is sadly out of practice, whether you believe it or not. Not to mention that he's hampered by a game leg. And we have a woman who's a base coward, terrified of heights and terrified of love. It seems to me a baby gate could keep us out."

"Blackheart . . ." she warned.

"Follow me, my love." He swung himself up into the first branch of a tree, then began climbing. "Unless you're too chicken."

"I'm too old to fall for dares," she said, looking up at him as he disappeared into the branches.

"I double-dare you, Francesca," his voice filtered down. "Hurry up, or you won't know where to go when you reach the top."

She who hesitates is lost, Ferris reminded herself grimly, reaching for the first branch. She wasn't as tall as Blackheart, nor as limber, and it took her a couple of tries to swing her body up and over the thick limb. She was just as glad she didn't have an audience. "Are you up there?" she called. "I'm coming."

"I know you are," she heard him say. "I'm waiting."

"I know you are," she muttered under her breath, hauling her body upward, mentally cursing the last few batches of Mrs. Field's Coco-Macs.

He was waiting for her, all right. Miles away from the dubious safety of the thick-limbed oak tree, lounging indolently on a third-floor balcony. She stopped her relentless climb, clinging to the branch for dear life, refusing to look down at the ground miles below her, and glared across the vast space. "How did you get there?"

"I jumped." He leaned over the thick stone parapet that was waist high and held out his hand. It was an eternity away from her reach. At least eight inches.

"Forget it," she said. "I'm going back down."

"If you go back down you'll have to look. And I'd advise against it."

She knew he was right. She considered a brief peek at the grass and gravel beneath her and thought better of it. "I think I'll just stay here," she said, clinging more tightly to the branch.

"It'll probably rain this afternoon. Don't you think you'll get wet?"

"That's all right. Then I won't have to worry about a shower."

"What about food?"

"I need to burn off a few of those cookies you've been plying me with. I'll be fine. Just send the fire department to extract me in a few days."

"Francesca," he said, his voice stern. "Come here." He reached out, crossing the space, and could almost touch her. "I won't let you fall. Trust me at least that far."

"I don't trust you, Patrick. I thought we made that clear." Slowly, carefully she pried one hand away from the tree branch and put it into his.

His long, brown fingers closed over hers. The leap would only be a couple of feet, and she'd land on the terrace with its nice high wall protecting her. He wouldn't let her fall. Would he?

"Come on," he said, yanking suddenly.

Caught off guard, she had no chance to do anything more than shut her eyes and leap. When she opened them she was standing safely on the balcony, Blackheart's arms wrapped tightly around her.

She pushed him away, brushing the clinging bark and leaves from her black clothes. "Well," she said briskly, "that was simple enough."

Blackheart's smile was devoid of cynicism. "Wasn't it, though? The next part will be even easier."

"We're going into the house and climbing the stairs, right?"

"Wrong. We're climbing up the outside of the house to the roof and going in through the attic."

"The hell we are!" Ferris protested, heading for the door.

His hand caught her before she'd gone two feet, spinning her around to face him. "Don't chicken out now, Francesca. I'll make a little bargain with you. If you can climb up the rest of the way without any more whining, then I'll let you go."

"You'll let me go back downstairs?" she said, not quite understanding.

"No. I'll let you go completely. No more breaking in to your apartment, no more leaving little gifts, no more cookies or movies or pickled herring. Just prove to me you're brave enough to do it, and I'll trust you to manage the rest of your life on your own."

She just stared at him. This was what she wanted, wasn't it? Finally to be free of him? Wouldn't she be willing to climb the Matterhorn for that freedom, never mind something as puny as Regina Merriam's stone mansion? "All right," she said breathlessly. "You've got a bargain."

His own smile was grim. "I thought I might. You first." He gestured toward the edge of the balcony.

She peered over it dubiously. "You want to tell me how we're going to manage this, or am I supposed to make it up as I go along?"

"No whining, Francesca, or the deal is off. Just be glad we're doing this in broad daylight and not the dead of night." He came up behind her, his body warm and solid, and she wished, longed for the chance to lean back against him and close her eyes, close out the dizzying heights and the miserable agreement she'd just made. His arm reached beside her, pointing. "It's not as bad as it looks. There's a stone ledge at least eight inches wide that will get us as far as that deep-set window, and you should be able to hoist yourself up the rest of the way."

"And if I can't?"

"There are boxwood below. They should cushion your fall."

Her reply was brief and colorful. "Why don't you go first?"

"I thought I should be there to catch you if you fall."

"I hate you, Patrick. You know that, don't you?" she muttered, climbing out onto the parapet.

"I know that, dear heart," he said gently, following close behind her, his strong hand within inches of hers.

Ferris edged out onto the narrow parapet, her sweaty hands clinging to the stones jutting out from the building. Once out on that narrow ledge there was no going back. With a deep intake of breath she put her brain on automatic pilot and began to climb, always aware of Blackheart close behind her.

Halfway up she realized she wouldn't fall. Blackheart wouldn't let her. Logic told her that there was nothing he could do to stop it if she started to tumble, but logic had nothing to do with it. He was behind her, his sheer force of will forcing her up, up, and that will would keep her safe. Even the dangerous slickness in her hands dried up in the soft autumn breeze that was playing around the angled roofs of the Merriam house, and as she reached up for the copper gutter she only allowed herself a brief moment to hope that Regina kept her gutter intact. Even that thought vanished. Blackheart would have checked it first, before he brought her out here.

She pulled herself up, landing on the roof with little grace and a great deal of relief, sprawling along the greenish metal and watching as Blackheart levered himself up and over.

"You did it," he said, his eyes alight with something she couldn't read.

"Yes, I did. Why?"

"I thought it was to get me to leave you alone."

"I'm not talking about that. Why did you want me to do it? No lies or evasions, Patrick. Why did you make me climb up here?"

"Because I wanted to be alone with you?"

"No."

"Because I hoped you'd fall and take my terrible guilty secret to the grave with you?"

"No."

"Because I wanted you to realize you do trust me, after all?"

"That's it," she agreed. "But you promised to leave me alone if I did it."

He grinned, his teeth strong and white in the glorious sunlight. "Francesca, dear heart," he said. "I lied."

Chapter Twelve

The Thirty-Nine Steps
(Lime Grove 1935)

At least he didn't make her climb down the skylight window, Ferris thought as she followed him through the dormer window into the musty attic. She wouldn't have put it past him. She knew for a fact that he was more than slightly partial to the old caper movie, *Topkapi,* and he loved the scene where the robbers were lowered through the skylight. While Blackheart hadn't been into fantasy games in the past, she'd still been holding her breath. After what he'd just put her through, she wouldn't have been surprised at anything.

He'd proven his point, unpleasant as she found it. She did trust him, and in recent weeks she'd forgotten that elemental fact. Not with jewels, not with worldly goods, but with her life, with her well-being, even with her love, she trusted him. She just didn't know how she was going to live with that knowledge.

She landed on the dusty floor with a soft thud, her ballet slippers pinching her feet slightly. There were dust motes in the late-morning sunlight, shifting shadows, and an odd assortment of science-fiction-type lights over to one side. "What's that?" she demanded, heading across the attic in its direction.

"The security system for the Van Gogh." Blackheart barely glanced at it.

Ferris stopped short. "It looks impressive."

"Trust me, it isn't. That wouldn't stop a determined teenager. For one thing, three people have keys to the system, and that's two people too many. For another, the technology is antique. That form of infrared detection went out several years ago."

"Who has the three keys?"

"It doesn't matter." Blackheart was poking around the boxes and trunks stacked by the doorway. "Any self-respecting thief could circumvent it, anyway."

"Is there such a thing as a self-respecting thief?" She was momentarily distracted.

Blackheart turned and grinned at her, and even in the murky light she could see the flash of his white teeth. "What do you think?"

"I think you're conscienceless. You still haven't answered my question. Where are the keys?"

"Regina has one, Phillip has the other," he said, turning back to his investigations.

"Need I ask where the third one is?"

"You needn't. It would probably take me less time to go through it without the key than with it, but yes, I have the third key. After all, I set up the system several years ago."

"An outmoded system."

"It wasn't outmoded then," he replied with great patience.

"What the hell are we doing up here, Blackheart?"

"I told you—we're double-checking the security. We have less than a week to worry—after that it's Nelbert's problem. I just don't want anything to happen in the meantime." There was a row of doors at the far end of the cavernous room, and Blackheart systematically began opening them, pawing through shallow closets filled with old clothes, boxes and trunks.

Ferris moved closer, drawn by a glimmer of deep blue silk, and within moments she was looking through an array of evening gowns dating back to the beginning of the century. The heavy stone Merriam mansion had survived the earthquake and fire of 1906, so it was entirely possible that some of these gowns came from that era. They were made for women shorter and far more buxom than Ferris, but the richness of the materials shimmered across her hands, and she was assailed with a sudden weak-minded and entirely feminine longing for something as beautiful as this to wear.

She turned to find Blackheart watching her, his expression guarded. He said nothing, closing the door of the closet he'd been delving into and advancing on her. She didn't know what she expected, and instinctively put up her hands to ward him off.

"Get into the closet," he ordered tersely.

"Blackheart, this is neither the time nor the place...."

"Someone's coming, you idiot. Get into the closet." Without waiting for a further protest he shoved her in, following her and pulling the door shut behind them, pushing the silks and satins back on the rod with a ruthlessness that caused Ferris to cry out in protest. The noise didn't get very far. He slammed his hand over her mouth and pushed her back against the partition. The dresses closed around them, still smelling faintly of faded roses, and they were alone in the cramped darkness, Blackheart's hand across her mouth, listening, listening.

At first she didn't believe him. It wouldn't have been beyond his capabilities to manufacture an intruder, just to give him the chance to back her into the closet. But a moment later she heard the sounds that had alerted him. After years of midnight invasions, Blackheart's ears were more finely tuned than those of a normal human being, and the footsteps, the muffled voices just outside the attic door were clearly not just an excuse for him to put his hands on her.

Slowly he released her mouth, but not his grip on her. His other hand was around her waist, holding her still, and she didn't dare squirm as she so desperately wanted to. Her fear of heights didn't extend to dark, enclosed spaces. She felt warm, cozy, and inexplicably excited in that cramped darkness with only Blackheart's heated body beside her, and she had to mentally slap herself for thinking what she couldn't help thinking.

There were three voices and presumably three sets of footsteps to go with them, though Ferris's hearing wasn't sophisticated enough to be certain. "As you can see," Jeff Nelbert's thick, fruity tones lectured, "this security system is laughable. Nothing compared to what I've set up at the museum for *The Hyacinths*, but then, Blackheart got into the business through the back door in more ways than one. One couldn't expect him to have the professional expertise I have."

Blackheart's low growl was inaudible to anyone but Ferris, plastered against him in the dark closet. She smothered a laugh against his shoulder, wishing he'd move away, wishing there was room enough to breathe without inhaling the scent of faded roses and sexy, impossible John Patrick Blackheart.

His mouth was somewhere just above her ear, his hand had reached up and loosened her hair, and all his attention seemed focused on the voices outside the closet door. She only wished she could be as single-minded.

"What makes you think Blackheart's going to go for the painting?" There was no mistaking Stephen McNab's deep tones, and if Blackheart's taut body started in surprise, it didn't stop his lips from nibbling on her sensitive earlobe.

Ferris stretched and preened like a stroked kitten. Her skin suddenly felt hot and very sensitive, and she wished those interfering voices from the attic would go away and leave her in peace with the man she loved.

"It's his only chance," Nelbert replied, his two-hundred-plus frame shaking the sturdy attic floor as he moved across the room. "He knows once it's gone from here and under my protection in the museum, he'll have a snowball's chance in hell of getting his hands on it. He's got to act fast, and he's going to use these circus goings-on as a cover up."

"Maybe," McNab said. "I'd like to believe it, but Blackheart's never had any connection to stolen artwork. It's hard to believe he'd change his MO so late in the game."

"Don't you believe it. What makes you think he hasn't done artwork before? Look at how hard it was to pin any of the jewel robberies on him. He could have been responsible for half the art thefts in Europe and those idiots at Interpol would have no idea."

"Maybe." Ferris could tell by the sound of McNab's voice that he was clearly unconvinced. She could also tell that he didn't like Nelbert that much, but then, nobody did. She wasn't able to make any more deductions because Blackheart had slipped his hands under her turtleneck shirt. "It wouldn't hurt to check."

Blackheart's mouth grazed her ear. "It's hot in here," he whispered, a bare thread of sound, one that would reach no farther than the tasseled silk wedding dress in front of them. "Why are your nipples hard?"

She turned to glare at him, but his mouth caught hers, kissing her with a complete dedication that in no way diminished the attention he was paying to the conversation in the outer room. She knew that, she hated it, but she kissed him back anyway, pressing her hips up against his, noting without surprise the extent of his arousal, wishing those noisy people would just go away.

"Listen, Lieutenant—" A new voice entered the fray, one surprising enough to make Blackheart release her mouth and listen. "We wouldn't be wasting our time if we didn't think there was something that merited your attention. I'm well aware of how overworked and underpaid our police is. I'm simply concerned about my mother's safety."

Blackheart's response was nothing more than an obscene, sibilant whisper in her ear.

"What makes you think your mother's in any danger?" McNab countered stubbornly, and Ferris found her feelings for the tenacious policeman warm several degrees. "Blackheart's never been involved in any form of assault. Cat burglars seldom are—it goes against their self-image. I'll tell you again, I don't believe Blackheart's going to change his ways this late in the game. He's not going to turn to art theft and he's not going to beat up old ladies."

"Are you willing to stake your career on that?" Phillip Merriam demanded. "And my mother's safety?"

There was a pause. The two in the closet listened intently, and Ferris was aware of an intense, sudden dislike of charming, noble Phillip Merriam.

"I'm not willing to risk anyone's safety without good reason," McNab said finally. "Maybe you're right. After all, you're the one who got the tip. And a painting like *The Hyacinths* isn't just a work of art, it's the heist of a lifetime, and when it comes to gall Blackheart has no bounds. Don't worry—we'll be watching."

"That's all I ask, Lieutenant," Phillip said smoothly, all belated affability. "That's all I ask."

They waited in silence, shrouded by the silk wedding dress. As they listened the footsteps faded away, the heavy clang of the metal door at the top of the stairs reassuring them they were once more alone.

Blackheart, thorough as ever, reached for her again, but she was one step ahead of him, pushing through the wall of clothes and out into the dusty attic before he could make her forget everything once more. "What's going on?" she demanded, keeping her voice down in case their visitors were still within earshot.

Blackheart shrugged, strolling over to get a closer look at the blinking, winking monolith that constituted the Van Gogh's security system. "Sounds like I'm about to become an art thief. Except that our friend McNab is going to catch me in the act. What does it sound like to you?" He seemed no more than casually curious, but Ferris knew he was intent on her answer.

"It sounds to me like a setup."

His smile across the expanse of the attic was beatific in the midday light. "Why, Francesca, you do trust me."

"No, I don't. I just agree with McNab. You're not about to start ripping off paintings this late in your career. If you steal anything, you'll steal Regina's jewels."

"She doesn't have any to speak of," he murmured absently, still watching her.

"You'd know that, of course."

"Just force of habit. When you've spent as many years as I have in the business, it's hard to let go of instincts. Besides, I've done security for Regina often enough to make it my business to know what's of value in this house."

"You don't need to keep explaining," Ferris said mildly.

"The hell I don't. You're enough to make a saint paranoid."

"You're no saint."

"No, it sounds more like I'm a fool. And a patsy."

"I can't imagine why Phillip would think you'd be planning on robbing his mother. He's usually such a fair, sensible man."

"Is he? Maybe he's got something else on his mind."

"I don't think he's pining for me, if that's what you're suggesting. He was very gracious about our engagement."

"Which engagement? Yours and his, or yours and mine?"

"Don't be obtuse. His and mine, of course. So I don't think his brain is clouded by latent jealousy. Especially now that you and I are no longer involved."

"Aren't we? What were you doing in the closet with me?"

She could only hope the shadows obscured the blush that rose to her face. "Kissing you," she said flatly. "Small enclosed places turn me on. Anyone would do in a situation like that."

If she'd hoped to goad him, and she had, it was obviously a waste of time, for he laughed, suddenly cheerful. "I'll keep that in mind. So if Phillip isn't intent on revenge, why is he setting me up and using Nelbert to do it?"

"Nelbert's obvious. He's your biggest competitor and he's always been jealous of Blackheart and Company. McNab doesn't even need an explanation—he's determined to nail you. Maybe they've tricked Phillip into thinking you're a danger."

"I'm not overly impressed with politicians' intellects, but Phillip isn't that much of a dunce. He's no one's dupe. If anyone's pulling the strings, he is."

Ferris couldn't rid herself of the suspicion that he just might be right. And since she could think of no motive for it but her own involvement with both men, she immediately denied it. "You're the one who's paranoid, Blackheart. Clearly you have nothing to worry about. If you're not going to steal *The Hyacinths* and sell it to the highest bidder, then you don't have to worry about what those three conspirators were doing. If they're busy watching the Van Gogh, you won't even run into them."

"No, I can steal Regina's jewels in relative peace and safety," Blackheart drawled.

"I thought she didn't have any jewels."

"Just testing. Do you want to go back over the roof, or would you prefer the steps?"

"Wouldn't we run into those three if we followed them into the house?"

"Maybe. Does that make a difference?"

"Not in the slightest. I'm not going back onto that roof for love or money."

"We can take the stairs," he agreed. "Regina knows what we're doing, anyway. If we run into the three musketeers we can refer them to Phillip's mother. That should put the fear of God into them." He moved to the door, holding it open for her. There was no sign of anyone on the stairs leading down into the third-floor hallway and *The Hyacinths*, and no sound of voices filtered upward.

"You don't like Phillip, do you?" she asked curiously, moving past him down the stairway. "I thought you two used to be friends."

"Amiable acquaintances," Blackheart corrected her, shutting the attic door behind them. "Polite relationships like that don't stand up to sexual jealousy on either side. The first time I saw him put his hands on you, I wanted to murder him.''

That violent statement shouldn't have started a small fire of pleasure burning in the pit of her stomach, but it did. She stopped on the bottom stairs, not even noticing the glowing, jewellike colors of the priceless painting, and looked up into his face. ''Did you really want me that much?''

He put out his hand and she couldn't move, mesmerized by the light in his warm brown eyes. ''I did,'' he murmured, his voice low and beguiling, the kind of voice that could seduce a mother superior. ''I still do.'' His fingers lightly touched her cheek, the rough texture of his skin sending tremors of heat across her face.

''Patrick,'' she whispered, her husky voice equally beguiling. ''I—''

''I didn't realize you were around here.'' Phillip's smooth voice came booming into their concentration, shattering it like a crystal figurine.

Blackheart raised his head, and his expression was frankly inimical. ''You weren't supposed to,'' he said.

Phillip's response was the epitome of the professional politician: a hearty laugh, a genial smile, and all the charm that was second nature to him. It was hard to remember that that same cheerful voice had been implicating Blackheart only moments before. ''I hadn't realized you two were talking to each other. Is there any hope for a reconciliation? I know it would make my mother very happy.''

An edge slipped into his voice, so slight that Ferris doubted he was even aware of it—anger for her, anger for Blackheart, anger for his mother? She opened her mouth to say something, but Blackheart's hand caught hers and his fingers closed tightly over her palm, silencing her.

"No," Blackheart said flatly. "Ferris tells me I'm a lost cause. She's just been kind enough to help me check out some of the security on the house."

Phillip's blue eyes took on a slightly glassy tint. "I wouldn't think there'd be anything worth that kind of trouble in the place. Mother disposed of most of her silver and jewelry years ago. Said they were too dangerous. There's nothing anyone would want."

"Except the Van Gogh," Blackheart murmured.

"Except the Van Gogh. But then, artwork isn't really in your line at all, is it, Blackheart?" Phillip said smoothly. "It's the glittering colors of emeralds and rubies that excite your larcenous instincts, not the jewellike hues of a painting."

"Oh, I don't know, Senator. A man shouldn't be too set in his ways. A moment of avarice, a moment of anger, and a lifetime of rules can get swept away. Can't it?" Blackheart's voice was low and his tone taunting. Ferris listened with growing confusion. She tried to pull her hand away from his, but his grip was unrelenting. There was something going on between Blackheart and Phillip, something she didn't understand, but whatever it was she didn't like it. Something was simmering beneath the surface, and she couldn't even begin to guess what it was.

"You tell me, Patrick," Phillip said, his affability never faltering. "You're the expert on breaking rules. And laws."

"Maybe. Maybe not. Where's your mother?"

"Going to tell on me?"

"What are you two talking about?" Ferris had had enough of this fencing. She yanked her hand free from Blackheart's grip, moving down the last few steps and confronting Phillip.

"Tell her it's nothing to worry her pretty little head about," Blackheart suggested helpfully. "I'd like to see her deck you."

Phillip reached out a hand. By sheer coincidence his smooth, well-manicured fingers brushed the same spot on her face that Blackheart's rougher hand had. "I wouldn't think of saying such a thing," he murmured. "Ferris and I understood each other. We had a civilized relationship, based on mutual respect and caring. We could have it again."

The touch of his flesh left her unmoved, except for a faint regret that it wiped away the memory of Blackheart's touch. She swallowed, taking a step backward against Blackheart's waiting body. "You're very sweet," she said, searching for the right words. "But I think you're too good for me."

Blackheart's laugh was mocking. "Don't you believe it, dear heart. Your golden senator has feet of clay."

Phillip ignored him. "I'm sorry," he murmured. "More than I can say." His eyes met Blackheart's for a brief, telling moment, and once more Ferris thought there was something more going on than she was aware of, something dark and wicked gliding beneath the surface. "I'll tell Mother you're looking for her."

They watched him go, his broad shoulders and golden head disappearing down the next flight of stairs. "A graceful exit," Blackheart drawled.

"Do you have to be such a rat?" Ferris snapped, guilt and regret for what couldn't be slashing through her.

"Sorry, darling. We don't have a civilized relationship based on mutual respect and caring. We're rather savage about it, don't you think?"

"Don't, Blackheart." But the words were murmured against his mouth as he yanked her back into his arms. His

actions fitted his words. There was nothing civilized about
his kiss, nothing civilized about her response. His hands
threaded through her thick hair and held her still, his
mouth caught hers in a bruising possession.

This time she didn't hesitate. This time she shoved him
with all her strength, catching him off guard so that he fell
back against the attic steps. Seconds later she was gone,
running down Regina Merriam's broad marble staircase
without looking back.

Blackheart watched her go. Slowly, ruefully he picked
himself up off the stairs, shook himself off, and smiled.
"Run, Francesca," he whispered. "You can't run away
from yourself." And with a jaunty little whistle he followed his erstwhile love down the stairs.

DANY MANAGED very well for most of the day, staying in
the shadows, keeping her head down, her voice lowered,
locking herself into the Winnebago with the accounts and
keeping her back to the sun when anyone came to disturb
her. At least Marco had made himself scarce. She had no
illusions that he might be feeling remorse. His only regret
might be that someone would notice the bruises. And while
she was tempted to wash off her makeup, she controlled
herself. That kind of petty revenge would only make things
worse. Five more days, and she'd be home free.

She'd had more than a few curious looks, of course.
Rocco, the old clown, had been around long enough to
know what was going on, and without saying a word he
went out of his way to be kind. He brought her coffee and
fresh pastries and kept people away from her. If he hadn't
gone for an early supper, she would have made it safely
through the day.

But there was no faithful Rocco guarding the tiny door to the van at five-thirty in the afternoon, no one to stop Stephen McNab from sticking his head in.

He couldn't have chosen a worse moment. She'd let the room grow dark, not bothering to turn on a lamp, and as she sat there in the shadows, the account books no longer visible, she allowed herself the rare luxury of crying. Her head ached, her ribs ached, her entire face felt raw. And she felt alone, as she had always felt, alone and a stranger in a world of other people's friends.

She saw McNab silhouetted in the doorway and held herself very still, hoping he wouldn't realize she was in there. But her body betrayed her with a watery hiccup. McNab hit the lights, flooding the Winnebago with a bright electric glare, and his startled eyes met hers.

"What in God's name happened to you?"

Chapter Thirteen

The Lady Vanishes
(Lime Grove 1938)

"Go away," Dany said, turning her face away. McNab paid no attention, slamming the door behind him and advancing into the cramped quarters. She was cowering behind the tiny built-in table, but he simply swept the papers out of the way, reached in and hauled her out.

He was quite a bit taller than she was. Quite a bit stronger, too, but she knew instinctively that unlike Marco he'd never use his strength to hurt anyone. Instead, with great gentleness, he caught her chin in one large hand and forced her to turn her battered face up to his.

His swiftly indrawn breath told her just how much of her makeup must have washed off during her bout of tears. "Porcini?" he demanded in a sharp voice, and she quickly revised her earlier opinion. He would never use his strength to hurt *her*, but she wasn't sure Marco would be safe.

"I fell," she said, repeating the lie she'd told Rocco. "I was working on an old acrobatic routine and I didn't warm up properly. You don't know circus people—bruises are part of the business."

"And do they sit in the dark and cry about them?" McNab's harsh tone was at odds with the gentleness in his hands.

"I fell, Lieutenant."

"Stephen," he corrected her. "And you must have fallen into Porcini's fists. We arrest wife beaters in this country, Dany. You don't have to put up with that kind of abuse."

"I don't know much about American law, but I imagine you can't arrest him if I don't lay a complaint. And I'm not going to do that." She felt calmer now, a coolness overlying her desperation. She was very close to blowing the whole thing. And she wanted to do just that, wanted to lay her head on Stephen's broad shoulder and tell him everything. Then she'd be the one in jail, she reminded herself.

"Why not? Do you love him that much?"

"I hate him."

"Then why don't you leave him? Divorce him? We can get a restraining order to keep him away. You don't have to stay with a brute like that."

"I can't get a divorce," Dany said. "We're not married."

She was unprepared for his reaction. She expected disgust and anger, not a sudden, unexpected grin of delight. "That makes life easier. Get your things."

"Why?"

"You're getting out of here. At least for a couple of days, until lover boy manages to control his temper."

"Where am I going?" She eyed him warily.

"Well, there are any number of shelters in the city for battered women. You'd be safe there. But I thought you might come with me."

"Where?" she asked again.

"I have some time off coming. We could go north. And don't jump to any conclusions. I'm not trying to get you into bed. That's the last thing you need, after what you've been through. I just think you need to get away for a while."

"How do you know what I need?" she muttered under her breath.

"I beg your pardon?" Luckily Stephen hadn't heard her.

"I said I'll go with you. For a couple of days. Just so I can have time to think."

"Are you sure you won't swear out a complaint...?"

"I fell," she said firmly, heading for the door.

"If you say so. Don't you want to bring any clothes?" He stood still in the middle of the caravan, dwarfing its already cramped confines.

"I have a suitcase packed and stowed over by the track tent. I like to be ready to leave at short notice."

"Do you? I wonder why?"

For a moment she faltered. What in the world was she doing, turning to an enemy for help? Stephen McNab didn't realize he was the enemy; he thought he was the only friend she had. How would he react when he found out the truth, as he was bound to, sooner or later? His determination to nail Blackheart would be nothing compared to his fury with her. She'd have to burrow very deep into the American heartland to get away from him.

If she had any sense at all she'd stay. Marco wouldn't dare hit her again, not if he hoped to carry off the job with her assistance. Stephen McNab was too enticing, with his world-weary air and absurdly kind eyes.

But she was ready to be enticed, ready for kindness, for anything else a couple of days in hiding with Stephen McNab might bring. "You'll find out why," she said. "Sooner or later. Let's get out of here before Marco gets back."

"I wouldn't mind having a few words with your friend Marco."

The thought of such a confrontation made Dany dizzy with horror. "Let's get out of here before I come to my senses," she said.

That moved him. "All right. Maybe we'll be lucky and run into him on our way out."

But they ran into no one at all on their trip through the dusk and across the trampled lawns to McNab's beat-up Bronco. Not an acrobat, not an illusionist, not an animal trainer, not a soul saw them leave. Except Rocco. He watched them go, then headed into the mess tent, a smile wreathing his weary old face. He was a man who knew how to keep a secret—a man who would enjoy seeing Marco Porcini squirm.

THERE WERE NO PRESENTS in Ferris's apartment that evening. She told herself she was deeply grateful, as she fed an indignant Blackie a can of Seafood Surprise. As she soaked her weary muscles in her oversize bathtub and tried to forget the number of times Patrick had kissed her that day, she told herself she was glad he was finally leaving her alone. She told herself she could start concentrating on the rest of her life and forget about old memories and lingering desires. And pushing a tape into the VCR, she climbed into her bed and sat back to watch *To Catch a Thief*.

The first thing she did the next morning was to check her ring finger. The canary diamond hadn't been replaced. It was still sitting where Blackheart had left it, on top of the VCR. She told herself she was very, very happy as she stomped into the kitchen, her lavender silk kimono trailing around her Jockey shorts and tank top. She told herself life was going to be splendid as she made herself a horrible cup of instant coffee, searched in vain for any kind of milk product that hadn't soured, and tossed out several stale doughnuts she'd ignored in favor of cookies in the last few days. And it was only because she stubbed her toe on the step up into the dining room that she sank to the floor and began to howl like a spoiled three-year-old.

There were no deliveries to her office at the Committee for Saving the Bay's headquarters. No phone calls, no summons to the circus setup on Regina's spacious grounds. Nothing.

By three o'clock she was ready to scream. She'd been able to accomplish one thing during the day, clearing up a minor glitch involving the license for the circus performance. But for the rest of the time she'd pushed papers around on her desk and waited for someone to call.

If she'd ever had any doubts about the worthlessness of her job, that endless day put them to rest. She wasn't needed there, she was wasting her time and energies. At three-fifteen she wrote her letter of resignation, effective the day after the circus performance, at three forty-five she had copies in the mail to the five trustees who were nominally her employers, and at three fifty-seven she was on her way home.

No one called her that night. She brought Blackie herring and Brie, but even he didn't show up, clearly not trusting his distracted mistress. She unplugged the phone at nine-thirty, tired of staring at its sleek lines and begging it to ring. She'd stopped by a video store and rented three movies, two comedies and a gangster film. She climbed into bed with a large snifter of brandy and watched *To Catch a Thief.*

There was no canary diamond on her finger the next morning. On a Saturday there was no work, either. The rain was pouring down, sheets of water lashing against the windows, turning the middle of the day into a lightless gloom. By two o'clock Ferris knew that one more moment in her apartment and she'd start screaming. Digging out her peach silk raincoat, she pulled it on over her jeans and sweater, grabbed her purse, and headed out into the rainy afternoon with one thought in her mind. There was more than one way to skin a cat.

DANY LIKED AMERICA, she decided as she sat curled up in the window seat of the old cabin and watched the rain. She liked the rawness, even the tackiness, of the new towns that seemed to have sprung up overnight around the more elegant areas of San Francisco and Marin County. She liked the log cabin Stephen had brought her to, a place off in the woods up north of Santa Rosa in Sonoma County, with running water and electricity but not much more, not even a telephone. She liked eating hamburgers and pizza and spaghetti, the limit of Stephen's cooking, and she liked his oddly polite way with her. In the last day and a half he hadn't touched her. He'd taken care of her like a kindly uncle, and yet there was nothing avuncular about the way he looked at her. She'd been waiting, longing for him to make a move, a gesture, but he'd done nothing but wish her a polite good-night at her bedroom doorway before retiring into his own room. And while Dany told herself it was all for the best, she was beginning to long for those big, strong hands of his to touch her, anywhere, just touch her.

It had been a curiously peaceful time, considering how little they'd talked. She'd responded to his gentle probing about the past with evasions and outright lies, spinning him a story about her upbringing that was culled directly from Christopher Robin and the Pooh stories. Stephen had stopped pressing her, and had responded to her own questions with equal reticence. All things considered, she knew as little about him as he knew about her. She knew he had two brothers, that he'd grown up on the east coast, and that he'd always wanted to be a cop. But she knew nothing else.

Not that it mattered. She wouldn't have minded if he'd had a wife and six kids stashed away in one of those towns they'd passed through; she wouldn't even have minded if he was on the take. It would have equalized the sides a bit, making both of them cheating liars instead of just one of them. Herself.

She leaned her forehead against the glass, staring out into the afternoon rain. They'd have to go back soon, she knew that, though he hadn't said anything about it. He was intent on catching John Patrick Blackheart, that much she knew instinctively, and Marco was busy baiting the trap—the trap to catch her half brother and make him the scapegoat, while they got away free and clear.

She thought about Blackheart for a moment. He wasn't what she'd expected, but then, twenty-one years was a long time ago. She didn't hate him as she'd thought she would; as a matter of fact, she had to work to raise any kind of anger at his desertion. After all those years, it suddenly no longer mattered. She just wished he'd had enough family feeling to notice that she looked slightly familiar.

She was a fool to brood. Everything was moving along at its preordained pace, and it was too late to stop what had been set in motion long ago. She'd made her choices; now she had no option but to ride along to the bitter end. She should just be glad she hadn't ended up in bed with Stephen McNab. After more than two years of celibacy it might have proved her emotional undoing. She was far too attracted to the man as it was, attracted in a spiritual, emotional way as well as on a simple physical level.

She could hear him splashing about in the kitchen. He'd refused to let her cook or do any housework, insisting that she needed time to relax and think. *All right,* she'd thought, but it had been impossible to relax with Stephen so near and yet so far. She drew back, looking at her reflection in the rain-spattered glass. The bruises were fading—a light application of makeup would cover up the worst of them without her having to skulk about in the shadows. It was time to go back, before she did something unforgivably stupid.

She got up, stretching lazily, and put another log onto the fire. There was a slight chill in the air, but the vast fireplace proved more than adequate to the task of heating the cabin. The smell and crackle of the fire added to the coziness, and for a moment she considered curling up on the rug in front of it and taking a nap. *That's what a sensible person would do,* she reminded herself. But when had she ever shown any sense?

Stephen McNab had just finished shaving himself at the kitchen sink, the only sink the cabin boasted. There were a stall shower and a toilet in a small alcove off the back, but every day he'd shaved in the kitchen, and she'd studiously avoided the room while he was busy. He couldn't have heard her approach—she had the ability to move in complete silence, and bare feet on a wooden floor didn't make much noise, anyway. But he knew she was there, and he turned, dropping the towel he'd used to dry his face. His expression was wary.

His shirt was lying on the wooden counter next to the sink. Dany managed a shy smile, trying to avert her eyes from his chest. "I thought I might make some coffee," she said. "I was feeling sleepy."

"You should take a nap," he said, turning to reach for his shirt.

"Oh, Stephen," Dany whispered in muffled horror. "What happened?"

Stephen McNab had a beautiful torso. Lean and wiry, he made Marco's bulging muscles look overblown in comparison. But Marco didn't have any scars marring his artfully tanned flesh.

Someone had done something very nasty indeed to Stephen McNab—but long enough ago that the scar had faded into a thick white line that traveled from his back, around under his arm and ended up by his right nipple.

"Sorry," he said, pulling on his khaki shirt and starting to button it. "I know it's not pleasant to look at."

"No," she said, crossing the kitchen before she had time to think and stopping his hands. "It's not that. It just must have been so painful...."

He kept his hands still beneath hers. The bright kitchen light glared behind him, and outside the rain was pouring, sending shifting blue shadows through the windows and into the corners of the small room. "It was a long time ago, Dany. It doesn't matter."

"But you could have been killed."

"That's what my wife thought."

She hadn't really wanted to hear that, Dany reflected numbly, dropping her hands and letting him continue buttoning the shirt. "What happened?"

He was busy tucking his shirt into his jeans, stalling for time. "I had just made detective, and I wasn't too bright. I made the wrong enemies, pushed where I wasn't supposed to push, and someone decided to teach me a lesson. Unfortunately I'm not a quick learner. He's in jail, and I'm alive and well."

"And your wife?"

Stephen sighed, his wintry-blue eyes almost black in the glaring kitchen light. "She said she couldn't stand watching me take chances and eventually end up getting killed. She said I had to choose between her and being a cop."

"And?"

"I'm still a cop."

"I'm sorry, Stephen."

"Don't be. We were just kids, anyway. High school sweethearts aren't supposed to spend the rest of their lives together. At least we didn't have any children."

"Did you want them?"

"Not then."

"Do you still miss her?"

He shook his head. "I hadn't thought of her in months. Years, maybe. Until I met you."

Damn, Dany thought. *God's punishing me, all right. Here I am, falling in love with a man who's any thief's natural enemy, and on top of that I remind him of his ex-wife.* She backed away, plastering a phony smile onto her face. "You'll have to find someone else who reminds you of her," she said brightly.

"Dany," he said in a weary voice, "Lucille was a red-headed Valkyrie with a fanatical devotion to makeup and clothes and doing as little as possible. She was a prom queen who never grew up or faced the consequences of the choices she made, and when the going got rough she took off. Does that sound like you?"

Yes, she thought miserably. *I don't want to face the consequences of the choices I've made. I want to live happily ever after.* "Why did you say I reminded you of her?"

"I didn't. I said I started thinking about her when I realized I wanted someone else. More than I'd ever wanted anyone, Lucille included, in my entire life."

Dany shut her eyes, taking a step backward. "This won't work. You don't know anything about me, and if you did, you wouldn't like it. It's doomed before we even begin."

If she expected an argument, she didn't get one. He just stood there, looking at her in the bright kitchen light. And then he reached over the sink and flicked the switch, plunging the room into a shifting, shadowy darkness. "Maybe," he said, his rough voice curiously caressing. "We'll never know until we find out."

"Stephen..."

"He didn't rape you, did he?" It wasn't a question. It was more that he wanted to verify a suspicion.

"Marco? No. He hasn't touched me for over two years. Except to hit me."

"I thought you fell," Stephen taunted her gently, moving toward her across the shadowy room. She held her ground, her heart pounding in anticipation—and regret. She shouldn't do this; she knew better than he did how hopeless it was. But she couldn't resist. His big hands caught her narrow shoulders, pulling her gently toward him. "I've been afraid to touch you, for fear you'd been hurt too badly to want me. But you do, don't you, Dany?"

"Want you?" she echoed. "I shouldn't."

"But you do." His mouth touched hers, gently, brushing against her lips, teasing them open. "You do, don't you?"

She slid her arms around his waist and up under his loose shirt, her hands grazing the rough texture of that terrible scar. "Yes," she whispered against his mouth. "Yes."

BLACKHEART'S STREET was half-empty on that Saturday afternoon, and his battered Volvo station wagon was nowhere in sight. Ferris jiggled the set of keys that she'd tucked into her jeans pocket and hoped that Blackheart hadn't changed his locks. He'd have no reason to. He would never suspect, after her high-and-mighty exit from his life, that she might want to break in when he wasn't around.

If he had changed the locks there was no way she'd get in. The one person you couldn't steal from was another thief—Blackheart's locks were impenetrable to any normal human being. Maybe the thief in Europe would be able to handle them, but not someone with her limited expertise.

She didn't know when she'd come to the conclusion that there really was a thief in Europe, and it wasn't Blackheart still plying his trade. It might have been when he kissed her in the closet. It might have been when she followed him out over rooftops, risking life and limb to prove heaven only knew what. Sometime during the last few days she'd realized that Blackheart hadn't reverted to his former ways.

But he'd still been lying to her, covering up. He knew far too much about the thefts in Madrid, Paris and Lisbon, but he wasn't about to tell her until he was good and ready. And she wasn't about to wait any longer. She was going to go through his apartment, inch by inch, and when she finally came up with the answers she was seeking, she would curl up on his couch and wait until he came home, so that she could confront him with it.

She had the presence of mind to call his apartment from a pay phone at the end of the block. She had absorbed certain tricks of the trade; whether it was from Blackheart himself or from the various caper movies she'd been watching was a moot point. There'd been no answer, and the way was clear. She just had to hope she had enough time to find what she was looking for before he put in a reappearance.

She went to the kitchen first. There was just enough coffee left in the pot to make a mug—she put it into the microwave and drank it black, savoring every drop. She had to give Blackheart credit—he was neater than she was. Not by much—he went in for artless clutter and piles of books as much as she did, but he seemed to have a slightly better sense of order.

She strolled into his living room, past the overstuffed couch where she'd spent far too much time, and headed straight for the desk. If he'd locked it, she could use her credit card, she told herself, her hand on the drawer pull, her eyes glancing at and then dismissing the old photograph of Blackheart and his father, dressed for business in tails.

She stood there for a long moment, considering. This was her future at stake—surely unethical things were necessary, even justified when it came to her only chance of happiness.

Maybe. Maybe not. If she opened the drawer and started pawing through it, she'd be just as untrustworthy as she'd accused Blackheart of being. Even if the end of uncertainty lay just beyond that closed door, she couldn't do it. She dropped her hand, moved away and sank onto the sofa.

"I'm glad you changed your mind." Blackheart's voice drifted to her from the bedroom door. "Why are you here? Looking for proof of my guilt?"

"No," she said. "I wanted to find out who you were covering up for."

A cynical grin twisted Blackheart's face. "A step in the right direction, but not the confession of undying love and trust I was hoping for. Go away, Ferris, and come back when you've made up your mind."

She didn't move. "Go away, Ferris," he said again, moving toward her. "Or I'll make sure you don't want to leave."

Ferris ran. It wasn't until she was halfway home that she remembered the picture on the desk and realized something she'd never noticed before. John Cyril Blackheart, alias Seymour Bunce, Blackheart's father, looked very familiar. And it wasn't his compelling son who resembled him. It was Danielle Porcini.

Chapter Fourteen

I Confess
(Warner Brothers 1952)

Stephen slept heavily, his face in the pillow, one arm stretched out, holding her loosely even in sleep. Dany regretfully edged out from under its protection, climbing from the bed and tiptoeing into the deserted living room. The rain had stopped sometime during the night, and now in the chilly predawn light a faint mist was rising from the short grass around the cabin. It was going to be a long, cold walk into town.

She didn't even dare take the time for a shower. She didn't really want one. This was all she was going to have of Stephen McNab—fate and history wouldn't allow her more, and she had no intention of washing away the scent and feel of him before she had to.

So many times during the last twelve hours she had wanted to tell him the truth. Never had she felt so open, so vulnerable, her defenses and her secrets crumbling around her. So many times she'd bitten her lip to keep from doing just that. His determination to catch Blackheart was so all-consuming that she had no doubt at all if she told him who she was and what she was really doing in California, he'd let go of her, jump out of bed and start reading her her rights.

So she kept her mouth shut, except to kiss him. And when the night began to vanish, a fitful daylight crept over the hillside and dreams were over, she knew she had to escape. She didn't believe he'd let her go that easily, that he'd just assume she'd changed her mind about being involved with him and leave her alone. She was going to have to come up with an excuse, something plausible to keep him away while she finished her job with Marco. Then by the time she was gone, he might be able to summon up some gratitude that he hadn't become more involved.

She shivered as she stepped onto the porch. The temperature wasn't that bad, but the chill came from deep inside her soul. She wished she could tell herself she was being noble, but she didn't even have that solace. Denying herself Stephen McNab now was simply anticipating his horrified rejection. As a defense against heartbreak it wasn't much, but it was better than nothing.

Her sneakered feet were quickly soaked by the heavy dew on the grass as she crossed to the rough dirt road. She shivered, pulling her thick sweater closer around her, and headed down the road.

He caught up with her five minutes later. The battered Bronco pulled up beside her, the passenger door slammed open, and he sat there in the driver's seat, glaring across at her, dressed in jeans, an old sweater and nothing else, his bare feet on the brake. "Get in."

"Stephen..."

"Get the hell in. We'll discuss this when you're in the car."

"I really don't think I'd better...."

"I'm bigger than you, Dany. A lot. You're getting into this car."

He'd do it, too, she thought. He was angry, not the cold, biting rage he directed at people like Marco and Blackheart, but a hot, heavy fury. If she stalled he would grab her, then he'd hate himself for it. It was one thing she could do for him, she thought, climbing into the front seat and keeping her head lowered, and at the same time she could enjoy the pleasurable torment of a few more minutes of his company. While she thought very fast of a plausible excuse.

He turned the Bronco around on the narrow road, each turn of the steering wheel accomplished with much more force than necessary. Leaning forward, he flicked on the heater, blasting her damp, chilled legs with blessed warmth. The Bronco kept moving, past the empty cabin, on up the winding road toward the top of the mountain.

"I don't think kindly of one-night stands, Dany," he said after a while, his eyes trained on the road, his profile grim.

"I don't either." Her voice wasn't much more than a whisper, but he could hear her.

"Then why?"

She deliberately misunderstood him. "I couldn't help it. I'm very attracted to you."

"That's not what I was talking about, and you know it. I mean why did you run?"

"I don't suppose you'd believe me if I said I hadn't enjoyed myself."

His laugh was humorless. "No. I was there, remember? And I don't think attraction and enjoyment are the operative words in this situation. This wasn't a yuppie mating ritual."

"We had sex, Stephen."

"We made love, Dany. There's a big difference." They'd reached the top of the hill and a small turnaround with a graveled parking space. Stephen pulled up the edge and parked, but left the motor running so that the heat still surrounded them in a cocoonlike warmth. "What's going on, Dany? Don't you think you can trust me enough to tell the truth?"

It was Dany's turn to laugh, but she couldn't quite manage a dry, mirthless chuckle. In her ears it sounded definitely on the watery side, and she bit her lip, hard. "It's not you who can't be trusted."

"Are you feeling guilty about Marco? The man is pond scum—he doesn't deserve any loyalty or consideration."

"Stephen..."

"You don't owe him anything. I don't want you going anywhere near him again—he's too dangerous. I think you need police protection. Twenty-four hours a day. And I'm offering it free of charge. Move in with me, Dany. I promise you, you won't regret it."

"I can't." This was worse than she'd anticipated. She'd expected an inquisition, not enticement. She leaned against the door, away from him, hugging herself in her misery. "I just need to go back. My job's there, my friends are there. This was very nice...."

"Nice?" he echoed, clearly affronted.

"All right, it wasn't nice!" she exploded. "It was wonderful, heavenly, the best thing that ever happened to me. But it's doomed! Hopeless! Can you get that through your thick cop's head?"

She'd been hoping to anger him, but his gray eyes merely narrowed as he watched her. "Why?"

"Take me back, Stephen."

"Why?" he persisted, his voice softer now, less demanding. He reached out his big, strong hand to gently stroke her tear-damp cheek. "I hate to tell you this, Dany, but I'm falling in love with you. So you can at least tell me why we're doomed."

It was the last straw. No one in all of her twenty-four years had ever told her they loved her. Something inside her burst, a tiny bubble of anger and hope, and she turned to him, her eyes filled with despair. "Because I'm a thief, Lieutenant. Any cop's a natural enemy. My real name is Danielle Bunce, and I've spent the last four years in Europe as an accessory to a cat burglar. On top of that, I'm John Patrick Blackheart's half sister." She leaned back and closed her eyes, breathing deeply, waiting for those words she'd heard so often on the telly. "You have the right to remain silent," it began. She couldn't remember the rest, but it didn't matter. She was about to hear them.

What she heard in the cab of the Bronco was absolute silence. Just the sound of the engine, the noisy whirr of the fan as it spun heat around them. And the steady breathing of the man beside her.

When she could stand the quiet no longer, she held out her slender wrists in front of him, keeping her face averted. "Where are the handcuffs, Lieutenant? I won't put up a fight."

But it wasn't cold metal closing around her wrist. Warm, long-fingered flesh was encircling her, pulling her over the bench seat and into his lap. "Damn," he muttered. "You don't make things easy, do you?" And he kissed her.

It was a while before she surfaced from that kiss, but when she did, she was more confused than ever. "You can't, Stephen," she said breathlessly. "I'm everything you despise. Didn't you hear what I just told you? Didn't you...?"

"Hush," he whispered. "I heard you. And you're not everything I despise. I told you, I'm falling in love with you, and you could be a chain saw murderer and it wouldn't make any difference to me. We can work it out."

"Stephen..."

"I've spent my entire law enforcement career watching scum make deals and get off with a slap on the wrist. For once plea bargaining is going to work in my favor. Do you have any warrants out on you?"

She just stared at him. "As far as I know, no one has ever suspected my involvement. Or my partner's."

"That's a different matter. You can turn state's evidence, get off with a suspended sentence, but Blackheart's going away for a long time." The grim satisfaction in his voice did little to help her state of mind.

She pulled away from him, and he let her go, watching her as she scrambled back to her side of the car. Here would be the perfect revenge that she'd always sought. Stephen assumed Blackheart was her partner—she could incriminate him and disappear.

But the stupid thing was, it no longer mattered. Whatever Blackheart's reasons for abandoning her had been, they must have felt justified at the time. She no longer needed her pound of flesh, not when her own heart lay shattered and bleeding on the ground. "Sorry, can't help you," she muttered, staring out the window.

"Can't?" he said. "Or won't?"

"There's nothing I can tell you that will help you in your vendetta against my half brother," she replied with absolute honesty.

As usual Stephen was more alert than she'd hoped. "He's not your partner, is he?" he asked in a quiet voice. "Does he even know you're his sister?"

Dany's only reply was a strangled sound that was half a negation, half a sob. "He doesn't," Stephen said. "So that leaves Marco." Leaning forward, he threw the gears into reverse and began backing around. He headed down the hill at a reasonably sedate pace, and the brief glance Dany stole at his strong, world-weary profile told her only that he was deep in thought.

When they reached the cabin again he turned off the engine, staring out the windshield with an abstracted air.

Dany couldn't stand the silence any longer. "What are you going to do? What next?"

He turned to look at her then, and the tenderness in his eyes twisted her newly vulnerable heart. "I'm going to take you back into the cabin and prove to you that you don't have to be frightened of me. And then I'm going to try to figure out what I can do without incriminating you."

"And if it's impossible? If there's no way you can do anything without sending me to prison?"

"Did you ever see *The Maltese Falcon*?"

"I beg your pardon?"

"An old Humphrey Bogart movie—a real classic. He's a private eye and the woman he loves is a murderer who killed his best friend. Problem is, she loves him too."

"What does he do?" She was fascinated despite herself.

"He tells her he'll wait twenty years till she gets out of prison."

"What does she say?"

"Something along the lines of 'Go to hell.' "

It surprised a laugh out of her. "So what happens?"

"I don't know. That's where the movie ends."

"You can turn me in, Stephen. The most they'll do is extradite me back to Europe. If I tell the truth, I'll get off lightly for helping them nail . . . my accomplice. If I insist I'm innocent, they probably don't have enough to convict me on. So it's all right. Start the car, let's drive back to San Francisco, and you can arrest me."

For a long moment he didn't move. She could see his big hands clasped on the steering wheel, so tightly that his knuckles were white with strain. And then he sank back, sighing. "Can't arrest someone without a warrant," he said, pulling the keys out of the ignition and flinging them into the underbrush surrounding the cabin. "And there's no evidence on which to issue one. You're stuck."

"Stuck?"

"Here. With me."

"Stephen," she said, desperation making her normally rich voice high-pitched. "You can't turn your back on everything you believe in. For pity's sake, take me in and arrest me!"

He was already out of the Bronco, walking around to her side and opening the door. "Sorry, babe. The only place I'm taking you is to bed." And scooping her up into his arms, he carried her up the creaking front steps of the cabin, kicking the door shut behind them.

FERRIS BYRD was very, very angry. After days of stupidity, she'd finally put two and two together and come up with a nice neat package of four. Patrick's long-lost sister had appeared on the scene, probably with a burglar friend in tow, and Blackheart was doing everything he could to save the girl from her folly. *Including lying to and misleading his fiancée,* she thought bitterly. Her last, lingering doubts had vanished. Blackheart hadn't taken to a life of crime once more. He'd taken to a life of chivalry, *curse him.*

She sat in her messy apartment, staring out the windows into the foggy San Francisco afternoon. While Ferris sat on the living-room love seat and thought, Blackie had come in, eaten the Brie and disappeared again. She welcomed the quiet, welcomed the distant noise of the traffic, welcomed the cocoon of fog that surrounded her apartment. She sat alone with her dark and shifting thoughts, her hands clenched into angry fists.

She knew she should be reasonable. She knew she should be relieved at finally understanding what lay behind Blackheart's mysterious behavior. *After all,* she had six brothers and sisters, countless nieces and nephews, a vast, sprawling, affectionate family. She of all people should understand blood ties.

But she didn't. All she knew was that Blackheart had sacrificed her and her love, and was well on the way to sacrificing his career and possibly even his freedom for a spoiled, amoral young woman who had appeared out of nowhere to wreak havoc and destroy their lives.

She wasn't going to let it happen. She wasn't going to roll over and play dead, sit back and wait to see if Blackheart could pull it off. This was her own future at stake, not just her erstwhile lover's. She'd spent enough time crying, enough time eating. Now it was time for action. And the first thing she was going to do was confront Danielle Porcini and find out what the hell she thought she was doing.

The memory of Tarzan, the albino tiger, suddenly shot into her brain, and she hesitated. That had been no accident—someone had tried to kill her. Could it have been Blackheart's sister? Blackheart himself?

The absurdity of the last question made her laugh out loud, the sound soft and comforting in the shadowy living room. No matter what Blackheart's transgressions, and they were many, he would never hurt her. He loved her, she could at least accept that, and it made everything else, every danger, every tall building she had to leap, worth it.

But what about Danielle? Her appearance at the time had been fortuitous, to say the least. But she'd also helped Ferris lure the carnivorous beast back into the cage. It would have been a simple enough matter to leave her there, to lock her in and come back after her screams had died away.

No. Danielle's appearance hadn't been coincidence, but it hadn't been murderous, either. She'd known Ferris had been in trouble, and she'd come to save her.

So whom did that leave? Dany's mysterious accomplice, the current cat burglar himself. And there was really no mystery to it at all. Marco Porcini might not have the brains to plan and carry out the complex robberies in Europe, but he had the agility and strength. And Danielle Porcini had brains in abundance—not to mention her knowledge of the family business.

Was there a family tendency toward burglary, some sort of recessive gene or ingrained trait that was passed from generation to generation? Was she going to give birth to a passel of baby cat burglars?

The very thought boggled her mind—because she had no doubt whatsoever that she was going to marry John Patrick Blackheart, né Edwin Bunce, and give birth to their children. Maybe if he changed back his name and they produced a small handful of little Bunces, they might break with the family tradition. Or maybe they'd better make sure at least one of them became a lawyer, so she or he could bail the rest out of jail.

Ferris stretched out on the love seat with a sigh, relaxing for the first time in days. Now that she at last had a very good idea of what was going on, she could handle it. Whatever Danielle and Marco Porcini were here to steal, Blackheart would stop them. She was just going to have to make sure her once and future fiancé didn't succumb to temptation and steal it himself.

He needed her. He needed her to drill some sense into his head, to make sure he didn't take the fall for his sister. He needed her almost as much as she needed him. And if she found her need for him frightening, threatening, she was no longer going to fight it. She'd simply have to learn to live with her fear.

At least she didn't have to worry about Regina. The Porcinis hadn't been anywhere near that blasted Van Gogh, and the painting wasn't due to be moved until after the circus benefit, when the Porcini Family Circus would be packing and moving to the next stop on their American tour. *No,* it was something else, and Regina, at least, was safe.

IT TOOK DANY too long to find the keys where he'd tossed them. Even in the glinting early-afternoon sunlight they were hard to find, and she wasted precious time searching through the long grass surrounding the cabin.

Stephen was in the shower. She knew he took long showers—she'd already taken one with him, and while he didn't have her as a distraction just now, he still was a man who took his time once he got into the stall.

Still, she couldn't count on anything. The rest of the day had been spent in bed, glorious, endless hours that had apparently left Stephen sure of himself and their relationship. Once the pleasure faded, it had only filled her with despair.

She couldn't do it to him. She couldn't allow him to turn his back on everything he believed in, just because he imagined he was in love with her. She'd learned over the long hard years that she wasn't worth loving, and she certainly wasn't worth a man destroying his life over her.

Never before had she put someone else's needs ahead of her own. Never had she made any sacrifice for a greater good—the greater good had always been what suited her. But not this time. This time she was going to be sickeningly noble. She was going to do one decent thing to counterbalance the years of anger and selfishness. She was going to abandon Stephen up at this cabin, without a vehicle, without a telephone, miles and miles away from the nearest town. She was going back to Marco, going through with the job, then she'd be gone.

Someone else would be working in Stephen's place when he didn't show up. Someone else would be to blame when the Fabergé eggs turned up missing from the museum. And while Stephen would be filled with anger and regret, his life wouldn't be destroyed. It was the least she could do for him; it was the best she could do for him.

The keys suddenly glinted in the sunlight. She pounced on them, then sprinted for the Bronco, terrified that Stephen might curtail his shower and come in search of her. But her luck held. Five minutes later she was several miles down the road. And Stephen was still singing in the shower.

In three hours she was back at Regina Merriam's sprawling estate, darkness closing around her. She'd abandoned Stephen's Bronco on the other side of town, taken a taxi back and was making her solitary way across the grounds, when she thought she heard someone moving behind her.

A frisson of fear raced down her backbone. She couldn't forget Tarzan's evil, colorless eyes as he'd stalked Ferris. Someone, the same someone who'd loosed him on Blackheart's ex-fiancée, could have set him free again.

"Don't be ridiculous," she told herself. "Marco doesn't even know you're back."

She'd been certain she was safe from him. Even though she'd disappeared for days, he'd be too relieved to have her back in time for the job to even touch her. He wouldn't

dare jeopardize the steal of a lifetime out of rage for
someone he didn't even want.

So why was someone watching her, when she couldn't
see anyone at all on the deserted grounds? Why could she
hear the muffled sound of footsteps every time she walked?
Why—?

Darkness descended as a blanket came down over her,
smelling of something sharp and acrid and very dangerous. She struggled, but a pair of strong arms had encir-
cled her, holding the enveloping material over her, forcing
her to breathe in the fumes that were making her light-
headed and dizzy. The body holding her was short, squat
and unfamiliar. And the voice in her ears was unknown.

"That's right, me girl. Take a little snooze," the cockney voice murmured into her ear. And then the blackness
closed in.

HE DIDN'T LIKE creeping around in his socks, but he
couldn't rely on his tread being as light as Blackheart's.
The last thing he needed was for the old woman sound
asleep downstairs to wake up and hear an intruder wan-
dering around her third-floor hallway. Around her precious Van Gogh.

He didn't need to be there. He was tempting fate by
coming back for one last look, one last gloating appraisal
before they set their plan in motion tomorrow night. He
was risking everything, but then, he suspected that was
half the fun. This was his first dip into a life of crime, and
he was finding it strangely exhilarating. No wonder
Blackheart had so much trouble giving it up.

He could have had a thousand plausible excuses for
being there, but he'd used not a one of them. He had a key
to the house, but he hadn't used it either, sneaking in
through an unlocked window in the downstairs pantry.

He'd left his shoes just inside and had crept through the house, up the flights of curving stairs to the third-floor landing, his heart pounding, his palms sweaty, the adrenaline rushing through him.

The Hyacinths glowed in the moonlight, and he stared at the painting, knowing that in the future this was one flower he'd pay attention to. He'd have dozens of them planted around his house as a private joke, a silent toast to his one, extremely lucrative venture into crime.

"Tomorrow," he whispered to the painting, a promise from an impatient lover. And turning, State Senator Phillip Merriam silently made his way back down his mother's stairs.

Chapter Fifteen

Frenzy
(Pinewood 1972)

Ferris slammed herself back against the cage, hoping there wasn't an inquisitive white tiger behind her. She'd come in the back way, over the unguarded museum wall, to see if she could find Danielle Blackheart Porcini without running into her accomplice. She had every intention of confronting her future sister-in-law, though she wasn't quite sure what that would accomplish. Perhaps if Danielle knew her secret was public knowledge, she might give up her current plans. If she proved stubborn, Ferris had no qualms about decking the little wretch. She was a good four inches taller and probably twenty pounds heavier, and even if Danielle was an accomplished aerialist, she still would be at a disadvantage. Maybe all those cookies would come in handy, after all.

The one person she didn't want to run into was Marco Porcini. She didn't know which would be worse, being the recipient of his nondismissable attentions or being fed to a tiger. She might prefer the tiger, but she'd prefer to avoid both. Dinnertime seemed as good a time as any. She was counting on Marco being in the dinner tent, counting on Danielle keeping a low profile, as she had during the past three days. According to Regina, the lovely Madame Porcini hadn't left the Winnebago since Tuesday. Ferris had every intention of bearding the lioness in her den, to use an unpleasant figure of speech, and pointing out a few home truths to her.

But the Winnebago was empty. Ferris had hidden back in the shadows, uncomfortably close to the animal cages, and waited, jumping every time she heard a big cat growl, her palms sweaty, her heart racing. *Damn the Porcinis, and damn Blackheart.* She'd much rather be home and in bed, watching *To Catch a Thief* for the umpteenth time. But if she didn't do something now, she might as well spend the rest of her life looking at that movie. And she had every intention of catching her own particular thief, for life.

She heard Danielle approach, and breathed a silent sigh of relief, edging around the corner of the Winnebago with a stealth that would have done Blackheart proud. So quiet was she, in fact, that the dark figure behind Danielle didn't even notice he had a witness. Ferris watched in horror as a small, wiry figure dropped some sort of heavy cloth over Danielle's head. There was a brief struggle, then the woman's body went limp.

Her assailant hoisted the dead weight to his shoulder with some difficulty and headed toward the back boundary of the estate. There was something familiar about the way he moved, the way he held his head, the tuneless whistle that came to her ears as she followed him. But it wasn't until she saw the Bentley that she was able to place him.

He dumped Dany's body into the back seat, breathing a sigh of relief that was audible even to Ferris's distant ears. "You just stay sleeping, me girl," said Alf Simmons, Blackheart's old friend and occasional chauffeur. "And everything will be just fine."

Thank heavens, he'd parked only a short distance away from Ferris's Mercedes. The moment the Bentley began its stately journey from the parking lot, Ferris raced for her own car, yanking open the unlocked door and diving for the ignition.

It didn't start. She shrieked, a short, colorful imprecation that compressed all her despair and determination into a few four-letter words. She turned the key again, her hands shaking, and this time it caught. The lights of the Bentley were already fading in the distance, and she pulled out of the museum parking lot with a screech of tires and a silent condemnation of her upscale vehicle.

"Tomorrow," she muttered, "I'm trading you in for a Corvette."

In response the Mercedes sputtered, but Ferris was having none of that. Jamming her foot down hard on the accelerator, she took off after the Bentley, driving with her customary disregard for the rules of road safety.

Either Alf was unused to this sort of work and didn't notice that he had a very determined driver tailing him, or he knew and didn't care. When she finally lost him, they were within three city blocks of his final destination, and Ferris knew the area well enough to make it the rest of the way on her own, ending up behind the Bentley, slamming to a stop and jumping out just as Alf Simmons opened the back door of the limousine.

He looked up, startled, ready to shield his unwilling passenger, when he recognized Ferris's pale face in the lamplight. "Oh, no," he said, shaking his head. "'Is nibs isn't going to like this, not one tiny bit."

"Is she all right?" Danielle's well-being wasn't of prime concern to Ferris at that point, but she hoped the girl was at least still breathing.

"Fine. Just gave her whiff of stuff to put her out while I brought her here. She'll have a hell of a headache, but then, that's not me problem."

"No," said Ferris, looking up at Blackheart's fifth-floor windows. "That's her brother's."

"You've got a head on your shoulders, I've always said so," Alf Simmons said admiringly. "Patrick didn't think anyone knew."

"Patrick's problem is that he thinks he's smarter than everyone," she said. "But he's not smarter than I am. What are you supposed to do with her?"

"Bring her upstairs and keep her out of harm's reach until Patrick can get her safely out of the country." Alf glanced in at the unconscious girl. "I think he was going to lock her in the bathroom."

Ferris's brain was working double time. "I'll tell you what. You take her to my place, and I'll go up and talk to Blackheart."

"Are you nuts? He's paid me to do a job, and when a Blackheart hires you to do something, you do it."

"You're not scared of him, Mr. Simmons?"

"The boy's got a nasty temper when he's crossed."

"But I'll be the one dealing with the boy," Ferris reminded him, pushing past and kneeling on the leather seat. For a moment she remembered a ride in that very car, with the scent of white roses and the bubbles of her favorite champagne tickling her nostrils. Ruthlessly she shoved away that sudden weakening, and reaching down, took Danielle's thin shoulder and shook her.

The drugged woman batted at her, murmuring something. "Wake up, Danielle," Ferris said ruthlessly, hauling her into a sitting position. "Wake up."

Danielle's blue eyes opened, slowly focusing on Ferris's determined face. "Go away," she said, and fell back against the seat.

Ferris was having none of that. "Come on, lady. Wake up." She yanked her upright again, giving her an enthusiastic whack across the cheek.

That did the trick, a little more effectively than Ferris could have wished. Danielle's eyes shot open as she winced, and in the artificial light overhead Ferris could see the fading bruises adorning her pale face.

"Sorry," Ferris muttered.

"Where am I?" Danielle asked groggily. "What's going on?"

"You're going to my place for a while. If you promise to go quietly and stay put, Alf won't drug you again."

Danielle shuddered. "I think I'm going to be sick."

The beautiful Bentley probably had never seen such rude behavior, but it served Alf right, Ferris thought. "There's a silver ice bucket you can use," she suggested.

"What do you want from me?"

"Not a damned thing. I just want to keep your brother from getting into any more trouble."

"My brother?" Even half-drugged and very nauseous, Danielle managed a creditable confusion, Ferris thought to herself. "I don't know what you're talking about."

"Yes, you do. Now are you going to go quietly or is Alf going to have to drug you again?"

"No more drugs," she said, shuddering. "I'll go peacefully."

"Word of a Blackheart?" Ferris knew she was pushing it.

There was something akin to hatred glittering in Danielle's eyes. "Word of a Bunce," she snapped.

Simmons pushed Ferris out of the way. "That's me girl," he said cheerfully, putting a cashmere lap rug over Danielle's legs. "You come along peacefully and we can talk about old times."

"Old times?" Danielle echoed.

"Don't tell me you've forgotten your second cousin Alfred? For shame, girl." Straightening up, he closed the heavy door of the Bentley, taking long enough to favor Ferris with a broad wink. "Better go deal with his lordship up there. The two of us will be fine."

"Are you really their cousin?"

"I am."

"And you aren't a cat burglar?" Maybe there was hope for her offspring, after all.

"No, ma'am. In my spare time I'm a bookie." And with a tip of his hat he climbed into the driver's seat and took off into the night.

BLACKHEART DRAINED his glass of whiskey, looking longingly at the bottle that was more than half-full. He wanted another drink, needed it, but wasn't about to give in to temptation. He needed his wits about him right now. Everything was coming together, all the tiny little bits and pieces, and he couldn't afford to let even a tiny part of his brain sink into an alcoholic fog.

Where the hell were they? He'd sent Alf out hours ago. It should have been a simple enough matter. According to reliable reports, Danielle had been hiding out in the Winnebago for the last few days—Alf wouldn't have had to search around for her. If his sister had any Blackheart blood at all in her veins, she'd put up a hell of a fight, but Alf was experienced in these matters. He should have been back here at least half an hour ago. Where were they?

He wasn't really looking forward to confronting his long-lost sister with the gloves off. He wasn't thinking very fond thoughts of her at that moment. She'd cost him his fiancée, his peace of mind, and was well on her way to costing him his freedom. McNab had been watching him, sitting there and waiting like a fat blue spider, waiting for him to slip up. The irony of it was that now Blackheart was in more trouble than he'd ever been, at a time in his life when he was most guiltless.

Much as he'd like to wring his sister's pretty little neck, he wasn't going to do that. But he was going to find out exactly what she and that thick-brained accomplice of hers had planned. It seemed embarrassingly obvious to Blackheart, so obvious, in fact, that he couldn't believe they were planning it. But no one else seemed to have noticed, so perhaps it was only his professional expertise that made their target so glaringly conspicuous.

But he needed verification. He needed to know when, he needed to know how, if he was going to foil Marco Porcini effectively and not end behind bars himself.

As if that weren't enough, he also had Phillip Merriam's convoluted stratagems to take into account. While Blackheart couldn't believe the bland and noble senator was really going to try to lift his dear mama's priceless Van Gogh, everything, including the usually infallible word on the street, pointed to the fact that that was exactly what he intended to do. And he expected Blackheart to take the fall for it.

Apparently destined to star as scapegoat in not one but two robberies, Blackheart was getting just a little bit irritated—not to mention missing his Francesca. Celibacy didn't sit well with him, but he had no interest in any of the other available females around. He wanted his woman and no one else.

In the meantime, though, he was going to have to content himself with persuading his little baby sister to keep out of the way, and then he'd work from there. It was all coming together—it couldn't last much longer. Still, there were moments like these when he would have given anything to find Francesca waiting at his door.

He heard the pounding on his door with a grimace of irritated relief. *Back at last.* Alf probably couldn't manage the key with an unconscious female over his shoulder. Setting down his empty glass, Blackheart crossed his lonely, dimly-lighted living room and flung open the door.

"What kept you...?" The words trailed off. Francesca stood there, an answer to an unconscious prayer.

She was dressed the way he liked her best, in faded jeans and an old cotton sweater, her upscale clothes packed away with her discreet gold jewelry, her perfect makeup and her alligator shoes. Her black hair was loose around her face, her green eyes glittered with apprehension and vulnerability and the traces of anger, and her mouth was pale and tremulous. On her left hand was the canary diamond.

He just stood there, momentarily blocking the door, too bemused to even think of an excuse. Any moment Alf would return, Danielle's comatose body over one shoulder, and then there'd be no way he could get rid of Francesca.

"What are you doing here?" His voice was surprisingly rough. He wondered if she could hear the longing in it. Longing for her.

She met his gaze with a semblance of calm, but her voice was huskier than usual, and he could see she was nervous. He wanted to put his hands on her, to calm her nerves, to make her think of something else entirely, when her words stopped him. "I had Alf take your sister to my place. She promised to wait until she heard from me."

He'd been a fool to underestimate her. He'd been a fool to ever let her go, even for a few weeks, just to protect her if things turned out badly. "How long do you think she'll wait?" he asked abruptly.

"Till tomorrow, at least."

It wasn't a conscious decision. It was inevitable, overwhelming and right. "Good," he said. "Then we've got all night." And he pulled her into his arms, shutting the door behind them.

If he was expecting a fight, she wasn't the one to give it to him. She went willingly, gladly, flowing into his arms like a hummingbird to a flower, without a word of protest. Her mouth was warm and sweet beneath his, tasting of surrender and delight, and she leaned against the door, kissing him back, sliding her hands up under his turtleneck, running them along his back, her fingers touching, caressing, exciting him beyond belief.

He yanked her sweater over her head with more haste than deftness, unfastened her jeans and shoved them down her long legs. The dim light in the hallway cast strange shadows around them, and as his mouth trailed along the slender column of her throat, he could hear a muffled laugh beneath his lips.

"Are we going to do this again?" she murmured. "We've made love in your hallway once already. Why don't we use the bed?"

He lifted his head to look down into her eyes. There was a dreamy expression on her face, a smile hovered about her pale mouth. "Are we going to make love?" he inquired huskily, pressing himself against her body.

"Maybe I'm jumping to conclusions," she said, her voice catching somewhat as his hands brushed the soft, full breasts that were still confined in a lacy bra. "Maybe you were just planning to put me into the shower?"

"We've done that already, too. We probably shouldn't repeat ourselves. What about the kitchen counter?"

"What about the bed?" she whispered, her lips brushing against his, slowly, tantalizingly. "We're out of practice."

"Practice makes perfect." He lifted her, wrapping her legs around his waist, and carried her into the bedroom, laying her down on the bed with infinite gentleness. He stripped off his clothes in the semidarkness and followed her onto the queen-size bed, his hands reaching for her with a sureness that felt impossibly right. It didn't matter whether she trusted him or not. It didn't matter what she knew, what she didn't know, what she thought she knew. All that mattered was that she was here, now, lying in his bed, her wonderful green eyes glittering in the shadows.

Her hands on his body were the same, that heady mixture of wonder and delight. In their six months together she'd never lost that sense of astonishment, of discovery, and he hoped she never would. Twenty-nine years of virginity had made her particularly appreciative of sensual delights, and he could only hope that after fifty years of making love with him, she'd still retain that fresh attitude. He had every intention of being around to find out.

Her mouth was growing bolder, moving down his chest, kissing, nibbling, her hands sliding down his rib cage, trailing down to capture the heavy solid heat of him, her fingers deft, arousing him to a point dangerously near explosion while her mouth teased his navel, his hip bones.

She'd never before touched him with her mouth, and he hadn't pushed her, never even suggesting the faint edge of disappointment he'd felt when she'd come close, achingly close. He wanted, he needed her mouth on him more than anything he'd ever needed in his life, but he bit his lip, hard, rather than beg.

She moved her mouth away from his stomach, looking up at his rigid face in the half light. Her eyes were heavy-lidded, a sensuous smile curved her mouth.

"Don't you like that?" she whispered, her voice a throaty enticement in the darkness as her fingers stroked, caressed, bringing him closer and closer....

"Come here," he said, his voice a raw demand as he wrapped his hands around her upper arms, ready to haul her up and over him.

"Not yet," she said. And put her mouth on him.

His hips arched in sudden reaction. He couldn't help it: he put his hands on her shoulders, holding her there, terrified that she'd pull away. But she didn't. He'd had a brief, conscious fear that during their time apart someone else had taught her this, but that unworthy thought vanished beneath her clearly untutored, achingly delightful ministrations.

He knew he wouldn't be able to bear much more of this, and wasn't sure if Francesca was ready for the logical consequence of her actions. "Dear heart," he said, his voice strangled, pleading. "Come here."

She lifted her head, releasing him from the warm, enveloping prison of her mouth, and he almost cried aloud with the anguish of that sudden desertion. "Didn't you like it?" Her voice was low, uncertain.

"Like it?" His laugh was a bare thread of laughter. "Francesca, darling, I could die from the pleasure of it. But I want all of you right now." This time when he pulled her she came, sliding up his length and over him, her hips settling over his as he reached up and joined them, slipping into her with a deep, savage thrust that she greeted with a shimmering, inner tremor. If he'd had any fears that he'd been taking advantage, her body set them to rest. She'd never been so ready, so responsive.

She was so right for him. So tight, so warm, so attuned to his body that he wondered how he'd survived so long without her. She sank down onto him, whimpering softly in delight, and he felt himself expand, filling her, every inch of her, until Ferris-Francesca and all her doubts disappeared, until Blackheart dissolved, until they were just one in a joining that grew more powerful, all-encompassing, until it swept over them, a triumphant destruction, a destructive triumph, a beginning that was an end and a beginning again.

He could feel her face, wet with tears or sweat or both, pressed against his chest as the tremors slowly left her body. He could feel his own face damp, with sweat or tears or both, and he wondered how he'd survive if she left him again—if she lifted her weary head and told him she still didn't trust him.

"Oops." Her voice was soft, muffled against his chest, and he felt her sudden stillness with a sinking feeling. *Here it comes,* he thought.

He was nothing if not resigned. "Oops?" he prompted. "Is that your way of telling me you made a mistake?"

She lifted her head, looking into his eyes, and there was a rueful expression on her face. "A major one," she said. "I stopped taking the pill."

"Oops," Blackheart said. "Why?"

"Without you around, there was no need for it," she said simply.

"But what if you met someone else?" He knew the answer to that one, but he wanted to hear it from her lips.

"Give me a break, Blackheart. If it took me twenty-nine years to find you, it'll probably take me half a century to find a suitable replacement. I'll be too old to get pregnant by that time, so why fill my body with chemicals?"

"That makes sense. This way you can just keep it full of healthy stuff like Diet Coke and cookies."

"Exactly. Don't worry, though. It's the best possible time in my cycle. If I do get pregnant, it'll be something close to a miracle. And then I'll just simply have to accept my fate."

"Accept your fate?" he echoed, not liking the sound of that.

Her smile lighted the darkened room with its sheer, childlike pleasure. "Maybe I should have said embrace my fate. Wholeheartedly." Gently she pushed him back against the pillows, and there was a mischievous expression on her face. "The damage has already been done. Want to tempt fate again?"

He reached up, sliding one hand behind her neck and pulling her down to his mouth. "And again," he said against her lips. "And again, and again."

REGINA MET the bland, ingenuous expression in her son's blue eyes across the silver coffeepot, her expression troubled. "I'm so glad you could join me for breakfast, darling," she said, pouring him a cup and adding the sugar and cream he liked. "I haven't seen enough of you recently. How's the campaign going?"

"Wonderfully. I'm up three points in the polls, and we've still got almost two months till the election."

"Isn't this very expensive?" she inquired in a careful voice. "I keep seeing your face on television when I least expect it. It's very unnerving," she added with a soft laugh.

"That's the way campaigns are run nowadays, Mother." He laughed his well-practiced, genial laugh. "We're running at a slight deficit, but things should improve. I'm expecting a major contribution."

"From whom?"

He frowned for a moment, clearly having forgotten that his mother was a sharp old lady. "A Dutch paint company," he replied, a tiny, smug smile twisting the corners of his mouth.

And Regina, remembering a day some thirty years ago when her only son had taken her pearl necklace to buy a new bicycle and then lied about it, was filled with a sudden dread.

Chapter Sixteen

To Catch a Thief
(Paramount 1955)

"I think I missed your coffee almost as much as I missed you," Ferris said with a sigh, leaning against the refrigerator door in Blackheart's kitchen and drinking deeply of the rich brew. She was wearing an old T-shirt of Blackheart's and her jeans, and she felt weary, replete and ridiculously happy. It was almost over. The worst part was past, the time without Patrick. Never, never would she willingly go through that again.

"Thanks a lot." His tone was ironic as he devoted his attention to the croissants heating in the toaster oven. "If I'd known that was all it would take to get you back, I would have shown up every morning with a thermos of the stuff. I should have realized you weren't a woman to be bought with diamonds."

"Nope. Mrs. Field's Cookies and a great cup of coffee should do it." She pushed away from the refrigerator, coming up behind him and putting her arms around his waist. "Don't let me be stupid again, Patrick," she whispered, pressing her cheek against his back.

He turned in her arms, threading his own around her, but his expression was wry. "I don't think I have any say in the matter, dear heart. If you persist in ignoring your instincts and listening to your fears . . ."

She stiffened. "I think trust goes both ways. You refused to confide in me, you still haven't explained . . . ."

"And I'm not going to. Not until it's over. There are just too many little threads that could unravel and end up tripping everything up."

This time she pushed away from him, hard, and he ended up against the counter. "I thought we came to an understanding," she said, her tone dangerously angry.

"Not exactly. We came to a climax, several of them, as a matter of fact. But that doesn't mean that all our troubles are over. The fact remains that you still don't trust me. Or if you do, it's only after you've received concrete proof. You couldn't pay attention to your own instincts, you were so busy running away . . . ."

She was about to run again, to storm from the kitchen in a rage, when his words stopped her. "You'd rather have a confrontation?" she demanded. "Fine." And stepping back, she swung at him. But he caught her, his hand fastening on to her wrist and holding tight. They stood there, immobile, and then he slowly, deliberately pulled her toward him. She went, hating herself, feeling herself once more vanishing into a vast, impenetrable cloud of love and desire where everything she was disappeared. She couldn't fight it, wasn't even sure she wanted to. She pressed her body against him and put her head on his shoulder, shuddering lightly.

"Why do we always do this?" she whispered.

"If I told you, you'd try to hit me again," he murmured into the silken cloud of her hair. He reached a hand under her chin, tipping up her head, her mouth to reach his. "Let's stop talking." His lips covered hers.

He tasted of coffee. He tasted of love. She shut her eyes, willing this to go on forever, when the insistent buzzing broke through her concentration. Lifting her head, she cast a questioning look at the toaster oven, but Blackheart shook his head.

"The front door," he said, releasing her.

"Don't answer it," she pleaded. "It'll be nothing but trouble. If it's not someone to arrest you, it'll be someone to arrest me. Let's just hide in the closet or sneak out the back."

Blackheart grinned. "The only way to sneak out of here is up the fire escape and over the rooftops. Are you game?"

"For you, yes."

His eyes narrowed. "Francesca, I could almost believe you do trust me, after all."

"I—"

This time he silenced her. "Not now. Wait till we get rid of our intruder."

She trailed after him to the door. "Don't answer it."

He opened it anyway. Standing in the doorway was a rumpled, hostile-looking Stephen McNab. "What did I tell you?" Ferris demanded. "We're doomed."

McNab didn't even waste a glance at her. Shouldering his way past a willing enough Blackheart, his flinty-gray eyes searched the apartment. "Where the hell is your sister?"

"For God's sake!" Blackheart exploded. "Does everyone know we're related?"

"Everyone who counts," Ferris said smugly. "Why do you want Danielle?"

"I don't think that's any of your business," McNab said in a cold voice. "Where is she?"

"I haven't seen her," Blackheart replied with complete honesty. "Do you happen to have a warrant, Lieutenant?" His voice was silkily polite. "Because if you don't, I suggest you leave. The city of San Francisco frowns on police harassment."

"I'm off duty," McNab growled. "This is personal."

"You mean you don't want to arrest Danielle?" Ferris questioned.

"The only person I want to arrest is Blackheart. It doesn't look as if I'm going to have the chance."

"No, it doesn't, does it?" Blackheart said cheerfully. "So tell me, McNab, what personal interest do you have in my sister? As head of the family I think I have a right to question your intentions."

"Don't push it, Blackheart," McNab warned, his eyes mere slits in his angry face. "For one thing, your sister stole my car."

"Did she? How enterprising of her. That makes her the first Blackheart in history to go for something other than jewels. Are you going to arrest her, McNab?" he inquired politely. "Or simply deport her?"

McNab glared at him. "I'm going to marry her." And without another word he slammed out of the apartment.

Blackheart stared at the tightly shut door. "That's all I need," he mourned. "A cop for a brother-in-law."

"Who says Danielle will go along with that?"

Blackheart shrugged. "I suggest we ask her. That is, if she's still waiting meekly at your apartment."

"She'll be there," Ferris said, sure of no such thing.

"I hope so. I have a few things to say to my long-lost sister," Blackheart said grimly. "And I'm tired of having to chase around after her."

"She's the one who committed the robberies, isn't she?"

Blackheart just looked at her. "You figure it out, dear heart. I'm not going to tell you." And without another word he headed for the shower.

THERE WAS NO SIGN of the Bentley outside Ferris's modest, two-and-a-half-story apartment building. They'd driven over in Blackheart's aging Volvo station wagon, barely speaking, and Ferris was sorely tempted to say something—until she noticed the expression on Blackheart's face, the muscle working in his jaw, the darkness of his eyes. She kept her mouth shut, following him up the stairs to the second-floor hallway, struggling with a new realization. Blackheart, the bold, brave cat burglar, Blackheart, who always knew what he wanted and seemed to know what everyone else wanted besides, Blackheart the invincible was afraid. Unsure of himself, wound up and afraid.

The last icy little part of her wounded heart melted. For some reason she'd never thought of him as vulnerable—it was only Francesca-Ferris with her troubled background and her confused future who was vulnerable. If Blackheart could care so much about a sister he hadn't seen in decades, it proved he was human, after all, and not the invulnerable man of steel she sometimes feared he was.

"Do you want me to wait out here?" she asked, her voice low and husky, completely devoid of her previous sulky manner.

He looked at her in surprise, not expecting the sudden softening on her part. "What makes you think she's still here?"

"She's a Blackheart. Or maybe she's a Bunce, I don't know. Either way, she's here. Do you want me to go get some coffee or something?"

For a long moment he looked at her, his tawny eyes dark and enigmatic. And then he leaned over and kissed her, a brief, hard kiss. "I want you with me," he said.

The living room was empty. From somewhere in the distance Ferris could hear the sound of voices, and it took her a moment to place them. Grace Kelly and Cary Grant, bickering throughout eternity, as *To Catch a Thief* played on the VCR.

Danielle was sitting curled up in the middle of Ferris's big bed, dressed in jeans and a sweater, looking vastly different from the elegant European socialite she usually resembled. Her eyes were faintly red-rimmed, any makeup washed off long ago. In her arms, purring like a docile house pussy, sat Blackie, the smoky-gray alley cat.

Danielle was watching her brother, a wary expression on her face, a stubborn thrust to her lower lip. Blackheart stood motionless beside Ferris, and she found herself holding her breath.

"You look about three years old with that pout," he said finally.

"I feel about three years old," Dany said.

The light in the bedroom was filtered by the foggy day, but Blackheart was nothing if not observant. His eyes narrowed. "Who hit you? If it was that swine McNab..."

"McNab? What made you think of him?" She looked startled, hopeful and worried.

"He showed up at my apartment, demanding to know where you were. He said you stole his car."

"Borrowed it," Dany amended with a shrug.

"He also said he was going to marry you." Blackheart moved into the room, his lean body tense and edgy. "Which is, as far as I'm concerned, the worst thing you've done to me. I can put up with being implicated in crimes I didn't commit, I can put up with being framed for your latest clumsy attempt, I can put up with my professional reputation going down the tubes. I can even contemplate the idea of an undeserved jail sentence with a fair amount of equanimity. But the thought of having Stephen McNab as a brother-in-law is too much.''

A small, wistful smile curved Dany's mouth. A mouth that was almost a twin to Blackheart's, Ferris noticed with belated surprise. ''Don't worry, I'm not going to marry him. It wouldn't work. And I expect I'll be the one who's going to jail, not you. And I'm sorry, though that doesn't do much good. Does that improve matters?''

''No,'' said Blackheart. ''I want my sister back.''

Dany dissolved into hiccupy sobs, Blackheart took her into his arms, and Ferris wisely tiptoed out the door, closing it behind them. Blackie made it out just in time, having a typical feline disdain for heavy emotion, and followed his mistress into the kitchen, his spiky gray tail switching back and forth.

''All right, I've been ignoring you,'' Ferris murmured, searching through the refrigerator for guilt food. ''I've had problems of my own, you know.''

Blackie jumped onto the counter, his bulk landing with a heavy thud, and his only response was a haughty meow. ''Yes, I know,'' she said, dishing out the last of the herring and opening herself a Diet Coke. ''You don't care about my problems, you only care about your stomach. What I want to know, cat of mine, is why you were cuddling up to a stranger? The only other stranger I've seen you tolerate is Blackheart. Do you have a certain affinity for cat burglars?''

Blackie shoved his face into the herring, ignoring her. Ferris levered herself up onto the narrow counter beside him, swinging her long legs. ''Who can blame you?'' she murmured, half to herself. "I have a certain affinity for them myself."

She was halfway through her soda when Blackheart emerged from the bedroom, Dany trailing behind him. "What makes you think everyone knows what we're going for?" she demanded, crowding into the tiny kitchen with them. "The Van Gogh is the logical target. When something like that is available, why would anyone go for the eggs?"

"Eggs?" Ferris echoed.

Blackheart opened her refrigerator, clucked in disgust and closed it again, leaning against the counter, touching her legs with that casual gesture that bespoke complete ease with another's body. She only wished she could be so nonchalant with his. The feel of his arm against her legs was like a burning brand. "Dany and her heavy-fisted accomplice were planning to steal the Fabergé eggs from the museum. They naively assumed that everyone would be watching the Van Gogh. What I've been trying to point out to her is that McNab, even in his besotted condition, is no fool. He knows that if a Blackheart is around and in a larcenous mood, that Blackheart is going to go for jewels. And the most bejeweled things in San Francisco at the moment are the Fabergé eggs. Ergo, Blackheart's sister is going to go for the eggs."

"McNab never asked me what our target was."

"Did he have time?" Blackheart countered. Dany's response was a surprising blush, and Blackheart swore. "I guess I'm going to have to put up with a bloody policeman for an in-law. He's going to have to make an honest woman of you."

"I'm not going to let him compromise his principles for me," Dany said nobly, her eyes filling again with tears.

"Fine," said Blackheart, taking the can of Diet Coke from Ferris's hand and drinking. He shuddered and handed it back. "Then you can compromise your principles for him. After all, you're a thief, born and bred, and you're planning to give up your wicked way. I'd think you'd let him meet you halfway."

"Do you miss it?" Dany asked the question Ferris didn't dare put.

Blackheart placed an arm around Ferris's waist, drawing her closer. "Francesca keeps me distracted whenever I get a larcenous urge. I'm certain you can count on McNab to do the same for you."

"Maybe," Dany said, reaching forward to stroke Blackie's thick gray fur. If there was one thing Blackie hated, it was affectionate gestures when he was pigging out, but he lifted his sour-cream-dappled face, looked at Dany, and purred.

"I know what you're getting as a wedding present," Ferris said sourly. "Let's hope McNab isn't allergic to cats."

"I don't know," Dany said. "I hardly know anything about him. It would be a ridiculous mistake to marry him."

"It seems to me, sister mine, that you've made a great many mistakes in your life. This one just might turn out well."

"You're forgetting about Marco. He's not going to let me go without a fight."

"He's not going to have a choice in the matter. He can't pull off the museum heist alone, can he?"

"No."

"And at this point you haven't committed any crimes on American soil?"

"Except for stealing McNab's car."

Blackheart dismissed that minor technicality with a wave of his hand. "And you managed to confuse the European authorities thoroughly. As long as you stay in this country, safely married to your cop, you should manage to live happily ever after. I think we can count on McNab to take care of Marco."

"Make him see reason." Dany turned to Ferris for support. "There's no future for a thief and a cop."

"Blackheart believes what he wants to believe. Unfortunately, he's usually right."

"Maybe." Dany didn't sound so sure. "But I don't think so. Not this time. I'm going to take a shower, if that's all right."

"Go right ahead," Ferris said. "Blackheart and I will still be here, arguing."

"We're not arguing, we're planning," he corrected her as Dany disappeared. "And all we have to worry about—" his voice was a silken purr "—is trapping Ferris Byrd's thieving ex-fiancé."

She jumped, looking into Blackheart's tawny eyes. "I thought you said you were no longer thieving?"

"I'm not. You happen to have more than one former fiancé."

"Don't be absurd!" Ferris protested, sliding off the counter. Unfortunately Blackheart helped her down, easing her body alongside his in a manner calculated to make her brain melt. They were alone in the tiny kitchen, and in the distance they could hear the muffled sound of the shower. She also noticed he'd said she had two former fiancés. If she wondered where they stood after last night, he'd just obliquely answered the question—still at an impasse. "Phillip wouldn't steal anything. He doesn't need to—he inherited a fortune from his father."

"He also has substantial campaign debts and a very tight race with a Hispanic congressman from San Diego. He needs more television time, and that's very, very expensive."

Ferris stared at him in disbelief—a disbelief tempered by the fact that she'd learned to trust Blackheart. If he said a notorious straight-arrow like Phillip Merriam was straying off center, he was most likely right. "What's he going to steal?"

"What else? His mother's Van Gogh."

"That's ridiculous! He wouldn't steal from his own mother. I don't believe you."

"Don't you?" It was a mild enough question.

Ferris hesitated. "I suppose I do. But why would he take such a risk? Couldn't he just ask his mother for the money? Why would he jeopardize his reputation and his career like that?"

"I've been doing a little checking in the last few days. He's borrowed everything he can, legally. And Regina, bless her heart, supports Congressman Diaz. Not to mention that she wouldn't sacrifice a treasure like the Van Gogh for the sake of her son's ambition. She wants it to belong to the people, and that's what will happen to it, if Phillip doesn't get there first."

"I still can't believe he'd take the risk," she said stubbornly.

Blackheart put a hand under her chin, forcing her eyes to meet his. "You know as well as I do how seductive danger can be. Your bland and boring Phillip is just about to be deflowered. Unless, of course, we stop him."

"Why would you be willing to do that? There's no love lost between you and Phillip. I wouldn't think you'd care what happened to him."

"I don't. But I do, however, have a fondness for Regina, and Phillip's disgrace would be hers. And there's one other little problem. Phillip's planning to frame me for the theft."

"Don't be ridiculous!"

"He had me recheck the security system yesterday, when you and I both know he went over it with Nelbert and McNab not three days ago. He made sure I left my fingerprints all over everything. He's also asked me to meet him at the house tonight at midnight, to discuss certain events in Madrid. I'm sure I'm supposed to arrive and discover the painting missing, with even more clues leading directly to me. If it weren't so obvious, I might be irritated. But with a clod like Nelbert helping him, he was bound to be fairly basic in his planning."

"Nelbert's in on it, too?"

"You can't trust anyone nowadays," Blackheart said with a soulful look. "Nelbert is as sleazy as they come. He's just managed to keep a lower profile than I have in my past indiscretions."

"That's a polite term for breaking and entering."

"Oh, I'm always polite," he said.

"So what are we going to do about it?"

"We aren't going to do anything. Tonight's the night of the circus performance. I'll be there anyway, but instead of watching the pickpockets and housebreakers, I'm going to keep my eye on the good senator. If I can't catch him in the act and stop him, then I deserve to take the fall for it."

"And what will I be doing?"

"You'll be circulating among the crowds, doing what you do so well."

"What's that?"

"Being charming. Of course you reserve that charm for everyone but me."

"Maybe I keep my charm for those who deserve it."

"Maybe," said Blackheart, pulling her into his arms, his mouth very close to hers. "And maybe you trust me enough not to have to charm me. Maybe you know that your very presence on this earth is charm enough for me." He brushed his lips over hers, a brief, glancing caress, one she reached for, pressing her mouth against his, deepening the kiss.

His hands slid down her back, catching the seat of her jeans and pulling her up tight against him. She could feel his arousal, feel the taut, hungry heat of him, and she moaned deep in the back of her throat.

"I wish your sister wasn't here," she whispered against his shoulder when he finally broke the kiss.

A sudden irritated expression crossed his face, and he released her abruptly. "How long has it been since you heard the shower?"

"I wasn't paying any attention." She followed him out of the kitchen, down two steps into the dining room and up another two to her bedroom. "She couldn't have left, Blackheart. She would have had to go past us."

Blackheart had already yanked open the bathroom door, exposing the empty room beyond. He swore, sharply and succinctly. "Do you think a Blackheart has to worry about things like front doors and stairs? If *you* can climb up your balcony and break in, it would be child's play for Dany to escape that way." He climbed across the bed that filled the small room, yanked open the terrace door and stepped out into the fitful spring sunlight. "Damn!"

She'd followed him, leaning against the open door watching him out of somber eyes. "Where do you think she's gone?"

"That's one question," he agreed. "The other one is why?" He came back into the bedroom, no longer interested in the rumpled bed or Ferris's heated body. "I think, dear heart, we may be in for a rough ride."

Chapter Seventeen

Sabotage
(Lime Grove 1936)

The evening was a zoo in more ways than one. Ferris threaded her way through the glittering, absurdly bejeweled crowds at the circus, a perfect smile plastered to her face, her eyes darting into shadowy corners, alert for the reappearance of Dany Bunce. There was no sign of her, though she kept running into a glowering Stephen McNab. Clearly his luck was as bad as hers, or he would have worn a more pleasant expression.

She was leaning against the side of the grandstand, watching her old friends the white tigers go through their paces, when she felt someone breathing down her neck. She looked up into the lieutenant's steely eyes with the unflinching courage born of complete desperation. "I haven't seen her," she said, forestalling his obvious question.

"If I find you have anything to do with her getting away, I'm going to put you in the slammer along with Blackheart," he growled. The sound was fiercer than her old friend Tarzan's theatrical roars from the center ring.

Ferris thought about it for a moment. "I might prefer that," she said finally. "If you're going to arrest Black heart on trumped-up charges, I'd just as soon go along with him."

"They won't be trumped up. I'm going to nail him for grand larceny, breaking and entering and obstructing justice, and I'll get you as an accessory."

"You can also charge me with littering," she added politely.

"Don't push me."

"Don't push *me*," Ferris countered. "Blackheart hasn't done any of those things in years, certainly not within your jurisdiction, and he paid for his earlier crimes."

"Six months in jail is not paying for more than fifteen years of crime."

"Are you a cop, McNab? Or are you God?"

He didn't say anything for a moment, his jaw working in rage and frustration. He was able to swallow it, a shudder leaving his body. "I need to find her," he said in a quieter voice. "I can't let her disappear. I need her."

"Do you think there's much of a future for you if you hound her brother into jail?" She refused to feel sorry for him.

"Her brother can do anything he damned well pleases. He can knock over Fort Knox for all I care. I'm not on duty tonight, and I'm not on his case anymore. It's somebody else's problem."

Marco Porcini was beginning his high wire act. Ferris looked up and shivered. "I'll do what I can. So, as a matter of fact, will Blackheart."

It must have galled him to accept aid from his nemesis. But he swallowed his pride. "I'll be around if you see anything."

She nodded, her attention on Marco's muscular form. She felt rather than saw him leave, so enrapt in watching the strong body overhead that she couldn't pull her eyes away. She didn't want to look. Even the sight of someone braving such great heights made her heart pound and her palms sweat in empathic fright. The net beneath offered no comfort. She watched Porcini's slippered feet dance along the high wire and wanted to throw up.

She heard a murmur of appreciation from the crowd, a ripple of laughter, one that she couldn't identify. Marco was doing nothing more than dancing lightly on the wire, nothing to encourage such a reaction. The reaction was growing, and Ferris reluctantly pulled her eyes away to the side, where a clown with oversize shoes, a gigantic purple wig, glowing nose and preposterous figure was making his way up the rope ladder to the high wire.

"What are you doing?" Blackheart breathed in her ear.

"Damn!" She turned her complete attention to the man who'd materialized behind her, grateful for the distraction. "You do creep up on a person, don't you? I was doing what you ordered me to do. Watching the circus and keeping an eye out for suspicious behavior. You told me I wasn't allowed to help you with your trap. For that matter, why aren't you lying in wait near the Van Gogh?"

Blackheart shrugged. "Nothing was happening. And I didn't order you. I suggested you might be more constructive down here. Particularly since I planned to go in over the roofs. It was hard enough for you in the daylight. Trust me, you wouldn't have liked it at all tonight."

"Did you go in over the roofs?"

"Actually, no," he admitted, keeping a wary eye on her. "But I might have had to. I still might have to, and you know you don't want to do that. You can barely stand to watch Porcini." He glanced up, and Ferris followed his gaze. The clown had reached the opposite end of the tightrope, and with a great show of incompetence and trepidation the figure started edging out onto the taut line.

Porcini reacted with theatrical rage, gesturing the clown to go away. The audience was in stitches, Ferris's palms were soaking, and she pulled her attention away from the spectacle. "No, I wouldn't want to climb over the roofs," she agreed.

"So why are you dressed like that?"

Ferris looked down at her black silk jumpsuit, an outfit that effectively covered her from wrist to ankle. An impressive expanse of pale breast was visible, but she only had to do up a couple of buttons to cover up even that amount of white flesh. "Don't you like it? It cost a small fortune."

"It's also brand-new. I know your clothes well enough to know you just bought it, and I know as well as you do how effective an outfit that would be for a cat burglar. Forget it, Francesca. You're not going to have anything to do with the festivities tonight."

"Why not?"

"Because I don't want you getting hurt."

"Why not?"

"Don't be obtuse. You know why not," he growled. "Even if there's no future for us, I want you to be alive and well enough to enjoy a future with someone else."

Ferris's fear of heights vanished, replaced by a new apprehension. "There's no future for us?" she echoed.

He pulled his eyes away from the act overhead for a brief moment. "Is there?"

It was her turn to look away to the figures of Porcini and the clown. They were engaged in some sort of mock struggle and the audience was eating it up. "Blackheart," she said, her voice raw with emotion, "I—"

"Oh, my God!" It wasn't a shout, it was a strangled gasp of horror as Blackheart effectively forgot her existence. "That's Dany up there."

Just at that moment Porcini lost his formidable balance. Clutching at Dany he fell, yanking her off the wire. Then losing his grip, he tumbled toward the net. Instinctively tucking himself into the proper position for falling, he landed smack-dab in the middle of the net.

The net should have rebounded, sending him into a standing position. It didn't. With an ominous rending sound it pulled free from one of its supports, sending Marco hurtling to the sawdust floor.

Throughout the tent, the laughter had been replaced by frightened screams. But Marco rolled into the sawdust, performed a somersault and ended standing, his arms held overhead in the age-old demand for applause.

He got it in spades. The crowd went wild, delighted at being tricked for a moment into actual fear. They seemed to have forgotten the figure still up on the wire, clinging with gloved hands, swinging over the broken net.

The silence fell, as one by the one the audience remembered and looked upward. Ferris could feel Blackheart, taut and sweating beside her, could hear his whispered words, part threat, part encouragement. "You can do it, you can do it. You stupid idiot, climb up there."

Dany swung her leg around. The oversize shoe fell off, tumbling to the floor, and her leg missed the wire. She tried again, one hand slipping and then grabbing again, and the audience gasped. One more try and she was up, sitting on the wire, looking down at the cheering spectators with pantomimed surprise.

She then proceeded to crawl on her hands and knees across the wire, exaggerating every step to the delight of the crowd. When she reached the platform at the end of the line, Marco was waiting for her, a huge, toothy grin on his sweaty face, a murderous glare in his eyes.

Blackheart started toward the base of the pole, when McNab suddenly appeared out of nowhere. "I'll take care of this," he said in a determined tone of voice.

Blackheart let him go. "Do you think he's a match for Porcini?" Ferris questioned, watching as Marco half dragged, half carried the penitent clown out of the tent, with McNab just behind them.

"I wouldn't be standing here if I didn't."

"Maybe you can't resist me?" she suggested lightly. "That certainly was a terrific act, wasn't it? They had the entire audience going. I didn't realize Dany still performed."

"It wasn't an act."

"I beg your pardon?"

"What you just witnessed," Blackheart said in a glum voice, "was attempted murder. By my sister, of a man who doubtless deserved it. I just hope McNab didn't catch on."

"Patrick." Regina Merriam joined them, perfectly dressed as always in blue silk, her mane of white hair neatly arranged, her face perfectly made-up. "And Ferris. I wondered where you two were. Wasn't that simply marvelous? I had no idea the Porcinis were so talented."

"They are quite different, aren't they?" Ferris said, casting a worried glance at Blackheart's troubled expression. And then she noticed Regina wasn't looking terribly happy, either. As usual she'd put a calm face on things, but Ferris had known her long enough and well enough to realize something was wrong.

"Are you feeling all right?" Blackheart managed to pull himself out of his abstraction.

"As a matter of fact, I was a little worried about something," she confessed with a contrived laugh. "I know you'll think I'm silly, but I'm concerned about the Van

Gogh. It moves to the museum tomorrow, and I can't help thinking that this would be the perfect time to take it.''

Ferris felt her heart twist at the sight of her old friend's desperate dignity. "Are you worried about the Van Gogh, Regina?" she asked gently. "Or about Phillip?"

Regina shut her eyes for a moment, leaning back against the grandstand. When she opened them, they were glittering with tears. "Does everyone know but me?"

"Only Francesca and I have guessed," Blackheart said gently. "Don't worry, Regina. We won't let him do anything foolish. I promise you."

Regina smiled through her tears. "I think I must have spoiled him. He was always so charming. It was easy to give him anything he wanted. He's just used to having everything."

"Maybe. I may just teach him a lesson or two tonight," Blackheart said.

Regina nodded. "I think it might be long overdue."

"You stay down here, Regina," Ferris said, pressing the thin hand that suddenly felt frail. "I'll make sure everything's all right."

"I knew I could count on you both," she said simply.

The grounds were almost deserted as Ferris followed Blackheart out into the night, heading toward the mansion. She had to run to keep up, and her high-heeled black sandals sank into the damp grass with each step. "Wait a minute," she gasped, struggling along.

"I don't want you involved in this," he snarled, not slowing his pace. "I told you that. This thing could turn ugly, and I don't want you in the line of fire."

"Why didn't you tell Regina that? She would have kept me with her."

"I wasn't about to tell an old lady her son might be dangerous. It's hard enough for her to deal with the fact that he's turning larcenous."

"I hadn't thought of that." She stopped for a moment, pulled off her shoes and threw them into the bushes, sprinting to catch up with Blackheart's elegant figure. He was wearing evening dress, as were most of the men tonight, and Ferris couldn't help but think that a tuxedo was the perfect outfit for a society burglar.

"Well, think of it. And know that if Phillip does anything to hurt you, then Danielle won't be the only Blackheart capable of attempted murder."

"I can go back...."

His arm caught her, tugging her along. "At this point I think you're safer with me," he said, resigned. "Just watch out for Nelbert. He's even stupider than Phillip, and a great deal more ruthless. Keep quiet and do as I say. Understood?"

"Yes, sir."

They went in through the terrace door. The house was dark. Most of the servants were down at the circus, and only Nelbert's hired security guards were in sight. It was child's play for Blackheart to move past them, the work of two seconds to go through the solid lock on the terrace door. And then they were creeping through the darkened house, up the long, curving stairs, Ferris fully as noiseless as the more experienced Blackheart.

They stopped on the second-floor landing. Fitful beams of light were filtering downward from the third-floor landing, and Ferris could hear the muffled sound of voices. Without ceremony Blackheart pushed her against a wall and clapped a hand over her mouth. "They're early." Barely a trace of sound issued forth, and Ferris wondered if she was getting adept at reading lips. He removed his hand, still keeping his body pressed against hers, and the light in his eyes came from determination and an unholy excitement.

"What if they have guns?" She mouthed her response. Blackheart shrugged. "Then duck."

"How reassuring." It was hard to be icy when you were speaking in something softer than a whisper, but her irony managed to reach Blackheart anyway, and he grinned.

"Listen, angel, you chose to come along," he taunted her. "If it makes you feel any better, I don't think either of them are armed. Phillip is too smart for that and Nelbert is too dumb."

"There are just the two of them?"

"No."

"No?"

"Someone else just came in downstairs. One set of footsteps. So there are three."

"I don't hear a thing," she protested, not making a sound.

"That's because you don't listen." He tugged at her, pulling her under the curve of the winding stairs. "We'll wait here. The Hardy Boys will be down before long, carrying their ill-gotten gains. They're lucky *The Hyacinths* is so small. It would have served Phillip right if it was the size of a Bierstadt."

"How big is a Bierstadt?"

"Room size." The footsteps directly above them signaled that the thieves were on the move. "When they get down here you stay put. I'll confront them."

"With what? The force of your personality? Blackheart, this is dangerous!"

"Sweetheart, just because they won't be carrying guns doesn't mean I'm similarly inclined." Reaching down to his ankle, he pulled out a very small, very nasty-looking little gun. "And yes, I have a permit. It's very legal."

"I wasn't going to ask that. I was going to ask if it was loaded."

"There's not much use in having a gun if it isn't loaded. First rule of firearms, darling."

"What's the second?"

"Don't brandish it, if you're not willing to use it."

"And the third."

"I already told you that one. Duck."

They stood there, huddled under the stairs for a time that stretched on endlessly, listening to the steady advance of the felons from the floor above, the accomplice from the floor below. In actuality it couldn't have been more than a minute and a half, but the time stretched and pulled like a rubber band until Ferris was ready to scream.

Blackheart was in total control, only the glitter in his dark eyes betraying just how much he was enjoying all this, Ferris thought bitterly. He waited until the last moment, until beyond the last moment, when the shadowy figures were almost ready to start down the second flight of stairs.

"I think you've gone far enough," he said calmly. His hand reached out and hit the light switch, flooding the landing with light, and as he stepped into the hallway, his nasty little gun was pointed directly at the center of Regina's priceless painting.

Phillip swore, dropping the picture, frame and all, onto his toe. Nelbert backed away, an ugly expression on his ugly face, and began fumbling under his coat.

Ferris decided it was time to contribute to the situation. "He's going for his gun, Blackheart," she said, stepping out of her hiding place.

"Get back, damn it!" Blackheart swore, diving for Nelbert before his hand could emerge with the gun. The force of his one hundred eighty-some pounds, catapulted against Nelbert's two hundred forty, was enough to knock the larger man off balance. He began to tumble down the stairs, grasping for Blackheart. Blackheart stepped neatly out of reach, watching with no reaction at all as Nelbert fell down a total of seventeen stairs to end lying in a crumpled heap at the bottom. He was moaning slightly, reassuring anyone who happened to care that he was still alive.

Regina was standing there, a rueful expression on her face. She looked up at the tableau above her, and an expression of utter sorrow darkened her faded blue eyes. She started up the stairs, holding on to the marble banister like a woman whose life had been shattered. In one day she'd aged twenty years, and Ferris was sorely tempted to toss down her witless son after his accomplice.

Blackheart looked up too, into Phillip's expressionless face. "Put the painting back, you jackass," he said mildly. "You've done enough harm for one night."

"You don't understand," Phillip whined. Golden, handsome Senator Phillip Merriam whined. "It costs too much to get elected nowadays. I have to have the money."

"I want you to withdraw from the race, Phillip." Regina's voice was cold, her tone determined as she reached the second-floor landing.

"Mother..."

"I want you to withdraw from the race, or I will turn you over for prosecution."

"You wouldn't!" He gasped.

"I would." She cast a beseeching glance at Blackheart. "Can you dispose of that—that trash downstairs?" She gestured toward Nelbert's lumpish, groaning figure.

"Certainly. Are you planning to file charges?"

"That's up to Phillip. What's it to be?"

"Can't we talk . . . ?"

"No. Your decision."

Phillip hung his elegant blond head. Ferris almost thought she heard a snuffle of misery. "I'll withdraw," he said sulkily.

Regina nodded, satisfied. "In that case, just dump his accomplice someplace and leave it at that. I doubt Mr. Nelbert will be interested in pursuing our acquaintance after this fiasco."

"What about the painting?" Ferris asked. It was lying facedown on the carpet, no way to treat a masterpiece.

"Do you suppose you could put it in the museum on your way home? Just leave it inside the door. If someone else comes along and takes it, they're welcome to it."

"Certainly." Blackheart gingerly picked it up, eyeing the glowing colors with a mixture of admiration and distrust. "Come along, Francesca."

For a moment she didn't move—she stood there staring at the shell of what had once, years ago, seemed her most attainable dream. With a tiny, imperceptible shake of her head she followed Blackheart down the stairs, passing Regina's upright figure with a brief, sympathetic touch on the arm.

Trace Walker materialized from the shadows, a questioning look on his bland, beefy face. "Take care of Nelbert, would you?" Blackheart requested of his partner. "We've got something to do."

"Sure thing. Do I have to be gentle?"

Blackheart grinned. "Use your judgment."

They were halfway across the lawn, almost at the circus area, when Ferris spoke. Blackheart had grabbed a raincoat from a hall closet to drape around the masterpiece, and he strode along carrying his burden, seemingly lost in thought.

"What's going to happen to Phillip?" she asked, wishing she hadn't been so precipitate about tossing her shoes. The grass beneath her stockinged feet was damp, sending a chill up her back.

"Do you care?" Blackheart didn't slow his pace.

"For Regina's sake. And yes, for his sake. I was once rather fond of him."

"Pretty tepid emotions to base an engagement on. Do you always agree to marry someone on such mundane grounds?"

"Not always." She wasn't about to offer anything more, and he wasn't about to ask.

"I expect Phillip will run in the next election, and probably win it," Blackheart said, answering her previous question.

"Patrick, the man's a sleaze with no moral judgment whatsoever, a liar, and more than willing to frame someone else for his misdeeds."

"Yup," said Blackheart. "At that rate there's no telling how far he'll go."

"You're such a cynic."

"I know," he said, unrepentant. "There's just one thing that's worrying me."

"What's that?"

"Where the hell is McNab?"

Chapter Eighteen

Rope
(Warner Brothers 1948)

It took Blackheart less than a minute to crack the heavy locks that guarded the entrance to the Museum of Decorative Arts. He clicked his tongue in professional disgust as he undid the final bolt. "We're going to have to do something about these locks," he muttered.

"We? I thought Nelbert Securities was in charge of the museum." Ferris shivered lightly in the breeze that was picking up. There was only the barest sliver of a moon that night, a good night for going a-burglaring, Blackheart had always told her. The noise and lights from the circus seemed far away, almost on another planet, and Ferris devoutly hoped everyone that mattered was down there, including Marco Porcini, McNab and Dany. She had the unpleasant suspicion that they were all much closer than that.

"You don't seriously think Nelbert's going to keep the job, do you?" Blackheart countered, following her into the darkened main hallway. "Even without formal charges, word will get out, and very quickly. Nelbert's washed up in this town, as well he should be."

"And you think you'll get the job?" She shivered again. She'd never liked the museum. Regina's robber baron father had constructed it to house his collection, and it had been designed after an Italian castle dating from the early fifteenth century. It was built of massive stone, cold and damp and eerie, and the entire feeling of the place was oppressive.

"We're the logical choice." Blackheart headed for the checkroom, dumped the raincoat-covered painting behind the half door and turned to face her. "Regina already had me double-check Nelbert's arrangements for the Van Gogh, and I also did a once-over on everything else. Including the Fabergé eggs."

"Do you think they would have been able to take them?"

"I have no doubt at all they would. And I'm not sure we're out of the woods yet. I won't rest easy until I find out where McNab and my sister have gone."

A strange noise had been worrying away at the back of Ferris's brain. For a moment she'd been considering large, evil rodents, then she realized what the sound was. "I don't know about Dany," she said gloomily. "But I think we've found McNab."

He was propped up against a massive marble column just inside the Egyptian room. There was blood on his forehead, and he was moaning groggily.

"What happened?" Blackheart demanded with more tension than sympathy, pulling him up by his lapels.

McNab slapped his hands away. "What do you think happened? Porcini blindsided me. I followed them in here and just when I was about to arrest him, the lights went out. Damned fool."

"Porcini?"

"Me. I should have paid more attention. But he was hurting Dany, twisting her arm, and I got so mad I couldn't see straight."

"They're here?"

"They're here. They've gone after the eggs. He was dragging Dany, and she was putting up a hell of a fuss, but I imagine he was able to make her do what he wanted. Dammit, she was crying."

"Well, if she'd tried to push me off a tightrope, I might want to twist her arm, too," Blackheart said fairly.

Ferris glared at him in the shadowed room. "What are you planning to do about it?"

McNab struggled to his feet, swaying slightly. "I've got to find Dany."

"First you need to call in reinforcements," Blackheart corrected him. "There's a crime being committed, and someone's going to have to arrest Porcini."

"But what about Dany?"

"We'll have her safely away by the time your backups get here. Just tell them to be quiet." McNab still didn't move, and Blackheart gave him an overenthusiastic shove. "Go ahead. I'm going to do something about the alarm system."

"Why?" Ferris had the temerity to ask.

"Because I don't want the alarm going off if somebody makes a false move. Whether I like it or not, I'm in this just as deeply as Porcini and Dany, and it's my neck I'm saving, too."

"All right, I can accept that," Ferris said. "What do you want me to do?"

"I want you to go back to the cloakroom and hide down behind the counter. Keep your eyes on the Van Gogh at all times, and don't move until you hear my voice."

"The hell with that. I'm not going to sit passively by, doing nothing."

"Watching the most valuable work of art in the city isn't doing nothing."

"I'm not—"

"You are!" His grip on her arm was viselike, just short of bruising, and she had no choice but to allow herself to be hustled ignominiously back to the cloakroom. He shoved her down onto the floor, glowering at her. "Stay put. It will all be over in a few minutes."

"Go to hell, Blackheart."

He grinned, and once more she recognized the reckless excitement that was throbbing through his veins. "Only if you're there, dear heart." And he disappeared into the vast darkness of the museum.

Ferris hadn't even seen where McNab had gone to call in reinforcements. It didn't matter. She wasn't going to sit there and babysit an oil painting that no one seemed to want, no matter how much it was worth. The stone floors were icy beneath her stockinged feet, and the shadows and dark shapes looming up made her skin crawl. She had only the faintest recollection of where the fabulous jeweled eggs were kept, and in the dark they'd be harder still to find, but she was damned if she was going to sit and cower while everyone else had all the fun. She'd suffered too much already. She was going to see this thing through to the end.

At the center of the museum was a great hall that had once been filled with armor, stuffed elephants, Rodin sculptures, and anything else that wouldn't fit into a smaller room. That hodgepodge had mostly either been tossed or relegated to other spaces, and the great hall had been divided up into fifteen or twenty smaller rooms, their partitions reaching halfway up the stone balconies on either side. The Fabergé eggs were in one of the twenty, but Ferris couldn't even begin to guess which one.

Unfortunately she didn't have to.

"There you are, *bella*." A burly arm snaked around her neck, pulling her back against a strong, sweaty body. "I thought you might show up sooner or later. Where's the boyfriend? He's not going to do you much good, any more than that stupid cop could stop me. There are some things that are just meant to happen, and this is one of them."

"Let me go!" At least, that was what she tried to say. With his muscled forearm across her throat, the words came out in a muffled oomph.

Even someone of Marco's self-absorbed intellect could figure out what she was saying, given the circumstances. "I'm sorry, but I need you," he said, half carrying, half dragging her up a flight of stairs. They, like almost everything else in the damned building, were stone, and banged against Ferris's shins as she flailed and kicked.

When they reached the top he flung her forward, so that she sprawled facedown on the equally hard floor of what was doubtless one of the balconies overlooking the great hall. She stayed there for a moment, absorbing the impact of the unforgiving stone, trying to figure out how she was going to get out of this current mess.

Marco locked the balcony door behind them, then crossed to the railing and began fiddling with something Ferris couldn't see. "Now if your lover had just left well enough alone, we wouldn't be in this predicament. There was a heat sensing device surrounding the doorway to the room with the eggs, and it would have been a simple enough matter to use some fire extinguisher to pass through. But no, he had to add infrared. Therefore—" he reached down and hauled her to her unsteady feet "—we have to go in from the top."

A wire stretched across the vast, cavernous expanse of the great hall, reaching to the opposite balcony. Even in the shadowy darkness Ferris could see Dany's absurd white clown's face at the other end, standing by the wire. "I hate to say this," Ferris whispered, "but what's this 'we'?"

"But you're going with me, of course. Otherwise, how can I trust my lethal ex-partner not to loosen the rigging? Daniella!" he shouted across the room. "See who I have with me! Your brother's girlfriend decided she would help me out. Not that I gave her much choice, you understand. But if you unfasten the rope you don't just send me to my death. You send her, too. *Capisce?*"

"I understand." Her voice was dull, its tone accepting.

"So you will make sure the rigging stays taut, won't you, *cara*? Once I get the eggs and make it safely back to the other side, then you will be free. I'd love to teach you another lesson, but I'm afraid I don't have the time. But don't worry. Your handsome cop will arrest you, and you'll have plenty of time in American jails to think about all the mistakes you made—the biggest of which was thinking you could fool me."

He climbed up onto the balcony, balancing lightly over the great drop beneath him, and Ferris began to sweat. He'd changed from his spangled spandex into a loose-fitting jumpsuit, and he looked fully as graceful as Blackheart ever had. And then, to Ferris's absolute horror, he reached down and hauled her up onto the wide stone balustrade beside him.

"I'm afraid of heights," she said through chattering teeth.

"That is a great deal too bad. Because you're coming with me."

"Where?" she demanded, mystified.

"Out there." He gestured to the taut wire in front of them as if it were a boulevard.

"I can't. I'll fall."

"Perhaps. But not if you're careful. Don't worry, I don't intend to make you walk it yourself. That takes years of practice to perfect. I'll simply carry you. As long as you keep perfectly still and don't struggle, we should be fine. Otherwise I'll drop you. And it's a long ways down."

"You can't do this."

He jerked her arm, hard, and tossed her over his shoulder with effortless disdain. "I'm about to. I've done high wire acts with trained chimpanzees who don't weigh any more than you do. If they can survive, I expect you can. If you fall, just close your eyes and pray."

Ferris was already doing just that, praying with all her might as Porcini stepped out into space.

"Ferris, I'm sorry," Dany called in a low voice. "I didn't mean to get you into this."

Keeping her head down and her eyes shut wasn't helping matters, so Ferris lifted her head to look at the clown across the vast expanse that was slowly diminishing—too slowly. "Why did you run?" she asked, her voice a raw thread of sound. Porcini's shoulder was digging painfully into her stomach, and her fear strangled the breath in her throat, but if she was about to die she might as well die enlightened.

"I couldn't let all of you risk your futures for me," Dany replied miserably. "Particularly Stephen. I love him. I couldn't let him destroy himself over me."

"But we could have helped you," Ferris said earnestly.

"If I were you, *cara*," Marco wheezed into her ear, "I wouldn't shift around too much. I was mistaken—you're a little heavier than a chimpanzee." He stopped where he was, looking around him. A huge marble column stood nearby, some relic of an ancient temple. The flat, pitted top of it was perhaps twenty-four inches square.

With a sickening whoosh of air Porcini swung her limp body over his head and deposited her on the top of the column. For a moment she clung to him in panic, but he pulled away, and she felt her balance begin to give, could see the floor, miles away, looming up to meet her.

She pulled back, overcompensating for a moment so that she swayed backward. Finally she held still, clinging to the tiny bit of space like an angry cat, doing her best to control her rapid breathing, her trembling limbs, her very heartbeat.

"Now you be a good girl and stay there, *cara*. And if Danielle obeys my orders and doesn't try to murder me again, everything will be just fine." He looked across at the clown figure waiting on the opposite balcony. "Are you ready, Danielle? Send me the rope."

There was no further hesitation. Though Ferris's brain was fogged with fear, she could just make out the rigging Danielle was sending toward Marco's waiting figure. A rope and pulley sort of affair, sliding across the taut wire. Marco looked calm and alert, as casual as if he were standing on a boardwalk and not a thin line of wire. He caught the pulley when it reached him, tested it for a moment, then dropped off the wire, letting himself down the rope toward the room twenty feet below.

Ferris found herself holding her breath. The best thing in the world would have been for him to fall, but right now, in her precarious position, she didn't want to see anyone fall. She had the horrible certainty that if Marco fell, she'd fall too, in some sort of sick empathy.

She could just see him beyond the partition. He was within ten feet of the floor, within ten feet of the beautiful, intricate eggs that Ferris hated with a very real passion, when the building was flooded with light.

She blinked, swaying on her tiny platform, for a moment unable to see a thing. She heard McNab's voice, strong and sure and very angry. "Nice of you to drop in, Porcini."

Marco had already begun to scuttle back up the rope like a fat black spider. A few more feet and he'd be out of their reach, with the only hostage available a stupid fool stuck on the top of a Grecian column.

McNab reached into his coat and pulled out the biggest gun Ferris had ever seen in her life. "If you don't want a bullet right where it would hurt most, Porcini, you'll get your thieving, woman-beating butt down here," he drawled.

Marco ignored him, shinnying up the rope at an astonishing speed. Without further hesitation McNab cocked the pistol, and the sound of gunfire echoed through the stone-walled building.

Marco shrieked, tumbling to the floor. He landed as well as he could, an aerialist used to falls, but the stone floor knew no forgiveness, and he lay there, moaning, the rope still clutched in his hand.

A wave of relief washed over Ferris. McNab hadn't shot Marco; he'd somehow managed to shoot through the rope.

"Fancy shooting," Blackheart murmured, hauling Marco upright.

"I'm considered something of an expert," McNab said modestly. "I'd better read him his rights." Quickly he did so, saying the familiar television words that went straight through Ferris's brains. All the while Marco remained silent and sullen, glaring at his two captors.

"I think I hear your reinforcements," Blackheart mentioned.

"Damn," said McNab. "You realize he's going to get deported? He'll have a nice cushy ride back to Madrid to stand trial."

"Cheer up. Spanish jails aren't noted for their pleasant atmosphere."

"True enough. There's just one small problem," Stephen said politely.

"What's that?"

"If I hit him, I might jeopardize his arrest. Police brutality and all that."

"Oh, allow me," Blackheart volunteered courteously.

"Be my guest."

Blackheart advanced on the larger, quivering Marco. The blows were swift, efficient and downright dirty. "This one is for my sister," he said between his teeth. "And this is for trying to feed my lady to the tigers."

A second later Marco was back on the floor, groaning very, very loudly. The two men ignored him, just as they ignored the two women overhead who were watching them. "I never thought I'd have you for a brother-in-law," McNab said, shaking his head.

"We all have to make compromises in this life. My sister is worth it."

For the first time McNab looked up, into Danielle' white-painted face. "You know," he said, "I believe sh is."

"Blackheart." Ferris's voice was plaintive. Now that th worst danger is over, she could react to her own predicament with at least a touch of asperity. "Would you consider getting me down from here?"

His grin was absolutely heartless. "I'd consider it However, it's nothing more than you deserve. I told you t stay put."

"I know."

"What kind of future will we have, if I'm not able t trust you?"

"I know," she said miserably.

He didn't move for a long moment. "I guess you suffered enough. I'll get you. Stay right there."

"I'm not moving," Ferris said fervently.

She had a perfect view of the proceedings. She got to watch a moaning, whining Marco being carted away by uniformed police, she got to watch McNab race up to the balcony and pull a weeping, repentant Dany into his arms. She would even have allowed herself a sniffle or two of sympathetic pleasure, if the rest of her attention hadn't been concentrating on Blackheart as he climbed onto the wide stone railing with, she had to admit, not quite the consummate grace of a Marco Porcini.

"Maybe you shouldn't do this," she suggested uneasily. "I can stay here awhile longer. Why don't you go find a crane or something?"

"Nonsense, dear heart," Blackheart said, edging along the wire. "Sooner or later you're going to have to admit you trust me. I can't think of a better way for you to prove it."

"Blackheart," she moaned, hiding her eyes. If he was going to fall to his death on her account, she didn't want to watch it.

He stopped long enough to catch the end of the rope and pulley, then continued. Before climbing out onto the wire he'd taken off his shoes and socks, and his long, narrow bare feet clung to the wire with almost as much self-assurance as Marco's had. "What I liked best," he murmured in a conversational tone as he was about to reach her, "was when Marco kept comparing you to a trained chimpanzee. I'm surprised you didn't clobber him."

"I didn't dare. We both would have fallen."

"I've never known you to refrain from a self-destructive act when your temper is up," he said, stopping beside her. There was a space of some eighteen inches between them. Had they been on nice, level ground it would have been no trouble at all. Or even four feet up in the air. But halfway up in the stratosphere, such a distance was too far to cross.

"I'm not moving, Blackheart," she said fervently. "You can't make me."

"I'm not going on without you."

"Blackheart, Marco was used to lifting weights. A trained chimpanzee, an angry woman was nothing more than a challenge to him. You aren't used to it."

"Now's as good a time as any to learn."

"I don't want to die."

"Neither do I. Come on, dear heart. Just one tiny step. I'll catch you."

"I'll knock you over."

"I trust you, Francesca."

What could she say? He was standing there, seemingly at ease on the thick, coiled wire, watching her tenderly. "Damn you, Blackheart," she muttered, slowly, carefully straightening from her semicrouching position on the top of the column. "Maybe some things are worth dying for." And without another word she took the step.

He caught her, rocking back under the unexpected weight, and for a moment they swayed there, the wire quivering beneath them. When it finally held steady he moved his hands from their tight grip on her upper arms, slid down to hold her hand, and started edging across the rope.

"Just move very carefully," he said. "And don't look down."

Ferris looked down. Moaning, she jerked her head back up, and spied their destination—the far side of the great hall. "Why don't we go back the way you came? It's shorter." Her tone was still plaintive.

"You'd have to go first." He kept moving, a fraction of an inch at a time, and she followed him, trying to forget about the rooms beneath her, about the Rodin sculpture that could crush her fragile bones, the crusaders' pikes that could skewer her. "Besides, I have something better in mind."

They were halfway across the room. The police had left with their prisoner, and Dany and McNab were nowhere in sight. They were alone on the wire in that shadowy old building. Blackheart still had the end of the rope in his hand as he halted, looking downward.

Ferris allowed herself a brief, terrified glance. They were directly above her favorite exhibit, a bedroom transported direct from a Venetian villa. She looked up again at Blackheart, and she didn't like the meditative expression on his face. "Why have we stopped?"

He put an arm around her waist. "Hold on to me," he whispered in her ear, his eyes alight with pleasure.

"Why?" Even as she questioned she obeyed, wrapping her arms around his narrow waist and holding tightly.

"Because," he said, and jumped.

Her scream echoed through the building, cut off as the rope stopped their precipitous descent a scant four feet from the green damask-covered bed. Blackheart let go of the rope, and the two of them dropped onto the bed. A cloud of dust rose around them.

"I hate you," Ferris said passionately, sneezing. "I despise and detest you, I'll never trust you again, I—"

"You love me," Blackheart said, odiously sure of himself. "And you'll never distrust me again. So let's stop arguing and take advantage of this bed."

"I could scream," she suggested fiercely, not about to be cajoled, despite the fact that Blackheart was busy undoing the rest of the buttons on her black silk jumpsuit.

"You already did. No one heard you, no one came to your rescue."

"They might if I tried it again."

He'd pushed the clothing down from her shoulders, temporarily imprisoning her arms. "With our luck they might. Don't scream." He covered his mouth with hers.

It took her less than five seconds to help him rid her of the rest of the jumpsuit and another seven seconds to take off his clothes. Then they were naked in the huge Renaissance bed, lost in pleasure, in passion, in love. He was hard and strong and pulsing within her, and she wrapped her arms and legs around him, holding him tightly, rising, falling with him, lost and floating through heights that knew no limits.

When it was over he collapsed on top of her, hot and sweating as she was, panting, heart racing in tune with her own. It was a long moment before either of them spoke, and when Blackheart did, it was disarmingly prosaic. "This isn't really a mattress we're lying on, is it?"

"I don't think so. Cardboard boxes, maybe. You're just lucky we didn't land on wood," she said sleepily, nuzzling his damp hair.

"It was only a four-foot drop at that point. We would have ended up with a few bruises."

"I think you gave me a few, anyway," she murmured. "I do, you know."

"Do what?" He knew the answer as well as she did, but was waiting to hear the words.

"Do trust you. I was wrong to think you'd lie to me. I trust you almost as much as I love you."

"Almost as much?" he echoed.

"Nobody could feel anything as much as the love I feel for you," she whispered against his shoulder.

"In that case, maybe you'd better marry me, after all. You don't seem inclined to give up the ring, and I hate to tell you this, but I didn't bring any protection tonight.

either. I really didn't expect we'd end up like this. I don't suppose you did anything...?"

"Nope. I guess you're going to have to make an honest woman of me," she said with a sleepy smile.

"When?"

"How about tomorrow?"

"It'll take three days to get the license. Are you going to change your mind?"

"No. Three days will be fine. Somewhere along the way I figured something out."

"What was that?"

"You're right. It wasn't you I didn't trust. It was me. I would get so lost whenever I was with you. I felt I was disappearing. It frightened me."

"And what changed your mind?"

"Oh, I didn't change my mind. I do tend to disappear when I'm with you. Ferris Byrd and Francesca Berdahofski cease to exist. What I didn't realize is that instead of being me alone, I become joined with you. The two of us are one, stronger than me alone. I don't lose something, I gain it. So I don't have to be so frightened."

"Very wise," he murmured, his mouth brushing hers. "Does that mean we get a happy ending?"

She grinned up at him. "You bet, Blackheart. Happily ever after."

Epilogue

Mr. and Mrs. Smith
(RKO 1941)

"Don't tell me," said Stephen McNab. "I don't want to hear it."

"Of course you do," his wife of eight months declared. "You want my brother to be happy."

"Not particularly," he muttered. "However, I've gotten rather fond of Francesca during the last few months. I suppose for her sake I won't begrudge him."

"Noble of you," Dany McNab said.

"Yes, isn't it? So tell me. Mother and child safe, I suppose? Father recovering from the trauma of it all?"

"Don't be so snotty. You'll probably be going through it before too long yourself."

Momentarily distracted, Stephen pulled his wife onto his lap and indulged in a few brief minutes of passionate necking. "All right," he said finally. "Tell me the details—I know you won't be able to concentrate on more important things until you do."

"Francesca had a baby girl, Catherine Emilie, with lots of dark hair and greeny-blue eyes. She weighed eight pounds even, Blackheart was with them, and everyone is very happy. You're an uncle, Stephen."

"Great," he said morosely. "She's not going to grow up to be a cat burglar, is she? I know bad blood when I see it."

Dany grinned. "Who knows? You'll have to provide a sterling example for her."

"Catherine Emilie," Stephen murmured, trying it out. "What are they going to call her?"

"What do you think?" Dany murmured. "They're going to call her Cat."

TEARS IN THE RAIN

STARRING
CHRISTOPHER CAVZENOVE AND
SHARON STONE

BASED ON A NOVEL BY
PAMELA WALLACE

PREMIERING IN NOVEMBER